Quest for Kimchi

Raquel Look

A POST HILL PRESS BOOK
ISBN: 978-1-63758-500-9
ISBN (eBook): 978-1-63758-501-6

Quest for Kimchi

Cover design by Tiffani Shea

Post Hill Press
New York • Nashville
posthillpress.com

Published in the United States of America
1 2 3 4 5 6 7 8 9 10

For Grandma

CONTENTS

PART I

PART III - EPILOGUE

PART 1

CHAPTER 1

How It Started

"*Signor*, slow down!" shouted Magda over the growling sound of the revved-up engine.

"*Si, signora*," the driver answered, and I slid across the backseat as he rounded the corner. Why did I even agree to come, anyway? Zigzagging across Rome, slipping and sliding in the backseat of a musty cab in a foreign land, wasn't my idea of sight-seeing. Our driver Pinocchio—or was it "Antonio"?—had promised us the "bezt zenic route," but he continued to zip past every single structure. Pinocchio was the more fitting name, I decided.

At this pace, there was no opportunity to take in the majestic and historic sites...but every chance of getting a concussion. The driver blurred past a set of seemingly beautiful stairs, then zipped past what seemed to be a fountain. Fountains were everywhere in Rome. I thought we had just passed the Trevi Fountain.... Were those Roman gods bathing? Or important emperors posing in what looked like luminous lights drowning them? How would I know, I thought dryly. I was being tenderized in the back seat by a goddamned Roman. I wish I had a coin to throw in there so I could wish for this cabbie to slow down.

"Pantheon!" shouted the driver, before eventually rounding the ancient Colosseum with shrieking tires.

Was that an ancient court? A recently excavated Italian market? Glancing backward in the rearview mirror, I managed to savor another millisecond of these historical landmarks, exactly what I had envisioned and seen in guidebooks.

It felt like we were in some kind of Gravitron-like time machine that tossed us from present day to 179 AD with ancient aqueducts all around. I was thrown onto Magda from my end of the backseat, and then thrown back again, before we zipped by more ancient structures I didn't know the name of.

We had been warned about the cabbies.

"Mag, I don't feel so great."

"I think we just passed this place," she whispered, seeming to ignore my last statement. "I think he's taking the long route, Rach. He's definitely ripping us off."

"Mag," I complained again. "I wanna throw up."

We sped toward the middle of a dark—and what looked to be abandoned—alleyway, coming to a sudden stop. Both of us jerked forward. Magda was reluctant to get out, but I couldn't get out fast enough, almost tripping over the cobblestones in my haste. No sooner had I exited the taxi—my arms folded over my constricted stomach and my body hunched over—than I gagged uncontrollably. We both turned our heads to look at the audibly laughing cabbie.

I had known this trip wasn't such a good idea. I'd been nervous to come to Italy. Not only was it outside my comfort zone, but I had read about petty crime and pickpocketing, and I didn't understand a word of Italian (except for maybe *ciao*, which was useless when I really wanted to say, "Stop driving so fast, you lunatic!").

But when my college roommate Magda invited me to go to Italy with her—something about it being a "magical place that awoke your inner soul," which prompted her to buy two round-trip airfare tickets—how could I say no?

Plus, I needed a desperate getaway from work. Was I that unhappy at the law firm? I pondered, and then answered myself immediately. *Yes.* Yes, I was. I should have been happy with such a prestigious job. My peers were. Lynch & Burnham, LLP only accepted the top of the top from the Ivy League universities for their entry-level program—and I got in? I had secretly hoped I wouldn't, since I was becoming unhappy with my life. At the core of it was this job that erupted all sorts of damaging, volcanic ash into my life: regret, anxiety, insomnia, backaches, even carpal tunnel. Partners and bosses who simply expected you to give up life to serve them their documents in their corner suites while they overzealously billed their clients by the hour and paid you one-fourth of the one-fourth billed amount. As if suffocating from the dense ash of legal work wasn't bad enough, my college sweetheart, Nate, had texted me earlier in the week while I was redacting documents for one of the largest corporate scandals in US history. The text had read, "We need to take a break," which felt like the biggest scandal of my premature love life.

"We need to take a break"? What the hell did that mean? There was no elaboration. Just eighteen characters emitted into the universe that damaged my heart like an 18.0 magnitude earthquake crushing the ash still erupting from that aforementioned volcano. Was the "we need to take a break" followed by a measurable, quantifiable metric of time? I had more questions that began with—*Huh? What? Why?* I needed an explanation. I needed to understand this statement. And I needed to know why he couldn't call me.

Nate and I met the first week of college. During orientation he was trying to find his dorm room and accidentally ended up at mine, comfortably unpacking his belongings onto my desk. It was a co-ed dorm room with co-ed bathrooms, and room "410" looked like "416."

"Hi, I'm Rachel. We corresponded over the summer," I said, not even looking up and opening another jar of the spicy cabbage my mom had so neatly packed for me.

"What's that smell?" He paused, putting his nose up in the air to take another sniff. His canvas bag dropped off his shoulder.

"It's kimchi," I answered, reaching for a plastic fork and scooping a little bit from the jar. I handed it to him.

"What is kimchi?" he asked, pulling away.

I rattled off what sounded like a Webster dictionary definition of the vegetable. "It's a *traditional side dish made from salted and fermented vegetables, most commonly napa cabbage and Korean radishes, with a variety of seasonings including chili powder, scallions, garlic, ginger, and jeotgal (salted seafood).*"

Nate finally leaned in, face puckered, as he put the fork into his mouth. A little dropped off the side of his mouth. "That's the most disgusting thing I've ever eaten."

I could go on and on about the most disgusting things I've ever eaten: anchovies, blue cheese, mutton, crickets, pig feet, chicken feet, intestines, fish eggs, and ketchup on Doritos. Instead, I kept a polite face and only grinned.

"Is this suite 410? I'm Nate." He struggled to swallow the last bit of kimchi. He flashed a smile, and an unusually long canine tooth protruded from the side with a piece of kimchi on it.

At that very moment, my real roommate, Magda Kim, arrived. She was donned in a baggy, dark tracksuit, walked in, dropped her two big duffel bags to the floor, and let out a hostile, "Who the hell are you?" directed at Nate. And what the hell is that smell?

Our eyes met. "You must be Rachel See," she said, as she moved forward, her shoulders brushing Nate's arm. Nate's real dorm room was down the hall.

After that incident, Nate and I spent almost every day of college together (to Magda's chagrin). We were that couple other couples snarked at under their breaths to "get a room" because of all the embarrassing public displays of affection that would be totally acceptable in a place like Paris. We endured the tragedy of all-nighters together, studying subjects neither of us really cared for at the Student Union. We rushed Greek life during the same semester and moved into the respective fraternity/sorority organizations across the street from each other on Thorston Avenue.

Nate and I became more unified, vowing to be "do-gooders," whatever that meant, for the rest of our lives. We stopped eating out. With the rice cooker in my dorm room, and the packaged spicy cabbage I still had, Nate frequently came over. He learned to love kimchi…or at least to tolerate it.

"I can't eat this anymore, Rach," Magda complained. She didn't like kimchi, which was odd since she grew up with this stuff. She had a mom and a grandmother who spent summers teaching her how to make kimchi under the perfect temperature conditions. I wasn't as fortunate. My Chinese family preferred their futile attempts at making me memorize Chinese vocabulary during the summers. *Please, Magda, will you share your family's unwavering devotion and kimchi recipe with me?* "No," she would tell me, eyes swelling up. She opened the door and left us for the evening.

"Finally, the room to ourselves. I can't stand her." Nate moved closer to me.

I opened my chemistry book to the chapter I was struggling with.

"I love you, Rach," he said suddenly. My focus was lost, and I hesitantly looked up into his unapologetic eyes. And just like that, I felt the *whoosh* of air as his body approached mine. I'd never imagined our first kiss to be filled with kimchi-smelling breaths, but it was, and it was perfect. Every beat of my heart increased, and everything in the world seemed to freeze, like we were the only ones left in the world. The following semester, we adopted our little hamster, Jimmy Chew, together and moved off campus. Followed by a kitten named Miss America. I even met Nate's family. I'll never forget the first words Grandma Lucetta said to me: "You don't look like a slut!"

A month earlier, she had driven almost 250 miles in an '86 Chevy by herself to drop us off food because she "didn't think we were eating well." We weren't.

"What the hell is that smell?" she said, barging into our dorm room. She was holding a heavy cooler of homemade Italian, which was as fresh as any food could be after the four-hour trip.

"Grandma, it's kimchi." Nate moved the jar close to her.

"Gum, *who*? It smells like an elephant just died in here. Get rid of that stuff."

I took the jar from Nate and closed it. I couldn't believe I was letting this stranger who knew nothing about kimchi tell me what to do with my favorite comfort food.

"Now here…have some real food." Grandma Lucetta opened the cooler and pulled out carefully wrapped lasagnas, meatballs, ravioli, and Caprese salads. It was the most nourishing food we had all semester. It surprisingly tasted good (and for a fleeting moment, I forgot about my kimchi). Grandma Lucetta would continue to take regular road trips to see us and make us "real" food that rivaled the delicious spicy cabbage.

After college, Nate and I moved to New York City. He worked in banking, and I worked in corporate law. Admittedly, we each began growing more distant, but I attributed that to our intense, seven-days-a-week, "important" jobs. He thrived on the stress and hard-earned six-figure bonuses that followed the large corporate deals he helped ink (the same ones I would soon come to despise). Meanwhile, I seemed to spiral into a sad "Rachel" state and emit a toxic aura whenever someone we encountered asked, "What do you do for a living?" My response was almost always pleasant and politically correct, but whoever was asking seemed to sense the true toxicity of that response, which really reeked of *I hate my job. I hate my life.* Nonetheless, I never would have expected the way I felt about a job to warrant a "break" from Nate (whatever the hell that meant).

But I certainly needed a break from all of this. And so I gave Magda a reassuring, "Yes, I will join you in Italy"—especially since she got a good deal on what was now a non-refundable ticket!

The cabbie pointed straight ahead into the depth of a narrow, dark alley, and proclaimed in heavily Italianized and broken English, "It would be the most *bellissimo* of places." There was nobody else around and I felt scared. He saluted us by jointly placing his index and forefingers to his lips, then extending his arms with fingers pointing toward us and making an all too familiar sound: "Muah!" I heard him mutter the word "Americans" as he sped off.

"Are you OK?" Magda asked nervously.

"I'll be alright," I said, trying hard to believe myself. I could barely muster up the words between each gasp. "I just need to catch my breath. What a maniac!" I stood upright and composed myself, breathing a bit more calmly. I stretched my arms, and we began to sheepishly walk toward the alley.

The alley between the two ancient buildings grew narrower toward the intersection of what may have been either another alley, a dead-end, or the unlikely intersection of another street. I prayed to Pope John Paul the Second. Antonio the Cabbie had said it was around the corner, but failed to mention in which direction. Were we supposed to interpret his instructions by the motion of his well-defined, sleeveless, and hairy dark arm? We took what we thought was a wrong turn until we found a barely lit yellowish button adorning the right side of the doorframe and a bronze, three-inch number "8" nailed on the door at eye-level for a child. We had arrived. We pressed the button with some remaining hesitation, and a flamboyantly dressed young Italian dandy greeted us with an operatic baritone voice: "*Benvenuto*! Welcome! Mi Chinezze bellas! Comeee! Siiiit! Eat!" he roared.

As a Korean American, Magda usually took offense to being called "Chinese"—but for some reason she had a forgiving look on her face.

"Oh my gosh, he's hot, Rachel. So *hot*!"

"I'm guessing that's why you weren't offended by what he called you?"

"He could call me whatever he'd like," she whispered, and then he placed his arm around us both and escorted us in. "Have you *seen* those arms?" she added.

To our pleasant and relieved surprise, we were brought to the back of a large room with a spectacular vaulted ceiling, full of gregarious patrons—most of whom were speaking some dialect of Italian or another.

"Our *speciale* today iz il un *bistec*...you like the steak?"

"Magda, I don't want steak. We're in Italy. How about something more Italian? Like Mac 'n' cheese?"

"You must try the meats here, Rach!"

"Fine, fine. Just order."

Our poorly manicured and unshaven waiter dispensed the menus and promptly placed fresh homemade focaccia bread with Parmigiano Reggiano chunks and a bowl of large, green and black olives at the center of the table. Oh my God, it was unlike any Italian restaurant either of us had been to in the United States: this tasted as if it was just made by a short, medium-plumped, lovely Italian grandmother.

Shortly thereafter, Magda picked a variety of foods, including a parade of buffalo burrata, a sampling of a variety of local handmade pastas, slow-cooked wild game from the Italian Alps, and the appropriate Montepulciano d'Abruzzo. Our waiter took charge with his Italian machismo in a full peacock-like display, along with his surprisingly bare chest peeking through his mostly unbuttoned collared shirt.

"Magda, I can't eat anymore. I'm about to burst," I said.

"We are in Italy, Rachel. *Italy!* Eating real Italian food. Cooked by real Italians."

Magda won again, and we gluttonously ate more than what our waistlines permitted, necessitating the unfastening of our jeans and, I joked, applications to *The Biggest Loser* upon our return to the United States.

Our waiter, along with our vivacious friend who greeted us at the door, told us the covert establishment belonged to his family and that we were in the presence of the brothers, Vincenzo and Aldo.

"We...our very fabled rezipes are passed from generation to generation from our very large and old familia. Madre and Nonna would be so angry if we no take over. My nonna source and simmer the ingredients, all, slowwwwly, for many hours, and we dun open the restaurant until all il food is ready, uzually around one o'clock in the afternoon!" one of them proudly exclaimed.

"Rachel, this is typical of Southern Italy but unusual for Rome!" Magda exclaimed. "We've hit an Italian, food-served-by-hot-Roman-brothers, gem!"

I believed her. There were so many obvious signs this was not a tourist trap, nor was it for the impatient traveler. There weren't any English menus, and we had to rely on Aldo's elementary

English that sounded more like Italian to me. Even so, I loved being serenaded by the conversations of gregarious patrons surrounding us, like we were in the audience of their opera di Verona performance still going strong hours later.

Several hours later, we were under the psychedelic influence of a vino stupor. We laughed hard with our newly formed friends, as though we were alone and had shared many fond memories together. Soon joining our festivities was a lovely Irish couple who sounded like they spoke a hundred words a minute.

"'Oly Jaysus, Mary, an' Joseph, waaat are ye birds drinkin'? It looks loike ye 'avin' a gran' time! Where's our lad? Mario? Luigi?! Refill!"

Aldo—or was it Vincenzo?—came over and soon brought the group downstairs to the cavernous and gloomy wine cellar, complete with the prerequisite amount of mangled aging cobwebs amidst the hundreds of neatly shelved, dust-covered bottles. There were vintage wines. New wines. Wines from his family estate. The collection was simply breathtaking. It was also damp and cool and smelled of an equal mixture of fermenting, overly ripe fruit, and mold.

The Irish couple danced around a bit. Is this what the Irish like to do? I wondered.

They asked us to take their picture, mumbling in their heavy accents, "Wud ye take a photo av us? Make sure yer git de gran' gran' bottles av wine in de backgroun'. Me wife 'ere, she's a lush."

Were we asked because we were Asian? How about asking the Italian fellow instead, I wondered. They were kind enough to reciprocate, but the pictures were blurred.

"T'anks a million."

Upon returning to our table with two different wine bottles in tow and a corked, half-full bottle of grappa—Italian moonshine (or was it Italian oil-paint thinner?)—we laughed some more and exchanged stories.

"Rachel here was too nervous to come to Italy. I practically had to lure her with free tickets!" Magda balked.

The Irish gentleman laughed.

"Me name is Pat. Pat McGrowgan."

He slipped towards the edge of the seat. "Nervous? What's dare ter be nervous aboyt? Yer 'en er tried me wife's cookin'. Nigh that's somethin' ter be nervous about."

After drinking some more, we rummaged through our purses and gave them our business cards, something we should have given them in the first place. They reciprocated. One read: *Claire McGrowgan, Head of Recruiting, WilHeltek Commerz, GmBH, East Point Business Park, Dublin 3, Ireland.*

CHAPTER 2

But, But...

"C'mon...email her already!" Magda wailed from her yoga mat, fidgeting as she tried to balance herself on one foot; meanwhile, I was trying hard to ignore her and focus on Jillian's vinyasa yoga class (*if everyone can transcend into a child's pose and take deep breaths*).

It was cold for a spring day in New York City. Barely even forty degrees outside, but inside the studio, it was a sweltering combobulation of 100 degrees of sauna-like heat exacerbated by stings of instigation from Magda that came at me sideways. It was a new style of yoga—"Bikram Yoga" they called it—and Magda insisted "we just had to try it," mentioning that the heat would stimulate our metabolisms and enable more body fat loss.

"Email Claire," Magda insisted, now clumsily shuffling into a downward dog pose, her head upside down now, peering in between her bent legs toward me, and howling back as five other women surrounding us began giving her dirty looks.

"She's the Head of Recruiting at her firm, Rach. She could potentially get you out of your hell hole," Magda continued.

"No. I can't. I won't," I responded, letting out a deep exhale. My glasses were fogging up.

"Email her!" Magda exclaimed in a more aggressive tone. One woman stood up at this point, rolled her mat up, and moved to the opposite end of the room, clearly annoyed as she let out a passive aggressive grunt. Jillian didn't seem to mind the commotion; after all, classes were eighty-five dollars per person.

Jillian reached for the window and tried to open it, but the knob was still broken. It opened only slightly, and a burst of humidity exited.

"No, I won't," I resisted, in a slightly more aggressive tone this time. I bent forward with my hands touching my toes. I focused on my breathing, closed my eyes, and remained calm.

"Email her! Tell her how lovely it was to meet her and her partner." Magda's cantankerous voice grew louder, and soon muffled Jillian's instructions.

I wiped the sweat from my forehead and bent backwards into a bridge position.

"No. I don't know her. What did you expect me to get out of this, Mag? A job in Ireland?"

The humidity allowed me to flex even further backwards.

"I was tipsy when you and I exchanged contact information with her. I wouldn't even know where her contact info was," I said on an exhale.

"You need to get out of your shell, Rachel! Be uncomfortable!" Magda yelled. "I abhor when you get like this!"

Somewhere, lost in my luggage that was stowed away from our trip to Italy last year in the deep furrows of my cluttered closet, *maybe* was her business card. I took a deep exhale and closed my eyes, trying to follow Jillian as she positioned her body into a bridge.

"All your life, you've been taught to be submissive. To listen to authority."

I took a deep breath, trying hard not to succumb to the pressure Magda was sending my way in the middle of yoga class.

"...To never question anyone. To never speak up. To color in between the lines."

Jillian stood up on her mat. I followed.

"To never do anything different. To accept. To study. To work. To care for others first. To put Nate first."

I moved my head slowly in the opposite direction, blocking out any negative energy that attacked me by way of Magda's words.

"To never go to bed without first brushing your teeth for exactly two minutes and twenty seconds. The obsequious one. Never one to socialize..."

I loudly exhaled this time. I hated when Magda got like this. She was that best friend you loved—and hated—all at once. The one you wanted to wrap and embrace before choking to death. The one who slapped you with the harshest dose of reality, and you suffered from whiplash as a result.

"Fucking A, Magda. For fuck's sake! I socialize...especially if I have a bit of alcohol...." I lifted my head, retaliating back.

"You're not happy at the law firm. Yes? Yes."

I bent forward as Magda went into a child's pose. "I will be the one who will lead the revolution against yourself. I'm not going to stop protesting until you do something."

I pretended not to listen.

"Now email her!" Magda said, with some finality.

My head fell forward as Jillian raised the volume of the peaceful meditation music.

"Oh darling, listen to your friend here and email her." The voice came from a stranger sitting behind Magda. He was equally flamboyant and compassionate, perfecting his bridge pose and looking at me as he turned around.

"Listen to your friend, darling," he repeated. A moment later, we learned his name was Augusto and he had been a fellow Yogi for five years.

As Magda became the ferocious sesquipedalian person she was and started using words too big even for my legal (non) grandiloquence, I wondered if she—and our new friend, Augusto—were right. This was Magda, after all. I always listened to Magda. She was always right. She and I shared a camaraderie like two soldiers from the same infantry now deployed on the ground and embroiled in World War Nate, a war declared on me by an eighteen-character text message with the weapon of mass destruction being, "Let's take a break." GI Magda shielded me from artillery shells and torpedoes aimed at my heart when my will for self-preservation was too weak to fight back.

"What about Nate?" My head hung low.

"What about him? Has he called you?" Magda wobbled, and almost came crashing down on her mat, before turning toward Augusto and bringing him up to speed with World War Nate. I saw Augusto shake his head from the corner of my eye.

"No." I moved away, afraid to confront Magda—and now, Augusto. It was becoming increasingly difficult to breathe in that studio.

"Has he written to you? Offered some kind of explanation? Apologized? Stopped being an asshole to you?!" Augusto was nodding his head in agreement with Magda before jumping in with a "Girlfriend, he don't deserve you," before transcending into a bridge pose.

No, I thought, but if only you knew.... I had spent the last few weeks gripping the pendant Nate got me for my birthday, thinking about when he said, "You are the one," and trying to decipher his text message...but neither having Sherlock Holmes's knack for solving mysteries nor the strength to accept what had just happened.

Sweat and tears rolled down my face.

I didn't want to go to war with Nate anymore. But did I have a choice? It was really hard not to hear from him. He ignored every one of my twenty-one (and counting) text messages, emails, and voicemails thus far. On my phone background was a photo of the three of us: Magda, me, and Nate. Magda always thought I could "do better." But was I ready to "do better" and cut Nate out of my life? Out of that photo? Emailing Claire would mean "yes," and would be the first step in my retribution against Nate.

"Count this as a blessing in disguise, Rachel. You dodged a bullet. He changed after college. You and I both know that. And that gap between his two front teeth…*so* not attractive."

Jillian clasped her hands together and moved her right foot against her left thigh.

"But this was the year he was supposed to propose to me, Mag." I couldn't bear another moment in this war. My body had never been so beaten up in my life, and as much as Magda tried to protect me, my heart still felt captured and tortured by Nate.

The window suddenly burst open, and a gust of cold, wintry-like air blew into the studio.

"Rach, ask yourself. If the last year or so was this rocky, what do you think a lifetime with him would have been like? And think about what your children would have looked like with those buck, gap teeth!"

But it was Nate. It was still a life I wanted. I wanted his big, buck-teeth children. All three of them. I wanted to live in the suburbs with him. I wanted to marry Nate.

As I struggled whether or not to reach out to this woman I knew nothing of, an email arrived in my inbox that evening:

Dear Rachel,

It was lovely to meet you and Magda at Fabrizio's. We had a grand time in Rome, and an even grander time meeting you both. Wasn't that wine cellar just something? I was just wondering if you would happen to have any group photos from that evening. If so, I'd truly appreciate you passing them on.

All the best,
Claire

Feeling like this was the sign from the Irish Italian Goddesses I was waiting for, I hastily drafted a reply:

Dear Claire,

It was nice meeting you and Pat too! Most of my photos came out blurry (must have been the poor lighting in the wine cellar), but the best ones from that evening are attached here. I noticed you are an executive human resources recruiter in Ireland. ~~*I'm desperate to leave my job here in New York. It sucks. They're overworking me with all the tasks they don't want to do. And the partners are mean. So mean. And my long-time boyfriend sent me the meanest text suggesting we "take a break." It might as well have been a sticky note. Do you have any job openings—ANYTHING—over there? I need to get away—per-*~~

~~*manently. I can type fast, I am multi-lingual, and I hail from a top school in the United States where I learned to tip cows....*~~

I would love to chat with you about opportunities if you have a moment. Please find my resume attached for your review too.

Rachel

CHAPTER 3

The Offer

You have a very strong resume, and we'd love to speak with you! I dropped my half-eaten bagel, which was smeared with strawberry cream cheese. I scrolled through the email again to make sure the words were what I was reading. My medium-sized iced cappuccino was ready, but it wasn't until the fifth time the barista had called my name that I actually went up to get it.

Would love to speak with me? I had a million and one questions. What was the name of this company again? What did they do? Who was "we"? And where were they located again?

"Dear Claire," I typed out, taking a sip of my cappuccino before continuing.

"Thank you for taking the time to read through my resume..." I paused to look up at a couple who was quarreling over their coffee order (*grande, tall, grande!*).

"I look forward to connecting with you too. Please advise your availability for a call."

No sooner than an hour did Claire's assistant, Sinead, send me a video call request with Claire, someone named Hilda Künt, and me. It was scheduled for the following day. It went something like:

"Is this Ray-chul?" The one with the dirty-blonde hair asked (I think Hilda).

"Yes," I responded. I stared straight into the camera, without even a grimace.

"Tell me about yourself," Hilda continued. So, I did. I told them about my major, about my aspirations for law, about my hunger for new challenges that really disguised my desperation to *get out* of law. But, all the while, I couldn't stop thinking about Nate. Would he call me back? Was he just punishing me, like that one time in college when he ignored me for a week because I coordinated a prank with his fraternity brothers? At the time I'd thought our relationship was over, but he came back. I was secretly hoping that he would come back this time too.

Claire and Hilda hired me soon thereafter. Hilda was clearly a boss, likely a big boss, since Claire remained quiet most of the interview, jotting notes instead. I should have been happy. Ecstatic. Joyous. But I was utterly apathetic.

"Mag, you won't believe this. After a short conversation with Claire and someone from the global accounts team, they hired me on the spot. I got a job in Ireland." I was unfazed and walking down Fifth Avenue when I called Mags. Good things seem to happen on Fifth Avenue. But today, that good thing didn't seem like a good thing to me.

"What?! Congratulations! You're going to accept, right? Please tell me you're going to take it." Suddenly, Mag's phone reception was cutting out. A cloud moved in above me, and it started to drizzle. I didn't have an umbrella.

"I don't know." Magda could hear the trepidation in my voice, and I felt the wrath of Magda bubbling up to the surface of my mobile phone.

"What do you mean you don't know?!" yelled Magda. I wanted to create "fake static" so I could hang up on Magda politely, but instead, I retaliated.

"You know what 'I know' means? Well, 'I don't know' is the opposite. *I don't know.* They couldn't even give me a job title, Mag. Something about when 'you get here, we will place you.'" A loud clap of thunder roared above me. Tourists began fleeing under awnings.

"What did their offer letter say?" she asked. I dashed into a convenience store to pick up a cheap five-dollar umbrella, hoping to avoid the downpour that was imminent.

"You mean, email? Here, I'll read it to you:

> *"Rachel,*
>
> *We are so excited to extend you an offer with WilHeltek Commerz, GmbH! You will be joining our global Key Account Management team in a capacity to work on various matters as needed at a salary of [...] per annum (Mag, I love you, but*

I'm not telling you my salary). You will be reporting to Hilda Künt. Your job title will be determined accordingly. You will be required to submit to a criminal background check, and upon verification, your start date will be June 5. You will immediately meet with Helen Waite upon your arrival."

"So, they're more interested in whether you're a criminal than putting forth a legal document solidifying what you'd be doing for them?"

"Mags!" The owner of the convenience store looked at me as my voice grew loud.

"Thank goodness your worst offense was a twenty-five-dollar parking ticket in Ithaca...which technically wasn't your fault, it was Nate's! Oh, and chewing gum at the Metropolitan Museum of Art, where they so politely escorted you out of the newest exhibition. Luckily for you, such a heinous act would not be deserving of the highest capital punishment of canning in Ireland."

"*Mags...!*"

"OMG, I just did an image search for Hilda Künt.... This bitch looks scary, Rach!"

"Stop judging a book by its cover," I snapped. The clerk shot me a look of death. I hated when Judgmental Magda came out. She never gave anyone—anyone!—a chance if she thought they were below her standards.

"Uh...look! Look at those eyes! And that crooked, sorry attempt at a smile! Be careful." She paused, and then conceded,

"But you should accept the job, nonetheless. You endured the worst partners at the law firm. What's Stew going to say?"

Stewart, otherwise known as Stew Pitt, Esq., was my direct boss at the firm. The one who, more often than not, dangled that "partner" carrot above me so I would work appallingly long hours, redacting documents filled with heinous white-collar crimes while he had both his feet up on his desk. I wanted out.

But I still had a million and one questions. What was the Key Account Management team responsible for? What various matters would I work on? What did Hilda do each day? More importantly, what would she want for me to do each day? How big was the team? What did I need to pack? And where in Ireland was this job again?

But did any of this matter? I wanted to escape New York City, and this offer was the potential key to me "starting over" as Magda continued to remind me. The prospective reboot. The "control-alt-delete" to my heart and my career. Getting away from corporate law. Getting away from Nate, because the truth was, we weren't going to get married this year—or probably ever. Acknowledging this hard truth—as much as I vehemently wanted to deny it—pierced my heart. A piece of me still hung onto hope that this was a "break," not a "break up." But it felt like Nate was one step closer to declaring "checkmate" (or "checkNate") on me. I had no more pawns to protect me. He usurped any good left standing, one by one, and now, surrounded by his ego, his arrogance, and his newfound wealth, his insistence on wanting a break pushed me into an inescapable position. Moving to Ireland could be my escape, could be the solution to freeing me from being stuck in this miserable state of suckiness.

After much reading on the law job I was supposed to love, I learned something about Ireland. Ireland was experiencing something called the "Celtic Tiger" boom. That's why there were so many jobs in Ireland. Lots and lots of jobs. Companies were relocating there from all over the world to evade—I mean, save—on taxes.

Call it the reverse immigration (or, more accurately, emigration) of Ireland, where more Americans were moving in droves for jobs than Irish were emigrating out of the country. The Irish economy was booming so much that they needed workers fast. Hence why Claire virtually hired me on the spot, with a salary on par with what the law firm was paying me. I should have accepted right then and there.

Nonetheless, I didn't respond for several days. Even after receiving all of the answers to my endless questions in a packaged formal letter slightly smaller than the size of a car manual, I couldn't make a decision. Did I really want to leave the love of my life and a potential career at one of the best international law firms for a company I didn't even know the name of in a job I knew nothing about? It seemed like an obvious answer—at least for the old me. I was hanging on to the last thread of hope with Nate. Surely he would respond—eventually, at least—and we would talk, make up, and talk some more, because break-ups were always part of make-ups. I imagined it going something like this: a big bouquet of long-stemmed red roses would await me at the apartment. He would gush over me and apologize a thousand different ways in a sweet, little note, before showing up, getting down on one knee, and asking me to marry him with a two-carat, round cut, diamond ring. He would explain how he really needed the alone time to figure out how much he wanted me in his life. I would forgive him, say yes to his proposal, and live happily ever after with him. Of course, Magda would hit me upside the head with her Lauren Merkin clutch bag whenever I brought this fantasy up. I didn't blame her. I needed a reality check via some form of physical altercation, because Nate seemed to want nothing to do with me. And I wanted nothing to do with Lynch & Burnham. Was the solution moving to Ireland?

It felt like a quagmire more suited for a flip of a coin, or maybe a rose whose petals I pulled one by one—reciting, "I will go, I will not go," instead of, "He loves me, he loves me not," (although the more classic question would make sense too, since Nate still hadn't responded to my last text of "I love you").

I walked three hundred fifty steps to the bodega on my block and bought the only bunch of roses left. They were lifeless, but that didn't matter since I would pluck them, one by one, like the "happily ever after" that, too, had slowly wilted before me and Nate's eyes. In over one hundred coin flips, the answer came to an astounding "go," and with a dozen red roses whose droopy petals were scattered on the floor of my bare living room, the final petal said, "I will go," and Nate "loves me not." So, there you go—I sealed my fate with a quarter and a fifteen-dollar bunch of roses from the corner Bodega.

After exactly three hundred seventy-two days serving as an attorney for one of the top international law firms—which pitted Ivy League graduates against one another like roosters in a cock-fight, then bred us in demoralizing conditions to make us angry, ill-tempered, and more competitive and cutthroat against one another—I submitted my resignation letter to Stew Pitt, abandoning the heroic fight while my integrity and body were still somewhat intact.

"This won't look good on your resume, kid," Stew would say quickly, pulling his feet back before rising up over me as I sat there, dreading his every movement.

I'm not a kid! I'm twenty-nine years old! I'd hear my inner voice bicker back.

"I have a great opportunity ahead of me," I'd say, although I wasn't sure I did. All I knew was, it was getting me out of this hell hole.

It wasn't easy to quit. In fact, I felt defeated. There was a part of me still beating myself up, as if my opponent had snuck up behind me and I had abruptly surrendered to their fight with a giant white flag.

Only, it was me who surrendered to myself.

CHAPTER 4

I Love You, I Love You Not

When Nate finally emerged from the abyss of ghosting me—and I continued to map out what exactly triggered his silence—I was beyond ecstatic. He was to come over in a few hours, so I decorated the apartment quickly with rose-smelling candles and bought his favorite foods. I wanted to make sure he subliminally and subconsciously connected me to his favorite things in the world so he would apologize and propose to me tonight.

That's not what happened.

"It's not you. It's me, Rach," he said, as he fumbled through the closet collecting his button-down shirts and not making any eye contact. The kitchen timer coincidentally went off like sirens and muffled much of what he had to say.

"Do you want to stay for dinner?" I asked desperately. "I'm making roast chicken." Roast chicken was Nate's favorite. He shook his head.

"I do still love you," he said, "and it's because I still love you that I think we need to take a break." Nate stood halfway across the cold room, belting out these cold words as if banishing me to a dungeon to be locked up and starved of love.

I didn't usually give up. But this time was different. It was different because I surrendered to Nate too. Nate had come to my apartment, but not to propose. He came to collect his belongings and give a half-ass explanation of his eighteen-character text message.

"You need to focus on you," he continued. "I want you to be happy again. Let's see how we still feel about each other next time we see each other and if we can work things out then."

If we could work things out then? I had all kinds of questions. It just seemed too subjective to me. Was this technically some kind of trial period where I would take home this "break," feel it, play around with it, experiment with it, and if I didn't like it prior to the trial period ending, return it? Would we communicate to each other during this break? Would we see other people to better assess if this "break" was right for us? Could you elaborate and quantify how long this "break" would be? Will you remember to feed Jimmy Chew and Miss America during this break?

I wanted to speak, but nothing came out. Instead, I sat there, slumped over the corner of my bed with a lump forming in my throat, nose sniffling and heart bleeding as he packed up his belongings and so easily walked out of an eleven-year relationship.

It felt like I was on a gurney on the brink of death. Magda would be the one to administer my "last rites," seeking forgiveness for the sins I have committed:

Thou shalt not have given your heart to anyone, especially an unsure prick;

Thou shalt not make any one person (especially Nate) your God;

Thou shalt never, ever, ever, ever let a person into your heart again.

I was guilty—very guilty—of having committed the sin of gluttony (the gluttony of love) and was seeking forgiveness before my soul was shipped off to Ireland. More specifically, before Magda shipped my soul off to Ireland. Magda picked me up on the following Saturday afternoon for my one-way flight to Ireland. Nate didn't even know I was leaving.

She was late, as usual, doing everything and anything Magda-related before she finally arrived in front of my house.

"Hurry!" she said. "We only have an hour and a half to get to Newark."

"My parents want to come along and send me off," I said, and Magda opened the back door to let them in. They slowly climbed in, holding onto the arm rest of the backseat. I carried my heavy luggage and tucked it into the trunk of the van.

"Hi, Mr. and Mrs. See!"

"Herro Magda. Long time! How you do?"

Magda adjusted her rearview mirror and smiled at them.

"Don't drive too fast," my parents said as they reached for their seat belts.

We were stuck in a bumper-to-bumper, weekday, morning rush-hour-like gridlock with nowhere to detour on this sunny weekend afternoon. The sound of beat-up cars honking at each other drowned out any cries my heart still let out and any music blaring from the radio.

A driver in a red, two-door sports car with a New Jersey license plate crept up next to us and tried to cut into our lane without signaling. He was playing some concoction of Latin-reggae on the radio with his sunroof open, and Magda pressed the gas pedal of her mom's minivan to cut him back off. I tried my best not to look toward the driver and make eye contact; he made muffled sounds at us, and in the side-view mirror, I was able to make out that he was sticking one of his long fingers at us. He became relentless, tailing us in the adjacent lane and trying to cut us off again. I was too numb to really respond to, or care for, such aggressive behavior.

Magda sped up more and kept almost no distance between our minivan and the Toyota Camry in front. I just sat with my eyes closed, my right hand clutching the door handle, secretly praying the Camry would not come to a sudden stop and that my Nate would return to me someday soon.

"Douchebag!" she yelled from the driver's side seat.

"Ah, Magda, don't say that. No good. Now turn here. Turn here. Turn here. Turn *here*!" My father interjected.

"Magda, you drive too fast. Slow down. Why you no come earlier? So much traffic now," my mother balked from the backseat. My Chinese parents had a difficult time letting their Chinese offspring just move to another country. Even though I was born in Tokyo, Japan, my very Chinese parents *always* kept true to our traditions, to our roots and customs, and of course, to our general daily practices. Sometimes I still miss the cat cafes my mom would bring me to after school, and the gorgeous lights. However, we ended up in America, as most do. And somewhere during the past few years, they "became more American," as they would say, and embraced seeing their child travel more, even if it meant enduring a tumultuous ride in the backseat of a minivan.

My parents continued to let out several loud, nervous sighs in the backseat as their appeals went ignored and their efforts to cajole Magda failed.

My one-way flight to Dublin was boarding in about thirty minutes from Newark International Airport. My mother became frantic and tried to download check-in information from her one-bar-signal phone. My dad was shaking his head and insisted, under his breath, that taking the Holland Tunnel would have been better.

My heart was palpitating—not because of this morning's coffee, although that was some potent double espresso John the Barista made—because I wondered if this was the right decision. Was the universe sending me a sign? Should I have stayed behind to wait for Nate? Should I have stayed at the law firm and worked my way up to partner, like I had carefully planned? Carefully planned, unlike this move to Dublin where I unabashedly submitted my resignation to one of the most prestigious international law firms only two weeks earlier, after meeting an Irish human resources recruiter in a drunken state in an alley-way restaurant in Rome!

I missed Nate already. He should have been coming along with me. We always said we'd travel the world together. For my twenty-first birthday, Nate created a travel scrapbook for me out of a black and white composition notebook. It was complete with cheesy Millennial phrases spelled out in random magazine cutouts with alternating lowercase and uppercase letters, which to any ordinary person, looked like it came from a serial killer instead of a twenty-year-old romantic. On the first page was a photo of our college ID cards along with the dorm building we both lived at, and a caption that read, "Where it all started." On page two, he taped the receipt of our first date.

COLLEGETOWN BAGELS
607-888-8485
SvrCk: Adam 7:56AM 08/31/10
2 Coffees … $3.75
2 Cinnamon Raisin Bagels … $2.75
+ Strawberry Cream Cheese … $.75
+ Blueberry Cream Cheese … $.75
Sub Total: $8.00
Tax: $.64
Total: $8.64
NOW OPEN ON SUNDAYS 7AM-9PM

In the pages that followed, he pasted all sorts of famous travel icons: the Eiffel Tower, the Taj Mahal, the Leaning Tower of Pisa, the pyramids of Egypt. If he couldn't find a suitable photo, he drew it in a child-like manner with stick figures. The notebook contained all the places we had talked about visiting. He deliberately left the page around each location blank, so we could fill it in later, when we had visited these places together. In the middle of the notebook read 1 Corinthians 13 in his messy penmanship:

"Love is patient, love is kind. It does not envy, it does not boast, it is not proud. It does not dishonor others, it is not self-seeking, it is not easily angered, it keeps no record of wrongs. Love does not delight in evil but rejoices with the truth. It always protects, always trusts, always hopes, always perseveres. Love never fails..."

If love never fails, then why was it failing us now?

Everything felt wrong. Was the universe trying to tell me something? I wanted to believe the universe worked in strange ways to guide each of us to our fate. If I missed this flight, I would yield to the universe and turn around. Hopefully, Nate would be waiting for me, arms open. A part of me desperately wanted to miss this flight.

But Magda had other plans.

"We're going to make this goddamn flight even if it means I drive on the shoulder of the highway and we get a speeding ticket! You're going to Ireland today!" she said, stepping on the gas pedal—only to encounter traffic a few feet ahead and stopping short on the brakes once again.

"No speed ticket, Magda!" my parents both yelped in the backseat, hanging tight to the side handle bars and preparing to brace themselves for another rollercoaster ride. Two traffic cops donning bright orange vests stood near us and directed Magda to merge into the neighboring lane. Cars inched up toward the Lincoln Tunnel at glacier speed in this lane. Magda popped her head out the window, and in her abrasive manner, started cursing and telling cars to, "Go already!"

If there ever were to be a picture in Webster's Dictionary for road rage, a headshot of Magda with her limbs sticking out of this vehicle would be an appropriate example.

A Con Edison van stood a few feet away, and a manhole was covered with a tall, orange cone, steam piping out several hundred feet above it. Several more traffic cones lined the lane, and cars were merging into our lane. Magda relinquished, yielding to the drivers merging in front. The sound of faint sirens could be heard too. Magda looked in the rearview mirror and saw a police car a few miles away.

"Slow down!" balked my dad, as his head jerked back and forth with the motion of the minivan, before turning to my mom and saying things in Chinese I didn't understand, his tone aggressive.

Once through the tunnel, Magda floored the minivan. My parents fell forward, quickly ricocheting back thanks to their seatbelts. My dad let out a loud, "Aiyah!"—an expression a Chinese person makes when they are surprised, startled, scared, or have experienced something unpleasant…like riding in the backseat of Magda's minivan while she rushed to get me to Newark International Airport.

My father helped unload the minivan and bring my two extra-large suitcases into the lobby of Delta's terminal. They were calling my name when we arrived, and my father couldn't stop bellowing, "Your name! Go, Go, Go, Go, Go!" while Magda was illegally parking her minivan right outside.

"C'mon, let's take one family photo together," Magda insisted as she strolled into the lobby, ignoring the airport security following closely behind her.

With some hesitation, clearly vexed by Magda illegally parking the car the way she did, my father responded, "Hurrrry, hurrrrry."

In a rushed, awkward manner, we stood next to each other, my parents each embracing one shoulder. My father extended his arm as far as possible and hastily snapped a family photo with Magda's digital camera. Mom's face was partially cut out, Magda flashed the peace sign, and Dad's eyes weren't looking at the camera—he had struggled to hit the flash button—but hey, we were all kind of in the photo together.

"I'm going to miss you biatch. Don't forget to write. Call. E-mail. Fax," Magda said as she gave me a big bear hug.

Before I could turn around, she pulled a bottled jar of spicy cabbage from her purse. "It's from my mom and me. We know you're going to miss kimchi in Ireland."

I smiled, and hugged her. Then grabbed it, turned around, and ran toward the gates.

At security, after much begging with travelers ahead of me who were kind enough to let me through, I ran towards the gate, zig-zagging between other passengers, dodging luggage, and almost knocking over a toddler. They announced my name again. When I finally arrived, a young woman in her purple uniform gave me a warm smile and held her hand out for my ticket.

Out of breath and panting, I handed her my ticket with my head hanging low. She let me through with a silent nod. Soon after boarding, the door behind me closed. The universe was once again shepherding me in my move to Dublin, Ireland.

Six hours, one sore neck, and severely missing Nate later, I awoke in what was the middle of the night for me at the tarmac of Dublin International Airport in their early morning. Me—by myself—in a foreign country. This was really happening. Did I just leave everything behind? It hadn't dawned on me until the apathetic customs agent looked at me and requested my documents in a swift, Irish voice—like I was in line for some kind of inspection to determine if I was fit enough to enter his country.

"What are you doing in Ireland?" he asked.

My voice—too hoarse from being overly dehydrated on the seven-hour flight—attempted to speak, but nothing came out. I literally couldn't tell him about the job I had just accepted, that I didn't know much about, yet still moved across continents for... nor my hopes of getting back together with Nate, that moving here was all part of my long-term strategy of providing a distraction to Nate until he realized what he was missing before running into my arms across the lush, rolling green hills of the Irish countryside underneath a rainbow. Instead, I handed the officer my passport with my work visa folded and tucked into the first page, my airplane ticket falling out of my pocket as I fumbled for my documents. After inspecting it—comparing the photo of the girl to the photo in the passport whose name appeared in the documents—he said, "Welcome to Ireland."

Welcome to Ireland. *Welcome to Ireland?* This was the start of a new personal journey for me, surrounded by lots and lots of corned beef, cabbage, fluffy white sheep, Guinness, and rainbows. Maybe I would acclimate to all this rather quickly, as if I had some type of past life connection there that was calling me back, now reincarnated in this Asian body that also loved cabbage. Maybe I would get over Nate.

I showed the printout of the hotel name to my cab driver: Trinity City Hotel, Dublin, City Centre. The folded e-mail from corporate titled "Welcome" had specific instructions to check in and charge their corporate card while I looked for an apartment. Recoiled in the back seat of the taxicab with one of my large suitcases—which neither fit in the trunk or front seat of the car—the middle-aged Irish driver started making his way through what looked like a dreary, desolate city. He asked where I was from and what brought me there. He'd probably never seen an Asian American before because when I told him I was from New York City, he continued to ask the same question in different ways, "So, love, where ye parents from?" "Where did ye move from before New York?" "What language do you speak?" "What brings ye here?" "Where ye really from?"

Unbeknownst to me, my head fell forward, and I was soon rudely dozing off before responding to the remainder of his questions. The sound of light rain hitting the car windows startled me every so often. We passed what looked like an indefinite amount of vacant land with some trees, a handful of homes and commercial buildings scattered across randomly. Where were the rolling green hills?

Dazed and confused and being in a somewhat deja-vu-like state, I forgot where I was when I continued to look out the window: "Baile Átha Cliath." The cab driver followed the road signs and had stopped talking to me by this point.

Thirty minutes later, we passed a statue of a voluptuous woman wheeling something in a cart, and the driver dropped me off in front of a hotel with the same name that was in my notes: *Trinity City Hotel.*

The taxi driver helped with my bags and then drove off. I was alone—really alone. It felt like the first day of my freshman year of college when my family dropped me off at my dorm room in

West Campus and then drove off, leaving me behind. Only this time, there was no Nate or Magda.

It was lonely and scary. I shouldn't have been surprised. It was exactly what I wanted—or so I thought. A new chapter. A new chapter to get away from Nate. But part of me really didn't want to go. All I had left was the same thing that brought me here: myself. As my eyes wandered the four-story, prison-like brick building, I felt a warm tear slowly fall onto my cheek. Then another, and another…and another. I plopped onto a bench, sobbing and exhaling uncontrollably. What was I doing? What the hell was I doing? I continued until I remembered all the reasons why I left. In the depths of my cry, I allowed myself to smile. There was no one around me. It was too early even for the tourists. Shops were still closed, and few cars were on the road. I gathered my belongings and stepped into the Trinity City Hotel.

CHAPTER 5

The Nightmare

I was running away from something when I encountered a dense, foggy forest. I continued to run, turning my head every so often, getting lost in these behemoth trees with the biggest trunks I'd ever seen. My heart was beating quickly, and I had difficulty breathing, clearly scared, when suddenly, a venomous Burmese snake with Nate's head jumped out at me. He bit me in the leg, leaving me to slowly die. I awoke and sat straight up in the hotel bed, sweat breaking from my forehead, heart still pounding, at exactly 4:44 AM, an omen in Chinese that meant *death, death, death.*

Hours later, I still couldn't get out of bed. I couldn't escape the nightmare. The nightmare of Nate. He slowly killed me in my dreams, and now, in real life, he was killing my soul—all the way here in Ireland. It wasn't a good sign. *Please, Universe, please give me a different sign; a sign that I'm supposed to be here.* A sign that Nate still loved me and would come back to me. I felt sad and incomplete, wondering whether this move was my futile attempt at escaping "real life."

What made me think I would be any happier here, escaping the one person I was hopelessly trying to win back? And working with a woman whom I knew nothing about (except that she enjoyed getting drunk off Montepulciano wine) at a company I knew nothing of in a job I couldn't even describe thousands of miles away from the love of my life?

I lay awake in that bed, soaking in my own sweat from the cataclysmic heartbreak of Nate. This dream had to mean something.

I thought I still wanted to marry Nate. Why was I letting him kill me then?

I couldn't stop thinking of him. Nate's birthday was coming up. I wanted to send him something sweet so he would miss me and think about me—maybe a torn page from the scrapbook he made for me years earlier, with "Ireland" written on one of the blank pages and a photo of me next to the Spire, smiling, pretending to be happy, complete with a note that said: *Ireland isn't the same without you.*

Last year, at Nate's twenty-ninth birthday bash, he pulled me onto the dance floor when Alicia Keys's "New York" song began to play, and whispered into my ear, "We have to start shopping for rings." Somehow, Alicia Keys had been the inspiration to take our relationship to the next step (maybe I should have played this in the background when he came back to the apartment before I left). But how did we go from "we have to start shopping for rings" to "I think we need a break"? It was confusing, misleading, and most of all, disheartening. The last 365 days played like a loop in my head as I tried to analyze the scenes repeatedly, wondering if there was any single event that triggered Nate. Was it the pernicious influence of work? Did he do this because I was unhappy, or because *he* was unhappy?

I wanted to marry Nate.

We had built a life over the last eleven years—a good life, so I thought. Nate and I had meticulously discussed the big house in the 'burbs that we were diligently working toward. "Next year" would be the year we would get married and put a down payment on a four-bedroom, white-picket-fence home in Connecticut with an organic garden in the back where, finally, I could grow my own cabbage for kimchi. We had imagined our vast network of friends and family coming over every weekend, sprawled out in the lawn chairs by the infinity pool. Nate would grill as I filled up sangria glasses while our three children—Carrie, Larry, and Mary—ran around. On weekdays, I would drive the minivan and drop each of the kids off at school before making the hour-long drive into the city to the law firm. We had just moved in together into a one-bedroom in Battery Park City, making regular weekend trips to Home Depot for more DIY home projects. It was one step closer to that American dream—my American dream—of being the all-you-can-be, do-it-all, superwoman mom/housewife/attorney/homeowner/maid/gardener.

I wanted to marry Nate.

It was worth sacrificing my "career happiness" for—and completely normal to have ambivalent and hostile feelings about—

work. Right? I reconciled this thought with the fact that I didn't know one person at the law firm who really wanted to be there. However, the cost was greater to not be there, and I wanted this life so badly. Any other rendition of this life was foreign to me, and immediately rejected.

One afternoon, some mystical energy by way of Magda's voice forced me out of bed.

"Mag, I need to talk!" I said, slouched backward, unable to move even an inch and still in pajamas.

"You pop your Guinness Irishman virginity yet?" Magda was in an obnoxious line filled with dozens of eager people at a Jimmy Choo sample sale when she picked up my phone call. All I could hear was the muffled screaming, and then finally a victorious sigh of relief on her end when she told me she had scored the latest patent pumps (beige). I wondered if Mag found anything cute in my size.

"I haven't done anything—or anyone—here, yet, Mag. I had a terrible dream. Nate was killing me, and I haven't been able to get out of bed since." The sun was just beginning to set. The sounds of chatter were loud by the window, and the *Irish Times* still lay outside the hotel door, unread.

"Stop moping, Rach!"

It was easy for Magda to say. What did she know about heartbreaks? She only ever had one relationship and that lasted barely eighteen months.

"Do you know how lucky you are? Luckier than a box of Irish Lucky Charms! You're in Ireland, the land of beer, sheep, and magically delicious Irishmen. Put on your best outfit and go to a pub. Right now. Go. *Go*. You desperately need a drink. Talk to a cute guy while you're there too. Have a Guinness. For *me*. Each time you think of that bastard Nate, drink!"

What was wrong with drowning in a self-indulged state of self-loathing pity with a side of pessimism?

After mustering up a little bit of strength, I walked into Dublin's city center alone, getting lost and following the maze-like roads across the River Liffey. I was in search of a pub, which shouldn't have been difficult to find since I was in Ireland, but I was too distraught by the idea of not marrying Nate that I kept walking past several without realizing they were pubs. Finally, I walked into one.

CHAPTER 6

The Luck of the Irish

The first lesson I learned in Ireland was this: never turn down an offer of Guinness at a pub, especially if the National Futbol Team of the drink-offeror just scored. I didn't even have to order a drink each time I thought about Nate, because the beer kept flowing toward me.

Not that I knew anything about futbol—I normally spelled it "football"—or pubs or Guinness. I wanted to stay inside the hotel, much preferring to order room service, mope, and watch reruns of Irish soap operas I had never even heard of.

But something strange happened when I walked into the pub—a sort of epiphany overcame me. Magda was right. This was exactly what I so desperately needed. The Irish pubs were filled with something called "crack" (spelled c-r-a-i-c). Craic meant fun in Ireland, didn't refer to an illegal substance, and was used differently than, "It's not all that's cracked up to be." People said it often here—"Eh, what's the craic?"—and it took some getting used to.

At first, I'd look at them and bite my tongue, trying hard not to conjure up images of needles and tourniquets.

A young Dubliner with orange-green-white face paint and a prepubescent looking chest turned toward me, his hands holding up a larger-than-life Irish flag, started chanting what sounded like Greek to me, and raised his arms in unison with his other friends nearby, screaming, "Sláinte!" (pronounced "Slan-cha") into my face before slamming a pint of Guinness into my chest.

"No, thank you."

"I dun take no for an answer," he said. "It's bad luck, ye know."

I was reluctant. Unable to move, my body was sandwiched between an older woman donned in a shirt with the colors of the Irish flag and the warrior-painted, wannabe-soccer players, when one of them passed me his Guinness. "Sláinte!" he said, "Now, go on, take a sip," so that his team could score again.

My heart pounded. I grimaced unintentionally, but not because of the beer–more so because I had no idea where his lips had been. With bated breath, I took a sip of the super bitter, heavy beverage and promptly returned the stout to him—abruptly wiping my lips with my opposite forearm thereafter.

His team didn't score again, and I don't know if the Irish reveled in drinking more than the actual game of futbol itself, because they still downed a pint. When their team didn't score, they downed a pint. When their team did score, they downed two more pints. When someone walked into the pub, they drank. When their team lost, they lingered...to down more pints with each other in an obvious attempt to drown their sorrow. That was a whole lot of pint-drinking. No wonder there was a convenient mechanism to escaping this inebriating insanity. It was called the "Irish Exit."

When you were in the middle of a random pub, with strangers squeezed at each of your shoulders, exchanging saliva via their Guinnesses, if one left to get more said Guinness, that was your opportunity to leave. There was no goodbye. No thank you. No, "I had great craic."

And that's exactly what I did. I left. No goodbye. No thank you. No, "It was nice meeting you, I had great craic." Truth was, I did have great craic. My first Irish craic, despite the heaviness in my heart and the diseases I may have caught. I did not see that group of futbol lovers again, but wondered if in the distant future, some of them would appear in an Alcoholics Anonymous meeting.

I began walking back to the hotel room, alone, with only the faint sound of debaucherous revelers drowning out the evening behind me. I encountered the Ha'penny Bridge, named appropriately so because toll collectors used to charge a half-penny toll to cross it. It was a beautiful evening—and odd, seeing as the sun only began to set at 10:00 PM. Leaning against the railing halfway across the bridge, I looked across the River Liffey. The water reflected what looked like a double, orange-purple hue rainbow.

A weird, surreal feeling enveloped me. Was this really my new home? And did I just enjoy myself, even temporarily? I felt at odds, guilty if you will, as if I should've instead been serving a multi-year sentence for leaving everything back home...especially Nate. I wondered if—when—I returned to my real home in shame, the jurors, comprising of just my mother, would read aloud my guilty verdict of, "I told you so!"

Those first days in Ireland hit me like a tsunami with no warning, slowly gaining speed before intensifying on the shorelines of my new life. I kept wondering about the "what ifs" and the "what should have beens." I couldn't ignore the question gnawing at the pit of my stomach: Was my life, in fact, better here? It didn't feel better. It didn't look better. But this other part of me began to soon emerge. The part of me who introduced herself by saying, "Hi Rachel, we've never met before. I've resided here all your life—all *my* life—but I never came out. Well today, I am coming out, usurping back my territory, proclaiming an emancipation from my wicked contemporaries who have kept me enslaved all these years in the dark corner of your brain. I'm going to build a big Noah's—*Nate's*—ark for you. But Nate will not be invited to take refuge from the massive deluge of heartbreak happening. You shall bring your heart, your soul, your hopes, your dreams, and your dignity. For the next forty days and forty nights, you shall be shielded from the violence and destruction of World War Nate because it's *OK.*

"*It's OK to be selfish!* It's *OK* to put yourself first. It's *OK* to expect all the things you expected from Nate because that bastard made promises to you, but you should manage your expectations differently in life. Life is full of disappointments. There will be more, *trust me*, and you will be OK." I was beginning to like this new self. I thought Magda would too. She resembled a cross between a pious Confucius and a motivational coach when she started saying things like:

Wheresoever you go, go with all your heart.

Which meant Ireland. I needed to be here with all my heart and not let pitiful, dismal sulking distract me.

Remember that sometimes not getting what you want is a wonderful stroke of luck.

Of course, referring to no other but Nate himself.

Choose a job you love, and you will never have to work a day in your life.

I hope the job I chose—that didn't even have a job description—will be a job I love!

To my surprise, the double rainbow drowned my soul with a calming, reassuring energy, and brought out the Confucius in me. For the first time in my life, I felt like things would be OK. I interpreted it as a sign from the universe as 1) it rained *a lot* in Ireland, and 2) "Yes, yes you belong here. You belong here and you are ready for your transformation in life. Stop worrying. Stop sulking over Nate. Your new life begins here. *Now*. Your unknown job that starts on Monday will be full of excitement and new challenges."

An automated message soon arrived in my inbox from the human resources department: "Congratulations! You have chosen to work in a wonderful organization with a talented and successful team. We promise you a fast-paced, challenging workplace where your skills and abilities will be developed and challenged."

I was experiencing a wild gyration of emotions, my heart reacting in tandem with the uneasiness of wondering what this job would be like. Would I succeed? Would I have the right skill sets? Would they like me? Did some of those skills and abilities involve tolerating a bunch of beer drinkers every night and getting used to the more than seventeen hours of daylight descending into my room each day? Why didn't Claire warn me? Why wasn't there some kind of training manual that would have listed this as one of the pre-requisites of the new job? I would have come prepared with a bulk of melatonin had I known.

For the first time in my new Ireland life, I wanted to go to sleep early. Work started tomorrow, but I couldn't fall asleep. My circadian rhythm was completely thrown off by the sunlight coming in; it felt as if I just chugged a double shot of Red Bull vodka tonight. My mind raced at 100 mph with thoughts and anxiety about the unknown job, and of course, my future with Nate.

I imagined myself being in that big, protective ark. I pictured my new self replacing the "I want to marry Nate" mantra with "I want to succeed in my new job. I want to fit in. I want to be liked. I want to meet new Irish friends. I want to love Ireland! I want to go to sleep." Saying this over and over again acted as a sort of mental exercise—an effort toward and a hope of all these things actually manifesting.

In my feeble attempt to calm down, I stared at the sun shining relentlessly into my room, reflecting off my belongings and spilling onto the extra-large suitcases and my perfect "first day outfit," laying on top of the pile near the window.

But the loud, garrulous drunks laughing and "taking the piss" (Irish slang for joking, though with all that beer they were drinking, they would be taking *that* piss too) were outside my room at the pub that was "just a stone's throw away."

"Whet my whistle with a Guinness," I overheard one say. "While you're there, get me another too, you slag." It sounded like a cacophony of drunken discord, with the glasses hitting each other and a few, occasionally, being shattered on the cobblestone streets while the sun was just beginning to set.

Please, go home, I thought. *Please.* It's past ten o'clock, for God's sake! Some of us have jobs and early bedtimes and important things to manifest! Why are you drinking so much anyway? It's not healthy for your livers!

To my dismay, each one of them ignored my telepathic pleas and seemed to—instead—laugh harder in my face while they continued to imbibe more.

At some point in the middle of my internal condemnation, I fell asleep berating these strangers, who were clearly having Irish craic.

CHAPTER 7

The Job in Ireland

Getting ready for my new job the next morning felt like a multi-year war with my body. It refused to get up, ready to fight me off when my mind declared independence and condemned my body for trying to wrestle sovereignty away from me. I pleaded with my immobile body: "Get up!" It fought back with a powerful coup of rebels and told me to come back next week. My body lay there. This went back and forth until my own personal manifesto of independence overthrew myself in a distressed raid and I got up, successfully usurping the failed coup-d'état.

I wasn't ready for the first day of my new job.

It felt like the longest hour of getting ready, sludging through the pains and doctrines of sleepiness, fighting with my comb and toothbrush, too weary to shower, and wrestling the clothes that were already out. I applied tons of foundation in hopes of covering the obvious bags underneath my eyes, which looked like they had been part of a revolutionary guerilla warfare.

Coffee. I needed coffee. Did they drink coffee in Ireland? I didn't see any coffee shops on my walk, until I finally did—a feat in and of itself. Finding coffee was surely a sign I had emerged victorious from the sloths of war.

I picked up the desperately needed cup of coffee handed to me from over the counter and brought it close enough to my face to feel the steam going through my pores. I inhaled deeply then pushed through the glass doors as I attempted to rub away the obvious reflection of lack of sleep. I anxiously watched the street up and down each time, hoping a cab driver would drive by. God, I wish there were Ubers here. Just as I was about to let my hand that was out signaling for a taxi drop, I let out a deep sigh of relief as the car pulled over just a few feet away. I let my head lean against the window while I fidgeted with the top of the coffee cup, thinking about what was to come with the rest of the day.

I entered what looked like a corporate campus. Why was everyone staring at me? It was the bags under my eyes…I was sure of it. I should have worn more makeup. Two noticeably anxious recruits sitting opposite me tried hard to look away, but my peripheral vision was sharp enough to notice them turning back toward me, only to see them turn quickly and mumble things to themselves, assumingly pretending to rehearse regurgitated responses to interview questions. Were they there to meet with Claire too?

One looked vaguely familiar, and had a strange resemblance to me, which was certainly odd because I didn't know anyone in

Dublin. His face was flustered red, seemingly from nervousness. He had a pair of beautiful brown eyes, a full head of black hair, and southern-Asian cheekbones (a feature I've become apt in discerning with all the KTV karaoke music videos I had been watching). He was extraordinarily tall, with humongous hands.

He must have noticed me in a "I recognize your curious stare" sort of way, because he blurted out, "Hi, I'm Aaron. I'm from Seattle." I wanted to know where he was "really from" because those cheekbones didn't exactly scream "Seattle." He fidgeted and moved closer from his seat. Another few recruits sitting in the opposite end of the room were mostly ignoring this interaction, flipping through Irish magazines as if they were in some medical waiting room waiting to be called in for surgery.

One candidate sitting closer to us with dirty-blonde hair, who appeared to be a "Dubliner," (not that I had become the expert at discerning a Dubliner, but during my week here thus far, it was a skill I was quickly picking up) leaned in as if to eavesdrop. She anxiously looked away before our eyes could meet.

"My parents are from Hong Kong. I was born in San Francisco, and moved to Seattle when I was five," Aaron said. My eyes seemed to have lit with an "aha, I know your kind; I swear I'm not a racist" look. He was close enough to my kind of Asian that sitting nearby made me feel at ease. Aaron, an Asian American from the United States, became my first friend in Ireland.

The receptionist made eye contact with me and gestured that she'd be another moment. When her phone rang continuously, one right after the other, she gave me an apologetic look with her big, brown puppy eyes. She was so adorable, with rosy, pink cheeks, freckles you'd only find in Ireland, and long, golden locks. Her name tag read Sinead.

"Hi, I'm here for Helen Waite. I was told to ask for her upon my..."

She flashed a smile and a "hang on just a moment" look before I could ecstatically shake her hand.

Her boss's voice could be overheard on one of those calls, and it sounded overbearing. Perhaps this was what made some of the recruits look away in fear. The team who recruited me was led by Hilda. I was right; Hilda was the boss.

"Sorry 'bout dat. The calls dun stop, ye know?"

I nodded.

"Welcome to Ireland. Now, don't be intimidated by Hilda. Oh, Helen Waite, yeah, she transferred to the German office two weeks ago."

She gestured her hand for me to come closer, so I moved forward.

"Hilda fired her analyst last year because he called in sick after St. Patrick's Day...."

A new job recruit entered and took a seat next to Aaron. I leaned over the receptionist's desk intently.

"Poor guy didn't even know he was fired. He came in the following morning—still ill—only to learn his access had been shut off by IT. Couldn't get through any of the buildings, and security had to lead him out."

My heart started palpitating.

"Poor lad never even had the chance to retrieve his belongings."

I took a deep breath.

"She will cut you off in meetings and just stare at you with demon eyes. She thinks everyone else is *stupid*."

I gulped my own saliva.

"She actually tells everyone else that they're stupid."

I stepped back.

Before I could ask Sinead about the job description, Hilda approached me, extended her hand to shake mine, and said in a deep monotone, "Welcome to WilHeltek Commerz." She looked different in person. She was barely five-feet tall, petite, vociferously stout, wore her dark-blonde hair in a braid, and had heavy green eyeshadow to mask what appeared to be mid- to late-thirties wrinkles.

Sinead whispered "Good luck" to me, before she tensely turned away, pretending to pick up a phone call. The other recruits didn't dare look up to make eye contact. From a distance, Aaron picked up an Irish magazine and started flipping through it.

Hilda marched toward a conference room without saying a word. I followed not far behind. The photo Mag found of her online did no justice to the in-person "resting bitch face" I was experiencing. Her full name was Hilda Künt, and in three short years, she had expanded the company's EU offices to Dublin, Ireland, where she was the head of sales. In that duration, she tripled the company's revenue by winning the business of a handful of e-commerce giants. Hilda was known to be a pit bull at closing deals, and it was no surprise she rose through the ranks as rapidly as she did. She was recently appointed by the executive board to open their Shanghai office too.

Employees who walked by us kept their heads down low, clutching notebooks tightly to their chests as they brushed by. No one had a smile on their face.

I quickly learned that the teams that reported to her—already twenty people within the Dublin office—dreaded their weekly Tuesday morning meetings with her. She was curt, serious, tenaciously demanding, and demeaning. Some employees had panic attacks or drank themselves to sleep the night before (I saw why people here hit the pubs almost every day). Hilda didn't smile, laugh, or make any jokes. She wanted to see results—preferably illustrated in ROYGBIV colors laid out in PowerPoint decks. If she wasn't happy with the results or with your response, you'd know. She just kind of stared back blankly at you, her eyes and eventually her mouth screaming, "You're stupid."

Occasionally, her unfiltered comments—like "Vat the hell iz this?"—filled the room. But at least all team members were equally criticized in front of each other. It was her way of motivating the team and not caring about anyone's feelings. A few senior executives unabashedly left the room in tears. "Not enough thick skin!" you'd hear her scream.

If you were unprepared for these meetings or didn't show up, you best not bother attending the next one.

Hilda was looking for someone to assist with efforts expanding into China. It was still unclear what the department did or what my specific job title would be. She sat there, silent and expressionless for several moments, like a centuries-old limestone erect in front of me.

"What kind of Chinese do you speak?" she demanded, eyes still looking downward at the resume she pulled up for me.

"Cantonese," I abruptly replied. More silence followed before she glanced over to the second page of my resume.

"Is that the kind that's spoken in Shanghai?" she retorted, now putting on a pair of thick glasses and examining the "language skills" section of my resume. She pressed her lips firmly and frowned, her thick eyebrows pulling together closely.

"No, but I understand that kind too." This was sort of a white lie because I really was not proficient in *that kind of* Chinese, but I was nervous and couldn't tell Hilda otherwise. I really ought to have been proficient in that kind of Chinese, especially after a summer studying under "Master Chan" in Beijing, and the countless attempts of my Tiger Mom (if you have no idea what I mean by this, imagine being raised by the strictest, most overachieving parent, who will do whatever it takes, including removing any form of normal childhood fun, to raise a child to excel in the highest echelons of academic and extracurricular achievement, even if it meant sacrificing Saturday morning cartoons for more schooling). She would show me colorful pictures of dumplings, mountains, and horses—more suited for a five-year-old—instructing me to raise the accent on the third tone, not the fourth, "or else." She would then point to the shape of the photo—"You see? The Chinese character look like the horse." I didn't see it…at all.

The Chinese language just did not come naturally to me. Spanish did. Latin did. But Chinese did not, for my seemingly native Chinese tongue. When I was not in the presence of Master Chan or my Tiger Mother, I pretended not to know any Chinese because it was easier to get around in English, which explained why I was barely a B student in his class and had a habit of skipping his classes altogether. I could maybe order a bowl of fatty-pork dumplings in *that kind of* Chinese, but even then, a bowl of fatty pig intestines drenched in soy sauce might come out instead.

Was Hilda looking for a Chinese translator to place in one of her call centers? I didn't dare ask her. I was too scared. Richard Branson's famous statement, "If somebody offers you an amazing opportunity but you are not sure you can do it, say yes—then learn how to do it later," came to mind, though it was questionable whether this was an amazing opportunity or not.

My mind started conjuring up all kinds of "Chinese" from the depths and cavities of my brain where any Chinese vocabulary might uselessly be stored in. "你好你 要森麼?" There, I think I remembered something meaningful. It's supposed to translate into, "Hi, how are you?" Master Chan would be proud. It was a start, right?

CHAPTER 8

Sent from My Blackberry

"How are things going?"
Sent from my Blackberry

I received an e-mail from Nate in the middle of my third workday. I was sipping bitter American coffee—which I finally found in the small WilHeltek Commerz canteen—and found his email, curt and cold, just like the coffee. I placed the mug down. I stared at the email, motionless, feeling sucker-punched one too many times in the depths of my heart. It felt more like a message between two former acquaintances-turned-strangers, separated by an ocean of time and a signature that should have instead read, "Sent from the callous corners of my heart."

How are things going? *How are things going*?! I'll tell you how they're going. You pretty much paralyzed me since we last spoke. I haven't eaten. I haven't slept (though the amount of sunlight here may have also been a factor). I may have to learn a new kind of Chinese. I have been miserable. *Miserable!* It was the worst of times, and it was...well, the worst of times. I've wasted a good chunk of my new life here moping and hoping you would reach out to me, even if in a brusque manner, because I just wanted to hear from you. Even if you accidentally butt-dialed me, seeing your name appear on my screen would have been like putting a small bandage on the gaping hole in my heart. But now that I've finally heard from you, I don't *want* to hear from you! I am angry with you! Livid! Annoyed! *Really* angry! *I hate you!*

You put me through unimaginable pain, as if you went straight for my jugular vein, cutting off any circulation and leaving me on the streets of this foreign country to die.... But none of these words came out. I continued to stare motionless at those four words.

"Who's de lad?" asked Keil O'Grady, a nosey financial analyst on my floor who walked by my desk and read aloud the email I had open in fourteen-point font. Keil sat nearby, which meant he passed by my office about a hundred times a day whenever he went to the supply room, the kitchen, or the bathroom (the latter he went to frequently, thanks to all that tea). My screen was in full view through the clear glass doors.

The heavy winds of heartbreak threw my ark from side to side. I didn't respond to Nate. I couldn't. I was too numb—and angry—from heartache. Plus, I was distracted by Keil walking into my office, standing over me and waiting for an answer.

His curiosity didn't abate, even when I ignored him. He continued to press, "Who's de lad?" My newly triggered anger was redirected at other facets of life in Ireland, and I continued to ignore Keil as I stormed out for an early lunch. But it was difficult experiencing all these angry thoughts at work. I was still new, which meant I had to put on my "enthusiastic new employee face." A face completely obliterated by the recent world war I had fought—and lost—but I wouldn't dare reveal at my new job.

WilHeltek Commerz felt like a college campus, complete with twenty-somethings who thrived equally on social events and drama. This was a potential new start with new people who wanted to be friends. They were anxious to be friends. They were also starved of gossip and prepared for their new job by sharpening their ears and unraveling their mouths. The girl next to me came from Finland, and the girl who sat next to her came from Spain. They had just become roommates in the Ballsbridge neighborhood of Dublin—a fact I only learned of when Keil stepped into my office (again).

Did I really need new friends, though? Did they need to know about Nate? I was a very private person and tried my best to keep to myself. I didn't want to recap the details of that war, and thought I could avoid doing so. After all, I technically reported directly to Künt, who was based in Germany but was in Ireland frequently enough through Hendrik, her right-hand officer, to make me want to call out sick once a month for what would surely be perceived as painful cramps by my other colleagues. I was a satellite in Dublin. An orphan. An anchor. A nobody. I could sulk in sadness alone and not mingle with anyone. I still didn't know what I was doing, job-wise and life-wise.

The "Welcome to WilHeltek Commerz, please join our walk-athon!" and "Welcome to WilHeltek Commerz, please come for happy hour!" emails clogged my inbox, continuously marked as "unread." When random colleagues—whose names were as fleeting as the recent message from Nate—appeared in my office, reminding me to join these new activities, I gave them any excuse as to why I couldn't join: *I'm not feeling well. I have a long-distance call with my parents.... I can't. I can't. I can't.*

I needed an escape. I did what any new employee would do on her third day. I went shopping in the nearby plaza and pondered important things, like why didn't stores provide you grocery bags with your groceries? What the hell was the "value added" tax for? Why were portions here so small? My "Americanness" spoiled me. I missed the bigger-than-life, family-size items that I was so accustomed to seeing at the membership-only warehouse clubs back home. It made me wonder why in the world anyone would drink from a shot-glass-like, paltry, eight-ounce cup...or only eat three ounces of beef. The bigger, the better, right? Apparently not here. Stores weren't open seven days a week, nor was there a Chinatown with endless roast meats hanging from a window that satisfied your 3:00 AM post-drinking, duck cravings. (Yes, that was a thing, and the Irish didn't know what they were missing out on)!

I wanted big things. I wanted roast duck. I wanted grocery bags with my groceries without having to pay on top of the value added tax. I wanted, I wanted, I wanted.... I wanted to be left alone. How could Nate do this to me?

There wasn't time to be irritated by all these things, though. I still needed an Irish mobile phone, and I needed to file paperwork at some government office to register and officialize my Irish employment. In the middle of my vexed and vain attempt to settle back into my office, an email notification came in:

> *Rachel,*
>
> *You have your stay at the Trinity Hotel until this Sunday, June 19.*
>
> *Hilda*

Two weeks? *Two weeks*, Hilda? I couldn't respond.... I didn't know how to without engaging in political intercourse and, ultimately, losing. I imagined responding how I really felt:

> *Hilda,*
>
> *Umm, may I have a few more weeks, please? You only gave me two weeks to acclimate to life in a new country, find a new place to live, potentially learn Mandarin—a new kind of Chinese I was not even proficient in—get an Irish mobile, and to obtain my government ID number when virtually all offices were closed on Sunday! Here is a list of things I would*

need so I don't have to retrace the steps of Leopold Bloom himself along Dublin Bay to discern which neighborhood would be most suited for a girl like me to live in:

1- *A relocation stipend;*

2- *A map of Dublin with a description of each neighborhood;*

3- *A list of available flats and prices;*

4- *A moving service;*

5- *Furniture;*

6- *A new LG microwave.*

Did you know I was going through a breakup too? A nonmutual, completely his idea, kind of "break" that was causing the life to be depleted out of my non-Irish veins. And I still didn't know what you hired me for! No one from the German office has made contact with me since arriving and I dare not ask. So please, may I have an additional two weeks along with all the assistance I can have?

Rachel

There was an uncomfortable amount of uneasiness—and anger—pent up within me. Anger that led to stress—stress that created a Berlin Wall between me and my new work—which would ultimately eat me up from the inside out. Two weeks was not much time, and I didn't have the words or the willpower to ask for more time. It took me a long time to do things. It took two weeks to pack my life into two extra-large suitcases and a carry-on to move here. To leave a cushy, corporate job.... To wait for some form of (in)human contact from Nate. And now, I had two weeks to find a new flat?

Maybe I would end up with a roommate, a stranger from this office who would share with the entire office the devastating heartbreak the "new Asian Yank" was going through before they all pointed and laughed at me with some sort of Irish or European accent. I couldn't face them. I didn't want to. I had a terrible secret and needed to hide the sins of my sadness and morally weak character from everyone.

As my sadness intensified, my inner Confucius Coach began to emerge.

"Rachel, me again, overpowering the voices in your head once again. Calm down. Take deep breaths. Take really deep breaths. Don't be angry. The Irish are a good bunch. Keil is a good guy. He lives with and cares for his grandma. Your other colleagues are a good bunch too. They save on electricity, water, and waste. You Americans are all wasteful and don't need the supersized food/household items/beverages and double grocery bags for each item you buy. You're a do-gooder at heart. I know this. I met her. She still resides there and wants to do good. They recycle here, too."

I took a deep breath at my desk while my emails continued to come in and prayed to the WilHeltek Commerz heavens for even a little bit of "Irish luck" that would reverse this negativity I was experiencing. Would this luck be destined to rub off on me here? It was Ireland, after all. Or was I more apt to endure a spiritual famine of epic proportion because Ireland just wasn't my home? Either way, I thought: *Please, please guide me in my search here in Ireland. I need a home. A new home. A nice home. Preferably in a good neighborhood but not so good that the property taxes outweigh my financial ability to live here. Preferably close to my new job too. I also need a new mobile and to figure out where the customs office is. Please, if you could meet my moderately stressful demands within the timely timeframe of two weeks, I would be really grateful. If God built the universe in seven days, will he please, please, please grant a smidgeon of his superpower in helping me find a suitable flat, and finally setting my life up here? I promise it would make me happy—as if I know what that word means anymore, but still....*

Amen.

CHAPTER 9

The Orphan Employee

I reported to work promptly at 8:45 AM each morning, despite not having any clear guidance from Hilda or the team on what my responsibilities were. There was no Hilda or Hilda-equivalent to check in with at the Dublin office on most days. I was alone and had to figure everything out on my own. What made it more difficult was my sheer unwillingness to make office friends. It wasn't on purpose, necessarily, but I felt like everyone could sense my general negativity and had decided to avoid me like a newly discovered plague. My two colleagues—Tristan and Niamh—would make small talk with me at first. But after a week of utter silence from me, they ignored me.

I spent those days in the office searching for a flat. The Irish WilHeltek Commerz gods pushed me toward a prominent, Silicon Valley–created search engine. I started the search but became mired in my recurring thoughts—"Am I happier here? Am I not?"—and absently typed in a capital "C." A slew of hits appeared in the search engine, including "craic," which appeared right on top of: "Craigslist Ireland."

Craigslist Ireland. Of course! Craigslist had been my savior in college when I so hastily needed an apartment! I was relieved to see they had an international website.

But when I clicked to see what kind of "flats" there were, it was scantily populated. It offered a few houses for rent I couldn't afford, and a couple of advertisements for a "really good in-home massage." I guess they didn't *really* use Craigslist here. Was there some kind of Irish version of it I was not aware of? McCraigslist, maybe?

There had to be some other website, one that Irish locals used for letting out flats and advertising all sorts of nefarious and non-nefarious activities. My lack of intel about my new home was frustrating. I was frustrated. No searches seemed to return the more affable and affordable search results I so expected. I fell into another slump and deleted everything in front of me, as I did with most things I didn't want to confront in real life (like Nate, and the prospect-turned-reality of living in Ireland).

Once again, I didn't know where to start. I typed, then deleted, several key words before collapsing backward onto the uncomfortable chair and staring up at the bare ceiling of the office, letting out an exhausted sigh that prompted Tristan and Niamh to walk quickly by and pretend I wasn't there. An interminable amount of time had passed, and I still felt like I was chasing something I couldn't reach.

I admitted that I didn't feel any better being in Ireland.

The alarm I had set days ago went off loudly, like a car honking next to me, startling me out of my seat. It was a reminder that I had fewer than two weeks left at the Trinity Hotel.

I found myself in the women's bathroom of WilHeltek Commerz, and for the first time in a long time, I stared at myself in the full-length mirror. I didn't recognize her. She was ugly. I wanted to ask: *Who are you? What happened to you?* She stared back, fatigued—likely from her inability to sleep here—with heavy bags hanging under her eyes. Finally, from the corner of my eye, I watched her jerk the door open and attempt to flee back to her office downstairs.

That's when I encountered Sinead again. She was chatty and energetic, and unlike most of the people I had met in the office thus far, Sinead didn't appear to be a gossipmonger. She had this motherly aura about her when she asked, "You OK? Is everything grand?" before water started forming in my eyes. Right outside the ladies' room, I burst out, "No. No, it's not!"

Sinead took the rest of the afternoon off, risking her own employment when she told Hilda she had a family emergency to tend to. Was I "family"? I didn't even know Sinead's surname. Even so, the gesture was unexpected, sweet, and the kindest thing a stranger could do for me—throw me a lifeline while I slowly drowned at work. She brought me to a canteen off campus, and we sat in a corner with two fresh hot cups of Bewley tea.

"I'm going through a divorce," she disclosed as she slowly sipped Bewley's tea. There was no one around, and it felt like she lifted the weight from my shoulders when she confided first in our newly formed confession corner. She continued to tell me about her ex's growing abuse, and her desire for separation finally outweighing her longing to have a child. I would have never guessed. She had a completely different demeanor in the office, often with an infectious smile as she picked up the phone and greeted strangers in the lobby.

"I'm lost," I admitted in response. "I'm lost in my love life. I'm lost in my career. I'm lost in Dublin—literally—and don't know where to start with my apartment search. I'm lost and I've been terrible to everyone here…absolutely, abysmally, abominably terrible. I think moving to Ireland was a mistake." I started tearing up in a trivial attempt to clear my conscience and amend my life, hoping my confession to Sister Sinead would solve my conundrum.

When she said, "Give it time," I imagined Sister Sinead meant, "May the merciful Lord have pity on thee and forgive thee thy faults." Then she held out her hand and drew several lines that eventually emulated a map of something familiar: Dublin. She explained how this area would be "too family oriented" and not "craic enough" for a twenty-nine-year-old like me.

Sinead started telling me about the different Irish neighborhoods, pronouncing the names like soliloquies, easily rolling off her tongue: "Droichead an Dothra," "Dalkey," "Dún Laoghaire." I tried to memorize all of them, but my brain got tangled with the unnatural sound of a language as foreign to me as Latin (though

I involuntarily studied Latin for two years under the auspices of Ms. Landree, who would be filled with disappointment if she knew her best student had forgotten everything). I took a napkin, turned it over, and asked Sinead to recite the neighborhoods again. Like a studious student who would soon forget the pronunciations, I asked her to repeat them in an attempt to take copious notes this time. Sinead looked at me and chuckled.

She directed me toward a different website, Daft.ie, where she suggested I consider a roommate. It would be a "great way to meet new friends," she said. A soft jazz tune began playing in the background as I caught a glimpse of the barista shuffling her playlist.

"I...yeah, I guess that's true...." I hesitated, taking a sip of my Bewley's tea. At this point, someone from the office walked in but hurried away, only making brief eye contact in our direction. After taking his order, the barista went back to reading a book. It was just us again.

Sinead gave me a couple of names of employees she knew of seeking roommates too, which I reluctantly accepted. The prospect of living with a roommate crossed my mind briefly, but I would not make a good roommate. No, I knew I would not make a good roommate. I left a trail of shoes in the hallway, as if it were my personal mark and way of announcing, "I'm home!"

Besides, I did laundry once a month; all my clothes were more often than not piled high, scattered throughout different areas of the room, left inside-out. They were their own landmines waiting to implode. It's the reason Nate insisted on hiring a weekly cleaning lady. I didn't even shower every day, and sometimes, I drank milk out of the container. I ate out of plastic containers too! I was considered in the American culture a "lazy slob." What would these roommates think about me? Maybe I was being paranoid. Maybe in the Irish culture, this was perfectly acceptable, and they would embrace such household "manners."

We continued sipping on our Bewley's tea and talking. A light drizzle began hitting the windowpane we were sitting near.

"You may want to follow up with human resources too, when you return. They can help you in locating a flat. But in the meantime, check out Daft.ie," she said calmly, with eyes that promised she would not share my sacramental confession to anyone.

CHAPTER 10

The Flat

A short, brunette Irish man drove toward me in a used, white van and stopped short at the Custom House Docks area, rolling down his window and introducing himself as Colin, the broker from Daft.ie.

"You must be Rachel." His smile was crooked, and he arched forward as he unlocked the backseat door. "Get in! I have a wonderful, newly built apartment for you!" The door began to slowly slide open. A cigarette butt rolled out onto the floor, and I hesitated to step inside as he continued to grin.

My heart began to beat faster. What did he have in the back of that van? Shovels, gardening gloves, garbage bags, victims? The New Yorker in me was telling me to *get the F*** out* and to tell him he had the wrong person. The gullible and forgiving side of me was telling me he was a cute, Irish man—they're not known to be serial killers, right? So, with hesitation, I climbed in, keeping my right hand by the door in case there was a need to jump out.

The real estate here in Ireland was booming.

"Where ya from?" he said, chewing loudly, eyes fixed on the road as we soon merged onto a freeway.

"New York," I responded, holding the handlebar tightly.

"You won't find a luxury, furnished, two-bed and two-bathroom, 1,300-square-foot duplex for nine hundred euros." There were what appeared to be homeless kids playing with abandoned tires and a semi-deflated soccer ball nearby, their belongings and an old cardboard box sprawled on the pavement. They seemed happy, though—genuinely happy—as they chased each other and uttered chaotic jokes in Irish, unaware of the squalor they were in. One young boy, no older than five, was quick with his feet as he maneuvered passed his friend. An adult was close by but was passed out on the floor.

We continued to drive away from the city center and into a more desolate area with lots of construction built midway. It didn't feel like the greatest area. And it was far...*far* from the city center we had just driven from. Colin turned right, then left, then passed several exits on the freeway. I wasn't paying much attention—I still had my hand on the door.

What felt like hours later, my hand now sore from clutching so hard, we arrived at a sprawling, luxury, glass high-rise overlooking a desolate, empty playground below. The building was new, equipped with the latest stainless-steel appliances, was styled with furniture imported from a DIY Swedish furniture company, had its own washer and dryer in each flat, provided sleek marble-top kitchens, boasted crown-molding throughout, and offered an Olympic-size indoor pool below and a state-of-the-art gym upstairs. I was relieved. He didn't kidnap me, and this building appeared nicer than anything I had ever lived in.

This was tempting, especially coming from a 500-square-foot cramped apartment in Manhattan where our living room intertwined with our bedroom and a coffee table acted both as a dining area and our office. I tried convincing myself this new flat could be kind of like the next East Williamsburg, New York—with restaurants, hip bars, and cool coffee shops (please!) finally springing up. A shuttle bus to Clontarf Station where my job was, was just steps outside. But instead of the bus, maybe I could be that "cool hipster" who saved the planet by biking to work every day.

Colin must have seen my eyes sparkle, distracted by the newness of the building and completely ignorant of what went on outside, when he asked, "Do you want to sign?"

CHAPTER 11

The Most Gorgeous Man I Ever Laid Eyes On

"No, no, no, you absolutely *do not* want to live in Ballymun," chuckled Liam as he continued typing away at his desk. Liam was my newest friend in Ireland and the most gorgeous man I had ever met in real life. I've met gorgeous men, but then there was *Liam.* He was a brunette with short hair and large, angelic brown eyes. He could pass as the doppelgänger of the actor Colin Farrell. He had the cutest dimples with the most heavenly smile. He came to my rescue when I so hopelessly walked into human resources at Sinead's urging, lost, holding up the "reminder email" Hilda had left for me.

"I need assistance. I moved here from New York less than two weeks ago…." I fumbled for my blackberry, which quickly dropped to the floor and startled the small group of five in the human resources department, who now stopped and looked up.

Before I could finish what sounded like a whiny toddler about to burst into an uncontrollable state of emotional distress, Liam jumped in and said, "Rachel! I've been waiting for you!" He immediately stopped typing on his computer and rolled out of his chair with a gleaming smile, as if to welcome me on his red carpet. He reached his right hand out.

Waiting for me? Like, I could have come to you sooner and you would have taken me in so I wouldn't have had to pray to the Irish heavens about where to start with my housing search in this sprawling city, waiting for me?

My heart skipped two and a half beats when Liam took my hand and shook it, introducing himself as the deputy of the human resources department. He was striking in his perfectly fitted, custom pinstripe suit that remained unwrinkled as he stood up.

"The flat in Ballymun was beautiful, Liam. It's nothing I have ever seen," I boasted (as I looked into his beautiful eyes).

"There is no gentrification in Ballymun, honey. Those new skyscrapers will likely come crashing down in a few years. That is the place where junkies go to inject needles. If you're lucky, you might not get stabbed, mugged, or assaulted." He continued to chuckle. His colleagues were too busy and entrenched in front of their monitors to even look up.

"But...but...but Liam, that's what gentrification is! You live in a mixed neighborhood with the not-so-fortunate. That's what made it cool...and well...gentrified!" I replied, walking closer to his desk. At this point one of his colleagues, Niamh, looked up to see what all the commotion was. She quickly flashed a smile at me before going back to her monitor.

Thank God I heeded Liam's advice, though. No amount of "Wait, but won't it gentrify in a few years?" could convince him to ever live in Ballymun. Years later, that apartment in Ballymun did come crashing down—something about the loan defaulting. There were a whole lot of pissed off investors who thought it would become a gentrified neighborhood, but crime soared and ruined that prospect, so the banks took it back and tore it down to recoup any bit of losses.

Liam answered my questions. All of them. He told me even more about the different Dublin neighborhoods: the good neighborhoods; the not-so-good neighborhoods; the too-good neighborhoods that mostly only new parents moved to because they had "the best" kindergarten programs in Dublin. I was happy and relieved to have the insight, and felt regretful that I had not come to human resources—or Liam—sooner. He was the key to my happiness in Ireland.

"Do you want roommates?" he asked, eyes beaming. "We maintain an internal list of employees looking for roommates, and I could pair you up with someone."

"No, thank you," I said politely. He wasn't even a little bit offended by my gentle refusal, I noticed. We culled through several listings together. Me, pointing out the ones that "looked pretty," and Liam, isolating only those that passed his assessment—such as, how far was the Dublin Area Rapid Transit (DART)? Was there crime or petty theft? How close to shops was it, and most importantly, would it be suitable for one person?

Yes, it was just me. I made it abundantly clear to Liam. Me. Myself. And I. Single and completely by myself.

"This one. How about this one?" I said with excitement, peering over his broad shoulders.

The ad read: "Fantastic, charming one-bedroom flat on the ground level of an attached townhouse in Dublin 3, Clontarf—with parking garage and close to DART. Seeking immediate occupancy. Five hundred euros per month." With some promising hesitation, Liam nodded in agreement, as if he were shepherding me along for a blind date he thought may be "good enough" for me.

That afternoon, I scheduled an appointment and arrived outside a cute, residential townhouse. It was Colin-not-Farrell again. This time, he didn't shove me into a white minivan.

"Well, if it isn't Rachel! How ye' doing? You're guhna love this flat. And this one is close to East Point Park," he said with his crooked grin.

But inside, it was more like a house for "professionals" than it was for professionals. The entrance hallway had a dark, moldy, stale smell to it. The "white" wallpaper had not been changed or cleaned in decades and was tearing. An old, musky, stained mattress lay on the floor, bare with no bed sheets, obstructing the foul kitchen that looked more like something out of the movie *The Shining* rather than a flat in this beautiful neighborhood north of the River Liffey.

The floors squeaked when we walked through. It was its own Ballymun brought into the quaint neighborhood of Clontarf.

Even though it was an infrequent sunny Dublin summer day, no sunlight entered this beat-up apartment. The bathroom light almost did not turn on, and when it did, light flickered against the already broken walls.

I curled my belongings closer, avoiding the stained and peeling walls. A young woman in her early twenties then entered the apartment, and for a moment, her gaunt, blood-shot eyes met mine before she closed the door behind her. I preferred not to be mugged, assaulted, or stabbed, so when Colin-not-Farrell said there was another soon-to-be bidder on the flat and asked, "Shall we go ahead and sign?" I pulled my second Irish Exit as he went into the bathroom to close the flickering lights. Colin seemed to have the dodgiest listings and I decided right then to stop accepting showings from him.

After that debacle, Liam insisted I meet with his real estate broker, Cormac. "In Liam I trusted," and then learned Cormac was showing a brand new flat that afternoon—in Clontarf. Liam promised it would be nothing like the one I just saw. If it weren't for this very, very gorgeous man who made my heart palpitate and warned me not to live in the brash, non-gentrifying Ballymun, I would not have met the second most very, very gorgeous man in Ireland who introduced me to my new flat.

I arrived at a bright yellow door around the corner from Junkie Ville Townhouse, and was relieved to be greeted by the second most very, very gorgeous middle-aged, blond Irishman. My heart skipped two beats when he opened the door.

He led me up a staircase and opened the second floor flat to a simple, clean, renovated, fully furnished, one-bedroom, 700-square-foot apartment within the three-story Georgian home on a quiet, residential block just minutes away from the WilHeltek Commerz headquarters, all the while talking about how safe and family-oriented the area was. The place was *nothing* like its brethren from around the corner, which we both grimaced at.

You know that feeling when you just know it's *the* one? I looked deep into Cormac's bright, brown eyes, while the rare Dublin sunlight shone in. I told him this was the one. It was renovated with dull colors that screamed 1985, but I felt oddly at home. Cormac stood in the middle of the kitchen, and we gazed into each other's eyes.

"The owners currently live in Spain. Their daughter resides downstairs with her husband. They recently renovated it and are looking to let out the second floor immediately. This flat is perfect. It is just you, yes?" he said, as he stood tall by the bay window in the kitchen, the bright light illuminating his face and making him look more gorgeous.

Yes, yes, it was just me because I think I was single now. If I told you Nate and I were on a "break" but he had ignored me when I reached out to him—you don't need to know how many times I reached out to him—and then I ignored him when he reached out, even though I still desperately wanted to marry him, you would probably agree with me that I was more suited to be in the "single" category. So yes, Cormac, it was just me.

I secured my deposit with Cormac that afternoon and gathered my belongings from Trinity Hotel. My prayers were heard. I found a flat by the miracles of the Irish Gods in under two weeks! Liam was relieved. I was relieved.

This felt like a new beginning. No Nate. In fact, I had packed up all the things that remotely reminded me of Nate and sealed them into a box: the pendant, the scrapbook, the photos, and my heartache. For the first time in my life, I was OK not being with Nate.

CHAPTER 12

Charlemont Road

15 Charlemont Road, Dublin 3, Clontarf, Ireland. It took some getting used to, even after reciting "15 Charlemont Road" aloud twelve times. This was my new address, which boasted a charming second-floor flat in the middle of a residential neighborhood one station away from the city center. It wasn't far from two local pubs where I could easily walk to get craic.

There was a small nook with two red pillows on the bay window, which was perfect for curling up, sipping tea, and looking out. I noticed one person walked down Charlemont Road all afternoon. I knew this because I stared out my window for three and a half hours. Did I need a reason to do this? Nope, I just wanted to. I *wanted* to! That was good enough reason to stare endlessly down into an empty street for hours on a Sunday afternoon.

My Irish flat was beaming with newness and optimism and positivity. There were no "Nate" things in this apartment. Only "Rachel" things. My furniture. My decorations. My favorite art piece with bright words spelling out "Make it Happen" hanging from the wall in the middle of the living room, staring at me when I turned around from this blissful position on the bay window. I felt alive again, already radiating some renewed form of hope simply from sitting there.

In every way, my new place was the opposite of the small, cramped, Nate-loves-Rachel/Rachel-loves-Nate, Manhattan apartment I had moved out of, where the window stared into the brick wall of a walk-up building inches away. It was an old life filled with memories sandwiched between a cacophony of firetrucks, sirens, and date nights competing for my attention in the evenings. It was quiet here. Really quiet. I was beginning to like my new flat, and Ireland, and me.

My address would soon be updated on all my financial records, officially designating me as an Irish resident. That meant I had to send a courtesy email to everyone in my life (well, maybe not Nate) about this important update:

> *Dear Friends and Family (and sort of friends and family that I neither liked nor disliked but decided to include because I wanted you to see what cool things I'm doing in my life and how un-miserable I am today).*
>
> *I moved—overseas! Please update your records with my new address: 15 Charlemont Road, Clontarf, Dublin 3, Ireland. Make sure to spell out "Dublin,*

> *Ireland" as the US Post Office may easily confuse this with "Dublin, Ohio" in the United States, in which case I may miss out on your wonderful holiday card complete with respective updates from the Elf on the Shelf. Please send your correspondence to me here, and anything else you deem appropriate or think I may enjoy.*

The flat was missing something, though—something "Irish" to make it sparkle. Up the block was the neighborhood convenience SPAR shop. It was open, and I found Tayto chips—sorry, *crisps*—Cadburys, Irish cookie biscuits, and a six pack of Guinness beer. I found the prettiest flowers you'd only find in Ireland too. With a bouquet of these flowers—which I didn't even know the name of—in one hand, the *Irish Times* in the other, a bunch of Irish snacks, and a six-pack of Guinness tucked under my arm, I retreated to my flat and made it more "Irish." I sat there in the nook of that bay window for many more hours, drinking a Guinness and staring blankly outside the window for the rest of the day. It was the best day of my new Irish life, and I was ready to make new friends, finally.

I started to open up. It was easy to make new friends at WilHeltek Commerz. Most of my colleagues were under thirty and willing to socialize. Most of Dublin was under thirty and willing to socialize. I needed to stop wondering about Nate—especially at work—and wondering if he still wondered about me, or if we would still be together if I hadn't been so miserable at the law firm. I didn't know and I never would. All I could say was, I didn't feel miserable anymore...at least, as miserable as I had been. Was Coach Confucius winning my internal battle against Hopeless and Sadness, riddling them with enthusiasm, dreams, and aspirations? Was she sitting at the throne of my head, crowned as Victorious?

A new, recurring Outlook invitation came from Sinead. It read:

> *Please join me for lunch at noon in the canteen.*
> *Accept? Decline? Tentative?*

I accepted with enthusiasm. I wanted to see my new friend again. That day at lunch, Aaron joined us too. So did Liam and his office mate, Siobhan; and the woman who sat next to Sinead who moved here from Finland; and Matthias from Frankfurt; and Francois from Paris; and Mariela from Madrid. I didn't mind meeting all these new people. We formed our own multi-cultural, United Nations melting pot at the large roundtable of the canteen, talking about what we did at work (or *didn't know* we did at work), where we were all from, and our experiences leading up to where we were.

I talked about my law firm job and life in New York ad nauseum, except I omitted one fact: Nate. Did Siobhan really need to know about my relentless and failed efforts to win the love of my life back on our first encounter? The answer was no. Nate was not relevant in my new conversations with my new friends. Nate was no longer relevant. Period.

On most days when Confucius Coach was at the throne of my brain, I didn't think of Nate. I was too busy enjoying the company of my new, Ireland-formed comrades. The conversations were lively, educational, and fun. Like learning the Irish language. I got *so* into it, as if I were a kid learning how to ride a bike for the first time without training wheels, balancing myself before falling off and scraping my knee, only to want to get back up and try again. Sure, they spoke English in Ireland. But I didn't understand it all the time. It sounded like a hybrid of English and Old English. Sometimes, it sounded like its own language with its own vocabulary I had to learn with cue cards: "That eejit, wanker over there, the bloke was acting the maggot before bunking off work and taking the piss with that hen over there and wanted to get a johnny into her knickers. When I approached the hen to ask if everything was alright, she responded, 'It's grand, ye, it's grand.'"

Living in Dublin meant I had to embrace the way the Dubliners spoke—or at least understand it to avoid sheer and utter embarrassment, like the time I proclaimed my love for "Johnny" Rockets to my new friends. Downtown I had discovered the best hamburger, which reminded me a whole lot of an American, 1960s-esque, fast-food chain called "Johnny Rockets" except it was called "Eddie Rockets." One day at work, when I said to them, "I love Johnny Rockets!" it garnered a few chuckles before Sinead gave me a forgiving look. She whispered in my ear that here, a "johnny" was slang for a condom. Hence, I had proclaimed to my new friends, "I love condom rockets!"

Sinead and Liam bestowed upon themselves their moral Irish obligation to form an intervention to teach me all about the Irish language. They lured me into the canteen for separate, more intimate, one-on-one coaching sessions. I was the "chosen" one of the United Nations group, destined for Irish greatness over tea and Cadbury chocolates so long as I swore our rituals to secrecy.

We would meet at 3:00 PM each day, to go over common Irish phrases, words, and the most important Gaelic slang. They were like two patient parents teaching a child how to form her first words. They'd roll their tongues, repeating the pronunciations repeatedly until I "mastered" it. But Gaelic was dead, I proclaimed. Why did I need to know this?

"Cluain Tarbh." Come on; you can do it. Sinead's eyes beamed, like a proud mom, as she rolled this off so easily and waited for me to respond.

"Cluain Tarbh is the name of your neighborhood. Try Baile Bricin, Dun Laoghaire. Guardai," Sinead continued.

My knack for speaking Gaelic sounded like gobbledygook mixed with Spanish, English, and a drop of uncertainty. I loved the way they made it sound. They sounded sexy and polite, even if they were telling me to wank off when I inadvertently proclaimed my love for condoms.

"Bah-LEE Bry-son. Gor-dye." I'd jerk my head a little forward to see if Liam or Sinead gave any indication the pronunciation was right, and like two parents proud of their nascent experiment, would nod and scream, "You're doing grand, you're doing grand!"

But really, the pronunciation was deplorable and they didn't want to discourage me. They sent me back with homework. I was to return promptly tomorrow, same time and place, after having filled my mind with words from RTE.ie, Ireland's national news channel.

The headline from today's Irish Times read: "Garda criticised for not moving fast enough with seizing 950K worth of drugs, guns, and cash discovered in Co Meath."

It started to drizzle that afternoon, like it did most days in Ireland. There were no seasons here. Just one: the perpetual, annoyingly wet, twelve-month-long rain season. The kind you'd never escape if you lived in the Pacific Northwest of the United States. The kind where opening an umbrella seemed silly, but if you didn't do so, your spectacles got wet enough to blur your vision. So far, most of the days I had spent here had been like this. I entered the canteen, drenched in drizzle and with wet spectacles before I spotted Liam and Sinead waiting for me in the back.

"Father Liam, Sister Sinead, before I go on and ask my numerous questions about the RTE news I pulled up, bless me Father, and Sister, for I have sinned. It has been exactly thirty days since my last confession. I still don't know what my job is. I pretend to know in the office, but I do not. I log into my computer each day waiting for emails to come through from Hilda or the team whom I don't even know from Germany. Nothing. So, I sit there, having already read through the company's quarterly earnings, and re-learning my Chinese in fear of Hilda deploying me to some secret call center overseas to translate her highly classified documents."

Sinead took a sip of her steaming hot tea. Liam bit into his chocolate. The rain came down harder outside. Sinead turned to me, as if to make an equally consecrated confession, when Aaron walked into the canteen with someone none of us were familiar with. He was hunched over holding a binder of documents under his arm, as if he had just been bulldozed over by the administrative department. A young woman followed closely behind him and barked out a name loud enough for me to overhear: *Hilda Künt.*

"I hate her, Aaron. I hate her. I hate her. I hate her," the stranger repeatedly said. I looked up at Liam and Sinead, who at this point became utterly silent. I became more curious and deliberately moved closer so I would continue to eavesdrop, much to Liam and Sinead's chagrin. I wanted to go over there and introduce myself. But what would I say?

"Hi, I'm Rachel. I couldn't help but hear you say you hated Hilda Künt. You see, I report to Hilda too. And I've heard so many not-so-good things about her. I still do not know what my job title is or what my responsibilities are. My inevitable doomsday meeting with her will be soon, and I'm wondering, why do you hate Hilda Künt? Do you know anything about my job title? Can you tell me anything you know so I could prepare for my corporate suicide in advance? It's very nice to meet you."

But I didn't know how to go over there and introduce myself. As Liam and Sinead clenched their teeth and told me to stop staring at them, Aaron let out a loud, "Rachel!" from across the canteen, waving his lanky arm and motioning for us to come over.

Aaron stood up. "Rachel, we just got out of a video conference call with Hilda."

He pulled up a couple of seats next to him and motioned for the young woman to move over.

"This is Katharina, by the way. She was just transferred from the German office." Katharina popped her knuckles loudly, as if she were preparing for some brawl, before taking my hand and giving me the strongest "nice to meet you" handshake.

"Transferred" was a euphemism for messing up in some way, but not so egregiously that Hilda fired you. However, it was enough for her to transfer you out of her team—and apparently, out of Germany. Enter Katharina, Hilda's research assistant of five years. She translated all the North American reports into German for Hilda. Katharina knew something was wrong when Hilda stopped responding to her emails and refused to accept any of her requests for a meeting. She found out through another team member that Hilda was furious because one of the documents was "not up to par" with the client's request. Something about Hilda's bio not being up to date and them relenting to the client's demand for a 10 percent shave on their fee.

"Hilda has no heart. She doesn't possess an ounce of human decency in her." Katharina reached for her coffee as we sat across from her, listening intently as if this was a therapy session to cure her from the mental asylum she had just escaped from.

"What did she do?" I asked, curious and wanting to hear from her the trauma Hilda had unleashed onto her.

Katharina moved the cup of coffee away.

"She is not human. She is pure evil if evil was to take on a human form, unable to mentor or communicate…."

She turned towards the window and started sobbing. "And instead, she forces those around her to worship her for six hours a day, six days a week, beginning at 6:00 AM each day."

Katharina continued, "And she dinks Helen Waite would do a better job? HA!"

I lay my hand on her shoulder, in a small effort to comfort her.

"Who cares if she got lucky and brought in one big account? I am more disappointed at her higher ups who do nothing. Absolutely nothing about her except for promoting her!" Katharina quickly chugged a double shot espresso as she shook her head rigorously and prepared for a new office life in Dublin.

Aaron pushed his seat away and stood up. Katharina became my new office mate.

CHAPTER 13

Hilda Nervosa

It had been exactly one hundred days since I arrived in Dublin, and I still had not called Grandma Lucetta back. I returned to my office that afternoon, my heart racing when I saw the red light to my voicemail, wondering what Hilda wanted. But thankfully, it was Grandma Lucetta who left me the voicemail: "Hey kiddo! What do I have to do to track you down? Fly there to your office? You don't call. You don't text. You don't fax. You don't send smoke signals. I know, I know…I heard about "the break", and you moving to Ireland. What the hell is that about?! Ireland? And not Italy? We're *not* all that bad! Don't bother with my schmucko grandson. The schmuck gene runs deep in this family for some reason. Don't run away from life, though. Seize it by its brass balls and take control of it. And call Grandma Lucetta back, please."

But I couldn't bring myself to call her back yet. I was too distracted by Hilda. It was worse in the office sharing such a small space with Katharina. Katharina suffered from emotional deterioration, rightfully so as she had just been violently discharged from the asylum of Hilda. Most days Katharina came into the office emotionally numb and kept to herself. Occasionally, I would hear her labored breathing from my desk, a claustrophobic two feet away. I'd try lifting her mood by asking if she wanted to join me for tea, or lunch, or anything.

"No, no danke," she said, without looking away from her screen. She obviously wasn't ready to socialize by the way she shunned me, and preferred instead to type loudly at her desk, the noise of banging against the keyboard being overpowered by the occasional pounding of her fist against the desk.

If Hilda was this terrible, why had nothing been done about it? Would Katharina ultimately stage an abrupt coup d'etat, leading all the others who had been as wrongfully demoralized and cast aside to overthrow Hilda and declare a "Key Account Management" victory? Or would Katharina succumb to Hilda's penitentiary, gnawing at the corporate straitjacket so mercilessly forced onto her? I didn't get it. I convinced myself having worked in a big, corporate law firm with big, important partners, that it couldn't be that bad. Hilda *would not* be that bad.

And with things finally falling into place in Ireland, I wouldn't let her be that bad. I was making new friends. I had my own flat decorated with my favorite flowers and new, Irish things. I was beginning to like Guinness too, and I was finally OK with being by myself.

But the anxiety of Hilda continued to erode the core of my sanity. Sometimes, I'd wake up in the middle of the night in a weakened state with an intense amount of sweat dripping down my forehead, panting and out of breath, suffering from a new disease called "Hilda nervosa." It was always a nightmare of some sort that involved Hilda asking me again what kind of Chinese I spoke. I returned home from work one evening—lugging a heavy laptop that felt like I had carried the weight of my former self on my left shoulder—only to realize I locked myself out of my own flat because I had been too preoccupied with Hilda.

I didn't know what to do or where to go, or how to stop feeding off this fear that had so permanently permeated the office and been so chronically contagious. The symptoms of "Hilda nervosa" started off as benign denial. Then, over the course of a week, I developed an unhealthy and distorted perception of myself, starved of optimism, happiness, and logic.

I needed to recover. I wanted to recover. But I had no mobile phone to rescue me. Just a useless, corporate blackberry that couldn't make phone calls and had an internet browser that crawled to a halt because the company was too frugal to set it up with any decent type of data-voice plan. How would I reach my landlord? Or a locksmith?

I needed therapy. I needed to purge this preoccupation with Hilda. I walked aimlessly along Charlemont Road when a sliver of hope emerged in front of me in the form of Graingers Pub. Upon entering, the few locals immersed in conversations alongside the bar stopped and looked up at me when I took a seat. It wasn't an unfriendly look, but more of a curious look, like—"I've never seen a person like you in Clontarf, but you like beer? I like beer. You look like you've been deprived of life and could use a beer. Have a beer."

When the bartender—Connor, as I learned his name was—gave me a Guinness, my body felt it was being intubated to a ventilator. Slowly, it breathed positivity back into my soul. Then optimism. Then hope, logic, and a bitter aftertaste. Connor changed the channel of the telly from futbol to the American comedy series, *Friends*, which happened to be my favorite show. How did he know?

"I figure you Americans love this show," he guessed correctly, as he placed the clunky remote control down with one hand and filled another pint of Guinness for the patron sitting next to me with the other. I had a grin from ear to ear and a moment where I had completely forgotten about Hilda. The patrons scattered across the bar didn't seem to mind me or the channel being changed. They continued their conversations in their Irish craic language and rarely looked up again.

I remembered Aaron was staying in some castle-reformed-hotel in Clontarf somewhere. Clontarf Castle, as I learned from Connor after offering a fumbled description. It really was a castle built around 1172 AD, used by many lavish Irish Lords, then converted into a cabaret in the early 1900s, and finally, renovated as a luxury, four-star hotel in the middle of an affluent suburb, charging a small fortune to corporate travelers. It was only a few minutes from where I was.

I sent Aaron a quick but friendly message on the blackberry: "Hi, I'm at Graingers Pub in Clontarf. Do you want to join? PS, can you ask your concierge for a locksmith they could recommend? I promise to explain and pay you in pints." He immediately responded as I was in between conversations with Connor.

Connor was from County Derry in Northern Ireland, and he was the secret suicidal prevention number to my Hilda nervosa. We talked, and talked, and talked.

"You know futbol?" Connor asked. He reached for a tall Guinness mug behind him.

"Are you a Giants fan?" I replied. Connor turned the channel back to the sports game that was playing earlier. The few patrons behind me loudly jeered when the colorful green and orange one kicked the ball and scored.

"Futbol!" he repeated. Futbol was the American equivalent of "soccer," and Connor professed his love for futbol. He had played since he was a kid and watched it with his "mum and dad." I learned more about the candy-striped Derry City Futbol Club than I ever wanted. They were to play next week here in Dublin against the Shelbournes. He would have to "hide" his loyalty for D.C. at this game because of the "futbol hooliganism" that was so prevalent here.

I sort of understood it as a Yankees vs. Mets kind of rivalry; both were teams from the same area (Republic of Ireland), but each team had their own diehard, loyal fans that heckled each other. But it was more than heckling here. It was violent, especially if one of these teams was playing the country next door—England. It was life or death to them. Literally.

"Me best friend, he got his arse kicked. It was a bloody, cruel, violent blow. Dey lef him for dead. He was in a coma for weeks," Connor balked.

"There's a similar rivalry between the boroughs of New York City," I responded. "You got your ass kicked if you proclaimed you were from Queens when you stepped foot into the Bronx."

Fans here couldn't just "let things go." They beat you up, and beat you up *bad*. Connor stopped wearing any D.C. paraphernalia to these games and became more of a "closet" hardcore futbol fan. While I was living in Ireland, I didn't think I would ever, ever, want to go to a futbol game.

Moments later, Aaron arrived, equally inspected upon his entrance into the pub. He stood there, tall and lanky and scanning the room, not seeing me hunched over at the bar with my back turned toward him when Connor asked, "Is that your friend?"

"My friend?" I asked, confused, then remembered. "My friend!" I had almost forgotten I called Aaron to come here before I turned around and waved at him, only for the rest of the bar to now stop their craic-friendly conversations and look up to see what was going on. Aaron took a seat next to me while I was in a tipsy state. "They have futbol here! Futbol, the American version of soccer, in Ireland!"

Aaron was easy to talk to. After having Connor help phone the locksmith Aaron had scribbled on a piece of "Clontarf

Castle" notepad, and over the course of what felt like many more pints of Guinness, I felt an overwhelming sense of familiarity with Aaron. We just got each other. Maybe it was the Asian thing. Maybe it was the American thing. Maybe it was the Asian-American-being-in-Clontarf, Dublin-thing and never wanting to step foot into a futbol arena here in Ireland, thing.

"I'm petrified of Hilda!" I blurted, in the middle of a jovial conversation inside a jovial pub.

I reached for another pint of Guinness.

Aaron was the first person I shared my secret Hilda nervosa disorder with. He would not have noticed my maniac spiritual weight loss otherwise.

"Don't take it personally," he said in a stoic manner, followed by a sip of beer.

"Don't take it personally? How could I not take it personally when she stings me with her lethal poison in my dreams night after night?"

Aaron let out a chuckle.

Aaron was an independent contractor hired by Corporate to fix their technology issues. He was based in the US office and came to the Dublin office as needed. He dealt with Hilda whenever she made her semi-annual US office visits, and telling from his slurred speech and excessively hunched posture, there was much more to his "don't take it personally" statement than he was willing to share.

Aside from my life-threatening ailment with Hilda, there was this Asian American homesickness that resurfaced too, which only Aaron seemed to understand. Aaron was craving Asian food. Authentic, Asian American, Chinese food with rice and everything that accompanied any authentic Chinese food—like sweet and sour chicken. I felt relieved not to be the only one carrying the undisclosed burden of craving cuisine from the vicinity of China (Vietnam, Japan, or Korea). We made our own little Aaron-Rachel-Asian agreement of finding the best Asian food there was in Ireland. There had to be something here. There were Chinese immigrants here too. Lots of them.

They were everywhere in Ireland. The servers at restaurants. The hosts and hostesses at bars. The janitors inside the malls. The receptionists at the hotels. The sous chefs. The maids and caretakers of rich, Irish families. The sales ladies at the perfume counters of Thomas Brown. They looked at me with an innate smile. I looked at them, wondering what scent they just sprayed on me. Many adapted here the same way they adapted in other countries: working menial jobs or churning out late-night, post debauchery, greasy food—with a side of salty fried rice. I'm sure if I looked hard enough, I would find a few knock-off bags with the incorrect spelling of "Fendi" on it.

"I want rice!" Aaron said, slamming down his now-empty pint of Guinness.

Connor overheard us and took it upon himself to tell us to go next door for "the best Chinese food there is in Ireland," he assured us. It was owned by people who looked like me. But the first red flag to this "Chinese" place? The name of it was "Ireland's Best Asian Food." The next red flag? The menu had every kind of Asian concoction attempting to surreptitiously pass as Asian. Double fried Guinness batter chicken wasabi sushi? Was it coupled with an Irish river dance and Irish folklore?

But there were suddenly more of my kind when Aaron and I walked in. Two people who (sort of) resembled me and Aaron were engrossed in a conversation by the window, with one obnoxiously slurping a big bowl of noodles, letting the fragments riddle his plain t-shirt with broth while his partner continued to speak in some dialect of Chinese.

"It feels sort of Chinese. It smells sort of Chinese. It sounds sort of Chinese," Aaron said, reaching for a menu.

There was a menu with some Chinese words on it I could neither read nor write. It looked like I was peering into a mirror when the young, Chinese girl at the counter looked back at me, waiting for me to speak first, wondering if I was her distant eighth cousin from the province of Ningbo. Neither of us spoke. She looked at me. I looked at her. She continued to look at me, as if to say, "I know your kind—*our* kind. I can give you the authentic stuff, like pig feet or intestines, if you'd like." But I wasn't that kind of Chinese. *I could barely speak that kind of Chinese.* There was this drawn out, awkward silence between us. Should I speak to her in my broken, Sino-American Chinese? Would she speak to me in her Irish-Chinese-English? The girl continued to look at me, perplexed, until Aaron pointed to a bunch of things on the menu.

"We'll have two orders of this," Aaron said in perfect Anglo-American English, pointing to item number 15 on the menu.

What we got was an unusual bastardization of Chinese food: beef with black bean sauce drenched in a heavy, creamy gravy, deep fried, then doused in more starchy gravy and served with a side of heaping, thick-cut "chips" (or what us Westerners would call French fries). I didn't like it. Where was the rice? I wanted rice. Aaron wanted rice too. What kind of Asian restaurant, supposedly the best in Ireland, didn't serve rice? There was no rice. I looked at our Chinese waitress, hoping to psychically communicate with her our desperate pleas for steamed, white rice. She came back with another plate of thick-cut fries, as if mocking us as she turned her back toward us.

A group of young, red-headed lads sitting nearby soaked their wannabe Chinese food into the thick-cut fries. They appeared to savor it as they reached for more. Aaron and I watched, dumbfounded, as they continued.

"This looks disgusting," Aaron balked.

"I miss real Chinese food. This is *nothing* like the Chinese food my dad would bring home from Lum's," I responded.

"What's Lum's?" asked Aaron.

"Only the best Chinese restaurant ever known to mankind. It was the reason my parents moved and settled in Flushing, Queens, and the reason I cannot eat what is in front of me."

Did we suffer from some other type of unsubstantiated medical condition that prevented us from eating such a sacrilege mixture of Chinese food? I wanted something more authentic—like General Tso's Chicken.

Aaron put some of the beef and black bean sauce in front of me. I flinched. I couldn't. I wouldn't. I shouldn't. But at Aaron's pleas, I reached for a fry and soaked it up with this wannabe Chinese food. Aaron followed, and we bellowed out a drunken laugh that seemed to say, "This was so horribly bad, it was good." Our Chinese waitress peered over, not saying a word, and continued to ignore our inner plea for rice.

"I guess we're hungry...*really* hungry," I said, reaching for another fry.

We continued eating this un-Chinese food in Ireland until... until...who knows. Who cares? Because toward the end of the night, it was still good. Before the check arrived, the same girl who stared at me handed out fortune cookies. Aaron's read, "The fortune you seek is another cookie." Mine read, "You will travel to a distant land."

The locksmith finally arrived—accompanied by Connor, who was looking for us—when we were somewhere between our second and third fortune cookies. It was past 10:00 PM and most of the other customers had already left by now, having fulfilled their Chinese food cravings. The locksmith apologized profusely for being this late, explaining the family he was helping just now was an hour away in the neighboring county. I didn't feel great with all the grease and beer and fries (sorry, *chips*) and wanted to go to bed. There was an aftertaste of gratification because Aaron was there. He made me feel at ease in a way that not even Nate had made me feel. Even when I was this tipsy, and my stomach was gurgling in all different directions, I knew what I felt was different. We all rounded the corner to my flat together. The locksmith successfully opened the door to my flat before I tripped forward, clearly a little drunk, before Aaron caught me by the side of my hips.

Anne, my landlord's daughter, was in the hallway carrying her laundry. She dropped her laundry basket, and a light blue blouse fell onto the floor when she exclaimed, "Are you OK?" She moved closer to us, like a worried mom whose daughter had been missing and emerged with two strangers in front of her. Anne gave a protective glare at Aaron and the locksmith and insisted I call her if ever anything like this happened again. She stepped forward and hugged me in her warm arms, giving me her mobile number and promising she'd make me a spare key too.

I thanked her. I thanked the locksmith. I thanked Aaron. It was incredibly heartwarming for such strangers to watch over me in my parents' absence. My parents always worried when I traveled alone—dreading the knock on the door by a US Marshall announcing the untimely murder of their daughter, stabbed and strewn in the gutters of some foreign city they'd never heard of, or couldn't even pronounce, because she had asked for directions.

Or, collapsing in the middle of her room of a deadly asthma attack, too weak and lonely to reach for her life-saving medication. I imagined them asking and wailing why they deserved such a fate, praying for their God to protect their only child in Chinese.

"Don't leave—" My eyes began to water as my body jerked toward the toilet bowl, evidently wallowing in nostalgia as Aaron held the lid up for me.

I hesitantly tilted my head back up as I sought and found comfort in his eyes.

"Don't leave me, Aaron," I finally was able to make out through my faint, drained out voice.

And so, Aaron stayed with me that night, which explained the big hands that tucked me in. Nothing happened, though. Nothing except, those same big arms helping me out, then back into bed. Over, and over again. Even with all the helpless cold bathroom floor pleads for my mother (as I swore I felt my guts shifting all over throughout my body), and the horrid yacking sounds, he was there through it all. Aaron (barely) slept on the floor that night, awakened hourly by my stomach and me darting straight up in bed at one point, yelling something incoherent in Chinese that made him think I was possessed. He swore up and down I had some form of alcohol poisoning no amount of water could cure at that hour. So out of true concern, he stayed, nursing me back to wellness before my eye lids finally shut for the remainder of the night.

Aaron had been awake for hours on this beautiful Saturday morning when I emerged and saw him with a cup of coffee in my kitchen.

"Let's explore Dublin," he said, excitedly. "Like, really explore it for its history and famous buildings."

Dublin was as famous for its Irish charm as it was for its notable poets, musicians, writers, would-be-writers, their alter-ego characters, beer, wit, and whisky—perhaps the latter being the secret to making those great poets, writers, would-be-writers, and their alter-ego characters so fun and whimsical. How could I decline when he spent so much time with me the night before, nursing me back to health?

"Coffee. I need coffee to resuscitate me," my hoarse voice responded.

After a jolt of caffeine, that afternoon I accompanied Aaron on a multi-hour Writer's Tour under moderate duress.

While there, I had an epiphany. Maybe I could be a writer too, by virtue of being here. Something may rub off on me like it did these great writers. Call it "great Irish writing by osmosis," simply by living in Dublin and being inside those very same watering holes they'd spent so many hours in.

The Oscar Wilde statue smirked at me, hearing my thoughts loud and clear before responding in a brazen way, his bright green smoking jacket matching the bright green buildings behind him in Merrion Square.

"What makes you think you can be one of the greats?" he balked, leaning back, chastising Aaron as to why he would bring such an unworthy aspiring writer here.

"I never said 'one of the greats.' Just one; one of the amateurs, maybe. I could form some words and thoughts in a mildly coherent sentence most of the time, and I won a writing scholarship once. Did you know that, Oscar? I was a winner once in someone's eyes. Why are you judging me, anyway?!"

Oscar continued to look at me with devoted disdain, raising one leg up as he slouched backward, almost chuckling beneath his breath, doubting my confidence. Aaron misinterpreted my involuntary posture as wanting to stay longer and insisted we could if that was what I wanted.

I didn't mind, and so I led the way down Grafton Street, shoulders slumped and defeated in response to Oscar's criticism. When we encountered the statue of Thin Lizzy bass rock star Phil Lynott a short walk away, he seemed gentler, and more kind. I stopped. Aaron stopped shortly behind me. Phil looked at my tearful eyes, as if to read what was on the plaque by his feet directly to me: "To become wise about a subject means you must have been a fool at some time. I don't actually think you become wiser; you just get more experienced." Well thank you, Phil, those words are much more comforting than Oscar's.

Aaron picked up a pamphlet from the ground nearby that must have been left by a previous visitor: "Spend the afternoon as Leopold Bloom in *Ulysses* did and stop in for a glass of burgundy and a gorgonzola sandwich. Davy Byrnes, located off central Grafton Street."

Aaron looked at his map, and like a child on Christmas morning who couldn't wait to rip open his presents, he blurted out, "Let's go to Davy Byrnes! It's around the corner! Let's go! Let's go!"

I turned around.

"It's…it's where Leopold Bloom…it's where Leopold…where, where we can get gorgonzola sandwiches, and burgundy," he said with a nervous twitch I just noticed as I gazed at him, confused, still thinking of Oscar Wilde's silent, abusive scolding. Feeling apathetic to the idea of Leopold Bloom and ingesting lactose-containing foods into my lactose-intolerant stomach, I followed along.

Aaron and I spent four hours inside a quiet corner of Davy Byrnes taking turns biting into a heaping gorgonzola sandwich and sipping burgundy just as how we envisioned the famous Irish authors to have done.

"Aaron, there's something you ought to know." I placed the gorgonzola sandwich down.

Aaron stopped chewing and swallowed loudly. He furrowed his thick eyebrows.

I began to experience pain in my chest, which worsened when I leaned over and whispered into Aaron's ear, "I'm lactose intolerant."

Aaron seemed relieved and reached into his pockets, pulling out what looked like Lactaid and handed one to me.

"So am I," he said, before taking a sip more of burgundy.

But the painful, burning sensation in my chest didn't go away after ingesting a Lactaid. Was the pain caused by the backflow of overeating gorgonzola on this beautiful Sunday afternoon? Or was it heartache resulting from a palpable sense of loss and enjoying a moment with another guy...another guy who wasn't Nate? I couldn't seem to shake the bitter aftertaste—or afterthought—from my mouth or mind.

Aaron and I emerged drunk from Davy Byrnes, zigzagging and giggling loudly as we continued walking, weaving in and out of museums and numerous other pubs that we posed next to.

"I like you," I caught myself saying, giggling into Aaron's face, as he caught me from falling from a statue of a man on a horse who appeared to be defending this land from an invasion.

"I...I...like you too," he said, before we both burst out laughing and fell onto a nearby bench.

His head leaned over mine.

"Rachel, will you...will you come to Blarney Castle with me tomorrow?" His lean arm fell onto my leg.

Irish legend said if you removed even a pebble from the Blarney Castle, you'd be cursed with bad luck. Some have even tried, unsuccessfully, to return the pieces they took back to their original places at the castle to reverse the curse. The legend is said to have originated from an incident where Queen Elizabeth I of England ordered the Earl of Leicester to seize Blarney Castle sometime in the late 1500s. He never seized it because the head of an elite family in Ireland was so talkative, and successful at stalling, that the Earl failed his mission. The Queen was so disappointed by this, she called the Earl's failure "blarney," or "humbug."

On the contrary, if you kissed the Blarney Stone, upside down, you'd be given the gift of eloquence and persuasiveness.

"Yes, Aaron, yes! I'll come with you. I need to confront my inner fear of Hilda." And at the thought of Hilda, and ingesting too many gorgonzola sandwiches, we fell asleep on that bench.

Aaron woke me hours later, and like the gentleman he was, dropped me off first on the cab ride back to Clontarf. He kissed my forehead and said, "See you tomorrow."

The following morning, Aaron picked me up at 15 Charlemont Road and we started our three-hour pilgrimage to County Cork for the sole purpose of risking "life and limb" to lay on our backs at a ninety-foot drop, backward, and kiss the Blarney Stone so we could be "more eloquent and persuasive."

"What do you want out of this?" I asked Aaron, as he handled the clutch with his left hand and swiftly adapted to driving on the right side of the road. There weren't many cars on the freeway at this hour.

He turned on a roundabout and said, "I…I…behave cowardly in front of superiors. They see me as this lanky engineer who doesn't know how to respond to criticism." He shifted the gear. "And they're right. I want to relish in the 'luck o' the Irish' while I'm here." Aaron continued on the freeway toward Contae Chorcaí.

"Open the glove compartment," he said. "The map is in there." I unfolded a clunky map of the castle and directed Aaron toward the parking lot.

The castle was as beautiful in real life as it was on the clunky map. There weren't many times I relished mother nature, but this was different. It was different being in Ireland. Being with Aaron. This lush, green turf with a centuries-old castle in front of us was more apt for kings and queens and thieves and serfs than the casually dressed tourists who were queued up at the entrance of the castle, willing to pay eighteen euros and equally eager to kiss the centuries-old stone below the battlements of Blarney Castle.

Someone was there assisting, and by the time it was our turn, a quirky Irish guy dipped me backward while I held onto two rusty guardrails on the side. I closed my eyes and went first. The stone felt cold against my lips. Then, Aaron went. It was over very quickly. Did we each receive the gift of eloquence? Or did we only receive the millions of germs these other tourists left behind?

I was getting used to life in a distant land with Aaron, who made those first months better. I was finally over Nate, and Aaron made being in this country better. My regular routine soon began looking like this: wake up at 6:30 AM, have one scrambled egg with a dash of salt, look right first, then left to avoid being hit by a double-decker bus, meet Aaron for an uninterrupted thirty-minute walk along Clontarf coast before going to work together. Walking was my exercise and my vain attempt at saving the monthly obligatory gym membership that was so common back in New York. *Everyone* had it, and even though there was a sauna and pool at the gym, I rarely went, because I was always too tired. It was different here, and with someone rallying me to also walk, it was easier—and healthier.

Aaron and I met Hiroko one morning. She was a quirky Japanese girl who stared at me with a familiar excitement during one of our walks, that seemed to say, "Are you *my* type of Asian?" She walked along the coast with us for almost an hour in her recon mission to find out "what Asian I was." To her chagrin, she learnt I was Chinese American, not quite her type. Did being born in Tokyo count, though? She wanted more female "Asian friends" and I would make do, she said with an optimistic twinkle in her eye.

Hiroko had followed her Irish husband here from Tokyo and left everything behind. She had regrets that she "promised to share one day in future," she said in her best Japanese English. She looked at my sad Chinese American self up and down, and in a *You are good enough of an Asian to be friends with* way, she gave me her phone number and told me to "call her anytime." I was an introvert (mostly), so I felt comfortable crumpling up the piece of paper with her number on it and placing it inside one of the pockets of my purse I never checked, expecting to never talk to her again.

CHAPTER 14

I Want Kimchi

I mostly stopped thinking of Nate. I was surrounded by new things and new friends and new neighborhoods in Ireland now. And I was still too angry with him.

I knew my old self was reemerging when I suddenly craved kimchi again, like a nine-month-pregnant woman too voraciously hangry or moody to do anything except demand weird food concoctions. You either hated kimchi or loved it. I love it. I really, really loved it., I had an intense obsession with this food. Plus it was good for your health. Chock-full of probiotic, bacteria-fighting good stuff, kimchi kept me from falling ill from third-world street food—and dairy. I wondered how I was one of the only few who didn't succumb to some sort of E. coli after eating questionable organs in China. My stomach had the lining of the Great Wall because of my almost daily consumption of kimchi. Maybe I was reincarnated in this Asian body in this Irish land because Ireland had plenty of cabbage?

I told Aaron about it and how I paired it with everything. *Everything.* I put gobs and gobs of it on top of rice (my favorite!), eggs, barbecue, fish, whatever. I sautéed it, I boiled it, I baked it, I steamed it, I fried it, I grilled it. Sometimes—especially when I was too lazy to cook (not that I really cooked, anyway)—I just ate it out of the jar, cold and lonely, like I did today with the last remaining bits I had smuggled in from New York City. Kimchi may have been an addiction. OK, so, it *was* an addiction. I didn't dare share what I was doing that Sunday with anyone, except Aaron. It was different with Aaron.

Hello, my name is Rachel, and I am an addict.

"Aaron, I need...I need my fix. I'm almost out," I said, my lips trembling with humiliation as I admitted my insatiable cravings for kimchi.

"I love kimchi!" Aaron exclaimed.

Suddenly, it was like we were in our own addiction group where I was no longer ashamed to admit I had the "shakes" from withdrawals whenever my stash got depleted. I would begin counting the minutes until my next "hit" and imagined many harebrained methods of bringing it with me. I considered chopping it up into tiny bits and carrying it in small, pocketbook-friendly sized "baggies." I even thought about drying the kimchi, then grinding it into a powder and filling saltshakers with it. This way, I could conveniently bring it everywhere and sprinkle it over my food because that wouldn't make me look too insane to neighboring diners—or so I thought.

I prayed to the Irish American-Chinese-Korean gods for a revelation. Please, please, please gods, reveal to me what Korean neighbor—as passed down from generation to generation, just as their ancestors had done for millennia before—is fermenting kimchi and burying batches of it in clay vessels in their backyard.

Besides Guinness, there was cabbage in Ireland. Lots and lots of it too! There were also Koreans. The combination of Koreans, cabbage, and a climate similar to Northern South Korea ensured that someone, somewhere in Ireland had buried what to me was better than gold. Would my prayers be heard, or would I have to deal with what was clearly an unhealthy obsession to a healthy side dish? Would the Irish embrace the idea of a spicy version of their renowned vegetable mixed in with a bunch of other seasonings and fish sauce? Did they even eat spicy food? Would the good Father Patty O'Connelly of the Clontarf church haul me into a confessional and make me repent for considering something so sacrilege? What could possibly be the sentence for such a crime? Would he hand me a rosary and force me to recite fifty, a hundred, a thousand Hail Marys? I couldn't muster up the courage to ask an Irishman where to find kimchi, because it would surely reveal my diabolical plans for their bland, boiled cabbage.

My stash was low, and I still hadn't found kimchi in any grocery store. I needed it. Fast. Making it myself was out of the question. I cooked as well as I could skydive (I couldn't do either). Google wasn't any help. As an accomplished lifelong introvert, I went back and forth on the idea of calling Hiroko—the only other Asian I met in Ireland who might understand my incorrigible appetite for kimchi. Desperate times called for desperate measures, so I reached for the folded post-it note with her mobile number scribbled on it.

"*Herro, Hiroko san desu,*" sounded the other end of the telephone.

I gulped. "Hi, Hiroko. It's Rachel," I said, shame and embarrassment in my voice—as if I had dialed a kimchi addiction intervention number.

"Oh, hi Michelle..." Hiroko said calmly. It's fine she didn't remember who I was. As long as she could point me somewhere to refill my stash, she could call me whatever she wanted. I looked up when a faint knock came at my door. I covered the mouth of the phone to make sure no one was near enough to hear our conversation. I moved to the bathroom of my flat and locked the door.

In an uncharacteristic move, I proudly proclaimed my love of kimchi to her—sitting atop my toilet bowl cover—revealing to an almost complete stranger the mood swings and impaired judgment I would soon experience, confiding in her my unhealthy obsession and pleading with her...did she know anyone or anywhere that may have some? I wept a little, as I described how bland my breakfast was without the globs of kimchi mounded on top of it. After a long, patient silence—I honestly wasn't sure Hiroko was still on the other line or if she understood all my rambling—Hiroko finally said, in her barely audible, soft-spoken tone, "I think you have problem."

She was right. I did have a problem.

"But I need help, Hiroko!" I implored her. Finally, she mentioned there was a small Asian supermarket downtown near Henry Street.

"You might find kimchi there," she said.

A few minutes later, I hung up and sat in the bathroom for thirty more lonely minutes, wondering with hope again—could there really be kimchi in Ireland?

CHAPTER 15

Mr. Meanie

Headquarters surveyed the Dublin office on the fourth week of the month, every month. More specifically, they used their henchman, Hendrik Müller, a six-foot-six blond donning a jet-black suit more fitting for a funeral than this quiet little office in the suburbs of Dublin, to find out intel on all of us.

When I reached my office door, my eyes locked briefly with Hendrik. He didn't look like he was from here. I learned later that I was right—he wasn't. He had a stoic demeanor about him that suggested he came from the German headquarters (he did). He looked mean. He *was* mean. He told the truth and nothing but the brutal, honest, ugly truth. You made a mistake on Excel? You were "dumm," you "doof." Speaking to him in a friendly, Irish manner, wishing him a "grand day" did nothing but earn you a hard, cold, two-minute demonic look.

He was otherwise known as a "cute hoor." A cute hoor in Ireland was someone who quietly engineered something to his or her advantage—a shrewd scoundrel, if you will, especially in business or politics—and today, he usurped my office.

Hendrik was sent here by his capo bosses to block and tackle the Irish officers, knocking them down and kicking them to the sidelines, metaphorically bludgeoning them with his big, bare hands until the officers were too bloody to return to the battlefield. Künt sent him because he had this knack for pretending to be your friend so he could observe the operations more carefully, making you comfortable enough to reveal what you really thought about all the team members and managers, subliminally persuading them to throw others under the bus. Hendrik took careful notes—and like the loyal tattletale he was—reported it back to the headquarters in Germany, who used the intel to abruptly fire people. There was never a reason either. You'd suddenly be told your position was "eliminated."

He turned toward me just enough that his big hands were visible for me to see, and he held out his five big fingers to tell me—seemingly—he needed five more minutes. By the powers vested in him, he was drafting my job description, right in front of me, in my own office.

What the hell was he writing? I was nervous and flustered, ready to cry and head back to NYC, hoping Lynch & Burnham would still want me. My future career and fate were sealed in Hendrik's big, European hands. He took notes every so often, looking up at me with a grimace that seemed to suggest a kiss on his ring finger when he emerged from my office. Who was he and why was he writing out my job description? I was visibly annoyed and felt like I was my own defendant in his courtroom; he, the chief judge, was forming all sorts of opinions about me for our equally satanic bosses in Germany, until he was ready to read them his verdict and I was prepared to perpetually plead the fifth.

Gutentag. Next up, Rachel, Cornell undergrad, American, twenty-nine years old, 5'6", dark brown eyes, salary band—very, very low compared to the partners. Seeking a "very important position" within Key Account Management, WilHeltek Commerz.

Did I have the right credentials? The right experience? Know the right kind of Chinese? I was unqualified for whatever he was drafting up and I knew it. Self-conscious, I rose and took the stand like the vulnerable Asian apprentice I was, my asthma flaring up and my wheezing exacerbated with each glance he gave, exposing myself, wondering what talent I had—more so, what talent I *didn't* have—and waiting for Hendrik to tell me the whole truth and nothing but the truth (did he know I wasn't one who could handle the truth)? I didn't have what it took to be part of this department, and he would inevitably eliminate me. I was sure of it. I could be a writer, though, I thought. That would be my backup profession, because even Oscar Wilde believed in me (OK, well, sort of, if you ignored everything he said about me).

Hendrik exited my office, and in a deep, robotic, staccato-like German English, waved his gigantic hand for me to come in.

"Assistant Administrative Analyst to the Key Account Management Team," he said.

"Excuse me? What does that mean?" I asked.

"*Assistant Administrative Analyst to the Key Account Management Team*," he repeated, this time more loudly.

What would the job specifically entail? Was I an assistant? An admin? An analyst? Would I get coffee for the team? Would I crunch sales numbers? Assist with research projects? Assassinate our Irish counterparties and make it look like a self-inflicted suicide?

"Ve need someone who vill assist in all aspects of day-to-day verk. Künt needs all kind of help," he said, before dismissing me out of my own office.

I wanted to cry. The wide-eyed enthusiasm accompanying my relocation here was suddenly ripped from my chest and stomped on by this mean, German giant, and his ability to label me so quickly.

I have merit, you know. I went to an Ivy League university and graduated almost at the middle of my class! I could sort of write too. And I know a little more than the kind of Chinese Hilda expects me to speak.

Keil took me into his office like a battered rescue puppy, congratulating me on surviving the "cut." Hendrik's cut. I survived? I survived. I wasn't eliminated. I was staffed on a somewhat important position to someone somewhat important. It was like watching the World Cup semi-finals in a tournament between Ireland vs. Germany. Unbeknownst to me, they—and the rest of this floor—were rooting for Ireland, a country I now proudly belonged to and represented.

Hendrik Müller steals the ball from his Irish opponent, but Rachel quickly retaliates and scores.

Hendrik the Henchman pledged his unwavering loyalty to Künt by distributing assignments and writing the job descriptions on her behalf. The first job assignment I received from him was communicated through a memo he left on my desk:

> To: Rachel See, *Assistant Administrative Analyst to the Key Account Management Team*
> From: Hendrik Müller, Deputy to the Key Account Management President
> Subject: Germany Headquarters
> Date: September 18
>
> You are to report to the WilHeltek Commerz headquarters on Monday, September 21 for the monthly Key Account Management meeting with A. Künt. The address is below.
>
> WilHeltek Commerz SE & Co. KGaA
> Carl-WilHeltek Commerz-Straße 270
> 66611 Gütersloh, Germany

CHAPTER 16

Gütersloh, Germany

How the hell do I even type this into the GPS? The voice coming out of the loudspeaker was berating me—in German! The prompts on the screen were in German. The instruction manual was in German. *Nein*! Speak English! Please! By the mercy of David Hasselhoff and all the other equally chiseled German gods, which button?! There were so many controls in here, and the one I randomly pressed opened the hardtop to the convertible.

"Sorry!" I yelled, glancing in the rearview mirror at the growing queue of obviously frustrated drivers behind me who probably wondered just how long it had been since I had driven a vehicle, let alone one that subjugated me to the bowels of Germany. The answer was, it had been a long—very long—time since I had driven any kind of vehicle (bumper cars don't count). I lived in New York City, home of the notoriously, reliably, unreliable Metropolitan Transit Authority. Why would I ever, ever, *ever* need to drive and join the combative leagues of the yellow taxi drivers on Fifth Avenue, when instead, I could hop on the subway? I didn't drive, but I sure wish I had.

I sat still in the driver's seat, both hands on the wheel, too ashamed to turn around and confront the truth that was staring me a mere foot away—which, incidentally, came in the form of a driver turning toward his partner and motioning his lips, shaking his arm out at me. I could only imagine the expletives I could not understand, when a rental car employee clad in yellow and black rushed toward me with a clipboard under her armpit.

"Yah, do you need help?" she said, her voice nurturing yet rigid. She checked things off on her keyboard and examined the body of the car before fully making eye contact with me.

Good gracious, she spoke English!

You see, I am American, and do not even want to be here. But Hendrik made me. I haven't driven since I was seventeen years old and passed the road test on my Tiger Mom's '97 Pontiac. The gearshift used to be on the physical wheel. Where is it on this vehicle? What are all these buttons? I don't see it here. And I don't know how to type the address that I cannot pronounce into the GPS that I cannot understand.

None of that came out, though. Instead, I said, "Gütersloh. I'm trying to get to Gütersloh. How do you program the GPS to English…and where is the gearshift on this thing?" My voice tapered off, and I turned away to avoid eye contact.

Without saying anything more, the woman climbed into the passenger seat of the vehicle and maneuvered the GPS in a way a child outsmarted his parents when it came to technology. By the mercy of Lord Hasselhoff, she programmed it for me in

English (and then pointed to the gearshift, which was *nowhere* near the wheel).

"Danke," I said, and like a disciplined soldier, she exited the vehicle, then held out her arm for me to move forward and yielded for the next driver to move up.

Pressing the gas pedal too quickly, the convertible jerked forward before I was able to get a better handle on it. It was a brand-new Mercedes Benz SLK convertible, the only automatic rental they had left, which explained why Hilda's secretary asked me multiple times if I could drive stick—"Not even a little bit?" I couldn't drive stick shift, not even a little bit. I could barely drive a car newer than 1997 (a little bit).

I unknowingly floored the SLK on the autobahn several times while blindly following the GPS, which botched the German town names in English. I was on my way to my first team meeting with Hilda Künt—the devil boss herself—in person. If the rumors were right, my head would be severed in that first meeting for God knows what (maybe for not driving stick just "a little bit") and served to our German counterparts with a side of sauerkraut.

Distracted by how Hilda would chastise me at the first team meeting, I programmed the GPS for a quaint little town called "Gütersloh" and set off.

Walking into the WilHeltek Commerz headquarters on that sprawling campus at the ungodly hour of 6:45 AM the next day, I noticed that all of the employees were already knee-deep in work and laser focused. My "Good morning, how are you?" went mostly ignored, except when a medium-built gentleman with square glasses stopped his brusque walk down the hallway, looked up, and said in an apathetic manner, "Nice to meet you. My name is Lieberkühn Joern," before darting back toward what looked like a conference room. I didn't get a chance to fully introduce myself.

Künt preferred her meetings first thing in the morning, so when I walked into the conference room at a punctual 7:00 AM to find the meeting had already started and I was the last to arrive, she singled me out by exclaiming, "Be on time next time!" She didn't even make eye contact with me.

On time? Did meetings here start earlier than the scheduled time? The invitation you sent me said 7:00 AM, Gütersloh time, so go F yourself, I thought angrily.

"Uh...sorry," I muttered, shuffling into my seat. "It won't happen again."

"It certainly vill not," she said, as she turned back to the team.

Lieberkühn sat at the opposite end of where I sat, and was awfully quiet throughout the meeting. I hadn't met any of the other team members, and there was no small talk or introductions. I wanted to shout, *Hello! I just flew all the way from Ireland! After navigating your unfriendly city in a language I couldn't understand, driving at a dangerous speed on your autobahn because there was no speed limit, and then getting lost on this gigantic campus. It's nice to finally meet everyone too!*

Instead, I sat there equally quiet while Künt's team—her disciplined army—prepared to salute her with their weekly sales figures.

Uli went first. Her numbers this week were excellent, and she got the general's pat on the back. "Good verk," Künt said. Next was Heinrich; his numbers weren't as good as Uli's, but still a marked improvement considering he was penetrating an already difficult market—the Middle East. Künt nodded and gave him some advice, which he swiftly jotted down with military obedience. Hendrik, with his big hands, diligently tracked everyone's sales figures because he would compile the numbers into a colorful excel report for Künt by the end of the day.

From context, I learned everyone was addressed by their last name first, and first name last. If you were already acquainted, people often just referred to your surname. So Hilda Künt was "Künt" here. I wondered what else came oddly last and first in this country. Jokes? Morale? A smile?

When it was my turn to speak, I didn't know where to start. "See," I said, following the name protocol. They stared at me, perplexed. "See, Rachel. Nice to meet everyone." Still nothing. Hendrik gave me a look of impatience, as if demanding—"So, what did you achieve all week?"

I imagined myself saying: *Well, Hendrik, I found a flat to move into up the block from a different flat I almost letted that was previously letted out to a bunch of junkies. Then, I was offered some craic at an Irish pub in the suburb of Clontarf. Then, I discovered most stores in Ireland closed at the God-awful hour of 5:00 PM, so I had to wait until the weekend to find a store still open in downtown Dublin to get all the things I needed for said flat I just letted. And then I entered my office to find you sitting in it, only to write out my wretched job description, which, by the way, I still have no clue what the actual job responsibilities include, before you summoned me to this office (which I was on time for because I drove the SLK automatic that was booked for me). I did all of this, after dropping my entire life in New York City months earlier to accept this job I still only have a vague idea about. That's what I achieved all week.*

Hendrik shuffled some papers toward Künt. Künt read these aloud and said, "It says here you know Chinese. Your first werk vill infolfe resbonting to zis Request for Bropozal in Chineze. Zen vu vill lead ein team conference call vith zee brospecdiffe client vo is in Schanghai. Bleaze haffe zis comblete py zee next meeding."

How could I go back to Hilda and tell her I didn't know how to read the thousands of hieroglyphic characters that made absolutely no sense to me in this request for proposal?

After the meeting, I started typing an email that I ultimately never sent:

> Dear Hilda,
>
> Please reconsider a different project for me. There's been an obvious misunderstanding between the kind of Chinese you think I know, and the kind of Chinese I actually know. My aptitude for reading, writing, and speaking in Chinese was as good as a French bulldog's ability to speak fluent French. I can't do this.

But my attorney self couldn't, and wouldn't, give up. There were over fifty thousand Chinese characters, with the average Chinese person knowing about eight thousand. Three thousand was adequate to "read a Chinese newspaper and conduct business in," according to an internet search. I could do this, I thought. It required learning four hundred new words a day. *Just* four hundred.

But that's not what really happened. Instead, sadness, anxiety, and defeat found their way into my life again and crept up slowly, in the middle of Gütersloh, unknowingly seizing my newfound optimism from Coach Confucius. I found myself at the only steakhouse downtown, worrying, wondering how I would complete this assignment well...if at all. I ordered the most expensive bottle of alcohol on the menu because I wanted to pretend like there was nothing to worry about and something to celebrate.

I was the only Asian in this restaurant—maybe even in this city—who didn't know Chinese and looked the way I did. My broad shoulders, tall-ish 5'6" physique, strikingly straight, black hair and high, Mongolian-like cheekbones garnered stares everywhere I went likely because they, too, thought I spoke Chinese. I was ashamed to be the kind of Chinese I was. My veins pumped with heavy remorse as I reminisced on my Chinese lessons in Beijing. Why didn't I pay more attention? Why didn't I study it? Why didn't I know more?

I didn't fit in, and because of that, I may soon be fired by Hilda.

CHAPTER 17

400 Chinese Characters

I had just squandered the last three days in nocturnal hell attempting to memorize much fewer than the four hundred daily Chinese characters I ought to have, all in an effort to *maybe* understand the Request for Proposal (RFP) well enough to respond. I sat alone on campus the following morning and felt consumed by failure, low self-esteem, and the thick clouds of cigarette smoke the Germans were so eager to exhale near me.

Beyond the thick clouds of cigarette smoke was a tall, lanky figure walking toward me. He looked familiar. His long arms swung back and forth and he had large hands, one of which waved at me. I started gathering my things, afraid it would be Hendrik.

But no...it was Aaron! Aaron was here! In Germany! He bent over and wrapped his slender arms around me and gave me a strong hug. I let out a sigh of relief and exclaimed, "My American friend! I finally know what my job is, and I'm going to be fired very soon."

"No, you won't!" he exclaimed. "You kissed the Blarney Stone upside down! You have the luck of the Irish on your side to wrangle you out of any embattlement you get yourself into with Hilda and the German HQ." Aaron sat down next to me and my shoulders sagged. I didn't know how to tell Aaron my embarrassing secret, but I had to confide in someone.

"Aaron," I whispered, and immediately started bawling, "you don't understand. They think I'm Chinese. Like, *real* Chinese. Fluent in Chinese." I pulled out a manila folder with the neatly sealed, twenty-page RFP for him to see.

He took it.

"Hilda expects me to answer all of this—*in Chinese*—and then to host a call with the prospect—*in Chinese*—at our next meeting."

Aaron examined the documents quickly and turned to me to say, "This is easy. They're asking for the name of the company here, the address, the name of the team, your name…"

I sat up, listening intently.

He leaned over. "Essentially, the RFP is broken into three main sections. The first section is basic identifying information. The second section is company offerings, which you can pull from the annual report. The last section is a specific solution offering, usually tailored to their needs."

I was speechless. Aaron, the Chinese American I thought was like me, was fluent in Chinese?! Did the thick clouds above me suddenly split open, the grace of Aaron's big hands granting me mercy?

"You knew Chinese this whole time?" I exclaimed.

"I did," he sheepishly responded.

"But you never said anything," I retorted.

"You never asked," he said.

"You didn't order food—rice—from that Chinese place next to the pub that time I was locked out of the flat?!" I stared at him, confused.

"I don't like speaking it in front of native speakers. I have a weird accent and I'm self-conscious about it," he explained.

Soon after, Aaron and I formed our own study group. He was adamant about my Chinese lessons. Each morning for fifteen consecutive days, he'd sound off his whistle with a morning wakeup call to me at 4:00 AM, preparing me for the arduous marathon ahead.

"Rachel, *kuai dian, kuai dian*," he'd say over the phone, which meant "hurry up." With eyelids half closed, I dragged myself out of bed, determined to master the morning drills of the five Chinese tones. I trained like Rachel Balboa those days, punching back with adjectives, adverbs, and nouns—in Chinese, of course. I doggedly continued to fight through my soreness, pain, and humiliation, dodging maneuvers Aaron threw at me before I was finally able to respond to the RFP in Chinese. I entered campus with both arms raised high above me as I championed up the main building staircase with an invincible ability to absorb hundreds of Chinese words and a refusal to flounder under Künt.

"*Hen hao, hen hao*!" Coach Aaron would yell unanimously with Coach Confucius who took full control of my anxiety, low self-esteem, and defeat. "You did it! You did it!"

I did it. There were ten complete pages with all Chinese characters on it that seemingly made sense in response to the prospective client. Aaron examined it carefully, reading it aloud to me.

"You are ready to lead your sales call," he announced with a grin, "in Chinese."

CHAPTER 18

The Sales Call

It only took nineteen days of hard work and a "you can do it" attitude adjustment from Aaron, but I was ready. This time, I didn't wait to be called to the witness stand to be cross-examined by Judge Hendrik. I was the defendant—defending the victim, me, Rachel See, armed with Aaron's dictionary of Chinese vocabulary words, against losing the new job I so desperately had to demonstrate I could keep. I stood tall and in charge, with fourteen neatly bound RFPs stacked on the conference table waiting for the rest of the team to arrive. Hendrik arrived first. Followed by Lieberkühn. Then Uli, Künt, and the remaining team members. I was equipped with about one hundred index cards of the most common business phrases in Chinese in my briefcase in case the grand jury of prospective clients called for it.

"*Ni men hao. Wo you ji hui ken ni men di wen ti*," I said confidently into the teleconference phone, as if I just sucker-punched Hendrik in the abdomen. The main point of contact, Mr. Zhou, responded. We entered into a friendly dialogue with me responding to each of his questions in Chinese.

Hendrik reached towards the phone and tried taking a stance, "What are they saying? You need to translate to us right now!" before Künt declared "order in the call" and asked me to proceed. The rest of the team sat quietly, observing, listening, and unable to understand any of the Chinese dialogue.

Mr. Zhou said in broken English at the end of the call, "Hilda, you have yourself deal. We happy to do business with you." Künt flashed me a half smile. Hendrik scribbled something aggressively into his notebook.

It was over! I did it!

But…did Mr. Zhou just speak English?

"He speaks English," I balked at Aaron, later that day. "The prospective Chinese client. He speaks English!"

It was a quiet Wednesday morning on campus. The grass was still wet from yesterday's rainstorm. Aaron leaned in, extending his arms in an effort to console me…but pulled back as I continued to rant.

"Hilda didn't tell me!" I said angrily. "I can't stand her, Aaron! Her and that damn minion of hers…with the giant German hands who follows her around everywhere!"

It felt good to vent…so good, in fact, that Aaron and I quickly formed our own clique. Membership requirements? Non-German speaking, frequent complaining of said German culture, being humiliated by your boss, an inability to drive a manual car even a little bit, and an ambiguous understanding of your job. We inducted two more individuals that week: Luuk and Ulrich.

Luuk was from the Netherlands. Ulrich was a German-speaking German, but a defector. When he introduced himself by his first name first, followed by a "…and I hate my asshole manager" in his German accent, we echoed back, "Hi Ulrich," making an exception and welcoming him to our own little Non-German (and German) Anonymous Club.

Ulrich sat down, and Luuk placed his laptop down beside him. It was within this little group that I learned more about Germans and their demoralizing workplace.

"Did you know the formal resignation notice here is three months? Yah, you must give three months' notice," Ulrich explained to me when I asked why Maren on my team was still here a month later, although she had been introduced as "the one who just resigned" by Hendrik.

"Three months? *Three months?!*" I was in disbelief. Luuk chuckled. "Three months is way too long. How could any company allow them to stay that long? Aren't there privacy concerns?" The canteen grew busier as the lunch hour started and the rush of workers came in. A thick cloud of smoke soon formed in the smoking section.

Aaron was indifferent about the three-month resignation notice, although he still couldn't get over addressing Germans by their last name first.

"My surname sounds like a curse. Imagine I answered a call to Künt with 'Fuk.' My name is Aaron Fuk."

I giggled.

"This is why I'm staying with Aaron," he said definitively.

Hendrik spotted us from across the canteen. I turned the other way and convinced Aaron—and our newly formed friends—not to look up.

Ulrich didn't notice, anyway, and instead, responded to me. "Anything short of three months, your existing employer could sue you personally…which is what happened to me, and is why I had to rescind my acceptance offer and continue working for my asshole boss."

Ulrich continued to share with us that Germans called out sick for the slightest of ailments, like a runny nose or a sore throat. They were paranoid about getting sick or getting others sick, which may have explained why the air conditioning was never on in the office. They didn't want to get cold. It made them sick—or so they thought.

The past couple of days, Gütersloh had experienced a record-breaking heatwave. Even then, the air conditioners were off, and it was visibly uncomfortable seeing everyone walk around with obvious yellow sweat stains marked on their shirts. Germans loved biergartens, where they'd so willingly sit outside in such uncomfortable temperatures—drinking beer and sweating more.

This was where we ended up after work that day—my first biergarten. A *real* biergarten. Not the "wannabe" backyards that called themselves "beer gardens." Here, strong, adventurous, self-driven German men were strutting around and showing off their virility dressed in tight *lederhosen*, chugging *bierstiefels*—boot-shaped glasses—of beer. I secretly chuckled as they paraded by with a "who could drink faster, who could slam the beer down harder, who could hold the glass out with one arm indefinitely and not flinch" competitive attitude.

Undistracted by the manliness of the other beer-chugging Germans around us, Luuk sipped his own beer and announced, "I am going to Greece for holiday." Here in Germany, the Germans—and non-Germans who worked for the Germans—were rewarded for their ostensible hard work with six weeks of paid holiday time off. That meant six weeks of vacation time, even for newbies like me.

"Where in Greece?" I chimed in, feeling intrigued. "I've always wanted to go to Greece." It was, admittedly, an adolescent dream of mine after watching the classic *Shirley Valentine* movie. Shirley, the protagonist, uncharacteristically travels to Mykonos on a whim when her best friend wins two tickets. She meets a taverna owner, whom she has a fling with, falls in love with herself all over again, and ultimately, refuses to return home. Instead, she finds joy sitting on the shorelines of the Aegean Sea, watching the sunset because it makes her happy. Greece seemed to make people happy like that.

"You must get to Greece too, Rachel. It can be a quick weekend trip," Ulrich interjected, as Aaron reached for a beer. The music grew louder again.

I sipped my stein of beer, envious of Luuk as he described his itinerary of arriving in Athens first before island hopping with friends on a boat for two whole solid weeks.

Why hadn't I considered going? Wasn't this the whole *other* point of relocating—to discover new places and jet-set around Europe?

A woman dressed in a yellow *dirndl* holding nine bierstiefels—each equivalent to three pints of beer—slammed another bierstefel down hard on our communal table. An overflow of beer spilled onto the ground and splashed my brand-new sandals, staining them.

"I can't," I said with a frown. "I can't travel like that when I'm at a new job...."

Ulrich reached for the beer.

"And with all the work Hendrik and Hilda have staffed me on, I need to maniacally focus on my work," I continued. "I can't travel to Greece."

They ignored my excuses.

Soon, Luuk joined in the festivities, clapping with the dance troupe that formed around him.

"I can't go to Greece. I'm learning Chinese too," I added, but what I had to say began to be drowned out by the German euphoria happening around us. The music only grew louder, and now, more crowds of Germans holding up their bierstefels of beer congregated near us. There was *plenty* of beer.

Where were the kegs? The Germans engineered, arguably, the best cars in the world. Surely they could have manufactured something like a keg to keep the beer cold while we were outdoors imbibing, instead of forcing these poor, bulky women to carry the number of steins they did and spill them all over the place. I was emotionally overwhelmed by the thought of work and the prospect of travel, while also wondering who drank more beer—the Irish or the Germans?—and whether a Tide pen would remove the fresh beer stains on my shoes.

After another moment's thought, I decided the Germans won. Definitely. By a significant amount. The beer consumption per capita (and likely, subsequent liver disease) at this table alone exceeded the county of Dublin.

The barmaid slammed another bierstefel down for us at the middle of the table. Ulrich stood and reached for it, making this his...Honestly, I had lost count. A live band came on in the background, and a crowd soon gathered around us. The men we saw earlier strutting their lederhosen now formed a straight line and started kicking their muscular legs into the air, in unison, as if it was some Christmas Spectacular performance.

There was so much beer and only the four of us. I didn't normally drink beer, but all they had here was beer, so I joined in. Drinking it made me happy, and reminded me of my favorite season—autumn.

Every conceivable version of bratwurst, wiener wurst, blutwurst, currywurst, kinderwurst, sommerwurst, and fleischwurst was in front of us too, shared comfortably with strangers who sat with us at a long, communal table. Occasionally they would shout things like, "*Ich hätte gern ein glas mineralwasser!*" which I learned meant, "I would like a glass of mineral water!"

"*Meine neuen freunde!*"—*my new friends!*—I yelled at the top of my lungs, standing up and throwing my hands in the air. We stayed up late that night, drinking way more than we should have, to the point that Aaron and I could not drive the ten minutes back to the Appelbaum Hotel in Gütersloh. The four of us hauled ourselves to Ulrich's flat, which was a short distance away from the biergarten.

"You're my best friend," I snickered as I tugged at Aaron's arm. Aaron cradled me from the waist up, pulling me forward when my legs went limp, while my other arm was around Luuk's shoulders, who laughed in unison with my giggles.

None of us wanted to be in Germany. But we had all ended up there somehow, working within the same company, all within the same year, sharing the same grievances under the auspices of several steins of beer, and now, laughing together as we walked toward a building in a foreign land. I fell asleep on the floor of Ulrich's flat, right next to Aaron.

CHAPTER 19

Aaron

By the powers vested in Aaron, I woke up early and sober the following morning, ready to pronounce my Chinese words.

"What are you doing up so early?" Aaron moaned, his eyes closed. The sunlight was just spreading into the flat. Luuk was fast asleep on the floor, and Ulrich was presumably in another room, passed out too. The toll of a tall standing grandfather clock could be heard, with each second sounding like a clap of thunder amidst the silence of a post–bierstefel marathon morning.

"We have our Chinese lessons. C'mon," I pleaded, wrestling the blanket off me. Luuk moved one of his limbs in response to the volume of my voice.

Aaron was confused. "But you don't need them anymore. Mr. Zhou speaks English!" Aaron pulled the blanket back on, conquered by the morning and the depravity of sleep.

"I want to keep going. There's still about three thousand new words I want to learn. I *want* to learn this!" Aaron sat up and sighed. He had the look of, "I don't want to, but I'll do it for you *if*..."

Luuk let out a loud snore, and Aaron said, "I'll teach you more Chinese if you agree to take a road trip with me to Köln." I looked at Aaron apprehensively because...what was a "Köln"? Would it hurt me? Would it toss me into the German dams of uncertainty? Did it smell pleasant?

Although I knew nothing about Köln—except it was pronounced like "cologne," which I sprayed myself occasionally with when I didn't shower—according to Aaron's travel book, the one he had on "extensive borrow" from his local library, Köln was *the city* to visit in Germany because of its hip gentrification. He "really, really, really" wanted to go, he confessed to me. It was *only* one and a half hours away, and this was his last weekend in town before having to return to the States.

"Pleaseee," he begged, like a toddler who held out his hands, bargaining with his ability to speak Chinese and batting his big, brown, adorable eyes.

"Fine! I'll go with you. We can practice Chinese in the car," I suggested. We quietly left Ulrich and Luuk behind for our Chinese-Köln expedition and walked toward the biergarten in hopes the SLK was still parked there. Thankfully, it was.

We had unlimited mileage on the car rental, no speed limits in this country, a four-lane autobahn, a somewhat English-proficient GPS, and two equally eager Americans driving to an unknown destination who couldn't wait to get there.

"*Wo men qu naer*?" Aaron lived up to his promise and overrode the English GPS with over one hundred new Chinese vocabulary words, of which I picked up about eleven.

Once we crossed Rodenkirchen Bridge, we knew we had entered a much bigger and more vibrant town than Gütersloh. "*Ji ge hen da*," I shouted. I was even able to translate "This is a big city" into Chinese!

Aaron was ready to explore and brought this big, boxy camera to do so. There were tall buildings here, and if it weren't for the German language blaring from the radio station, the landscape made it feel as if we were in New York City.

Then came the sudden stop. There was local traffic ahead of us, and as we inched behind it, a growing music beat grew louder. We opened our windows to what sounded like a live band or outdoor music festival, along with a faint sound of crowd-gathers cheering them on. An MC was riling everyone up too, and every few minutes, you'd hear a crescendo echo of something in German followed by more cheering and clapping.

Neighboring drivers began rolling down their windows too. There was a group of young adults in the car next to us, sunglasses on, looking like they drove from another city to be at this festival.

One of the main streets ahead was blocked off, and like a queue of marching soldiers, each driver followed the one in front in impeccable order. Each car had to turn right. A short distance ahead, I caught a glimpse of a woman wearing a shiny, silver one-piece costume that fell to her knees, with gigantic platform heels.

"Oh, can we stop and see what's going on?" I begged Aaron, in an interesting reversal of our usual roles. He was curious too, and alternated between peering into the sideview mirrors and rearview mirrors. The music grew louder.

Aaron turned toward the event and squeezed the SLK tightly in between two sedans, where a smart car would more aptly fit. Before I could get out, Aaron exited and walked around the vehicle to open my door before taking my hand and bravely escorting me through the crowded festival.

"I'm glad we're here," he said, before he snapped a photo of me pointing to a random building behind him. He continued to take photos of everything around us. The lighthouse. The rail. The steel bridge. The group of multi-color-hair dancers. The cute city center square with pointy roofs.

"*Ni men hao ma*?" I asked, confidently, as German was being spoken around us. I asked Aaron if he was good. He was, then proceeded to take my heavy backpack.

"What is in here? It's heavy!" he exclaimed. He moved the strap from one shoulder to the other. The camera almost fell out of his left hand. I roamed around freely, as if a burden was lifted from my shoulders.

He carried it for me the rest of the afternoon.

• • •

"You take the bed. I'll take the floor," Aaron insisted. The hotel ran out of rooms with two single beds. There was a massive, romantic-looking king-size bed in the middle of the room and a small kitchen beside it. It was a "free upgrade," and the check-in clerk looked proud as he handed us the keys, mistaking us as a couple (because, you know, we were two Chinese people to them—and Aaron was holding my bag).

"No, you take it. You've been driving all day," I said back. I don't know if this was the very moment my feelings for Aaron started changing, but I desperately wanted to sleep with Aaron in that big bed. I was conflicted, though, because I was still technically in a relationship with a guy in New York who sent me a curt, one-line email that was more indicative of a distant acquaintance. Nate and I were on a "break" but not broken up…right? I wasn't supposed to be sharing a hotel room with another guy during the break…was I?

And Aaron was not even my type. He was a clumsy looking, 6'4" nerdy guy with big hands and long limbs, rectangularly shaped bi-focal glasses, and a slight hunch, who had an obsessive-compulsive order with cleanliness. He straightened everything in the bathroom (twice) and wrapped up my straightening iron cord neatly, like he had just watched one too many Japanese decluttering videos. He refolded and repacked my luggage, even though I was taking things out. He even packed his own pillowcases with him everywhere he went, because "you don't know when they were last cleaned."

While I tried prohibiting any new feelings forming for this guy—who I had only met a couple of months earlier—Aaron was making himself comfortable on the couch, wrapping the pillowcases onto the loveseat pillows that looked strikingly similar to a pillow I had from childhood.

"Can I trade you for one of those pillows?" I asked, as I crawled into the king-sized bed.

He stood up and walked toward me with the pillow he just tucked in, placing it carefully behind my head.

"Don't go," I whispered, hoping he would hear me. He must have, because Aaron climbed into the bed and stayed on his side, as if there was an invisible line of demarcation between us—before I crossed it. Then it happened. Aaron's hand brushed up against my cheek, and we kissed.

I had never felt my heart drop like this—not even with Nate. But it did.

Aaron and I made intense love that night. We didn't intend to…it just sort of "happened" because things felt different with him. He held onto me in an "I'm here to make you feel safe from Nate" sort of way. Even afterward, my heart continued to beat fast. He lay there next to me, one long limb hanging off the side of the bed, fast asleep. I felt secure again, and loved. He restored my damaged, splintered heart, which had been crucified too many times by Nate.

That morning, I did something I never, ever did (even when I was with Nate): I made breakfast. Not just kimchi from a jar either. I pulled out the one frying pan the room had. I washed the two non-disposable dishes that were in the cupboard. I turned on the stove and carefully placed a few slices of thick bacon, eggs and tomatoes we picked up at the farmers market onto the sizzling pan. The smell of bacon finally woke Aaron.

"I'm making an Irish breakfast without all of the Irish stuff." He walked toward me in his boxers—a colorful, uneven pattern of cats. He came over to me and kissed the top of my head, then sat at the small dining table.

Thinking about Nate, I wondered if I should feel bad. It felt strange that I didn't.

CHAPTER 20

I Think I Love You

I couldn't breathe. It felt like an intense asthma attack—the clutching-your-chest type of "I can't breathe" asthma attack.

I might be in love with Aaron.

Neither of us said anything to each other during the drive back to Gütersloh. Did he enjoy it? Did he still want to be in my company? Aaron wasn't saying anything to me. His eyes were laser-focused on the road. He cleared his throat a couple of times, the only sign there was another living being in that vehicle with me. I wasn't saying anything to Aaron either, but I felt a euphoric sense of freedom from the chains once shackled to the throngs of Nate memories. I didn't know how to express my new feelings to Aaron. Then he reached his large, right hand over and grabbed my left hand with it, pulling it toward his chest as he drove. His heart was beating fast. I presumed he was nervous. He planted a kiss on my hand before letting it go.

When we reached the lot of the Appelbaum hotel, he stepped out to open the door for me, outstretching his hand because it was such a low car.

"Are you OK?" he asked.

I stepped out.

"I'm fine," I said, but I really wasn't. I wanted to know if he felt like he just made the biggest mistake of our lives, or if this was the beginning of something new and exciting. He closed the door gently behind me.

Aaron walked me to my room and planted a kiss on my left cheek, before saying goodnight.

When I returned to headquarters the next morning, my mind kept flooding with the constant thoughts of Aaron. Aaron and all the things he made me feel, especially that night. There was an undeniable spark. I felt it in the way his skin felt against mine, in the way every stroke and every touch brought the comfort and security not even Nate could bring. But, I didn't want to mistake pleasure for love. Besides, he was scheduled to leave to go back to the States tomorrow with no return in the near (or far) future. I tried picturing what my days would be like without him, and found I didn't want to.

My thoughts were distracted by a deep-sounding laugh coming from the conference room. An evil, deep-sounding laugh. It was Hendrik. I would recognize his malicious intent anywhere. In my effort to show up early for another team meeting, hoping no one would be there yet, I encountered the demonic voice speaking to another familiar voice, "Ven shall ve turn off Vachel's access card?" It was Hilda.

"Next month, avter I put her on Japanese proposal deal," Hilda said carelessly. Meanwhile, I felt as if the fires of hell shot up from the depths and consumed me.

They were going to shut off my access? They were going to fire me? I moved away slowly, taken aback. Didn't I just learn Chinese and procure a deal for them? In my panic, the hot coffee in my hand spilled all over my blouse. I screamed in silence and started to sob, running into the ladies' bathroom where I couldn't stop.

I made no eye contact with anyone when the meeting started. But when Hendrik muttered, "And what did you do this week?" at me, I stared the demon directly in the eyes and told him exactly what I had achieved all week.

"I learned two hundred more words of Chinese. I learned Mr. Zhou enjoys a fine bottle of Caymus red wine. I learned his business is expanding throughout Guangzhou province along with several other competing businesses seeking similar merchant processing services. There is a tremendous opportunity for WilHeltek Commerz in China, and I pulled the figures to prove it," I answered swiftly.

"Good," Hilda responded, "because ve haf a proposal in Japan for you. Mr. Morimoto-san is seeking merchant processing services in Tokyo." She then flung a half-bound notebook toward me before saying, "Take dis and bring the business in. I vood vike for you to spicht his language."

Hilda obviously didn't know—or care—that Japanese and Chinese were two different languages, and for that matter, two different countries. She also didn't know Japanese was actually my first language, so I could "spicht" it quite well. Not only was I born in Tokyo, it's also where I spent the first five years of my life because my father was the head of credit risk for some major bank over there.

I couldn't wait to leave Germany tomorrow.

CHAPTER 21

It's Good to Be Home (Dublin)

It was nice to see the customs officer at Dublin International Airport. His words this time were, "Welcome home," instead of the usual abrupt, "What are you doing in Ireland?" that typically followed my disembarkment. Ireland was my home now, and it felt so this time, as if the blood of my Chinese ancestry were rooted somewhere deep within the luscious village of County Kildare instead of the village of Guangzhou (which I'd never even visited, so technically, Ireland was much more of a home to me).

Still, I felt anxious, as if a cancerous tumor had developed in Gütersloh and was now spreading to the throngs of my life here, unable to be cured by the latest round of Irish chemotherapy called the Dublin Bay that seemed to have been completely ineffective anyway.

"Where ye goin, love?" asked the cab driver. He turned the windshield wipers on as the rain became heavier. I turned toward the window, which was blurry. I had no idea where I was going.

Why did I even come here, anyway? Hilda was going to fire me sometime after I finished the Japanese proposal. I didn't know why. But I knew how (by having my access cut off like all my predecessors). The demonic conversation I had overheard was still fresh in my memory. I debated whether I should commit corporate *harakiri* by submitting my resignation by email now. Doing so would avoid defeat and salvage any honor still within me, I reasoned.

The cabbie pulled up to Charlemont Road and someone was sitting there, at the doorstep, waiting for me. Was it Aaron? It was definitely a man, and he stood up and started making his way forward....

Nate.

It was Nate!

What was he doing here? Why was he here? My heart began beating a thousand times faster. I fell into the backseat and silently implored the cabbie to drive elsewhere—anywhere. But he didn't hear my thoughts and had already gone outside to gather my belongings. Oh Lord, please, please, please tell me this is a dream. Nate is not here. Nate is not here. Nate *is not* here in Ireland waiting for me.

But there he was—Nate, notably mild-mannered and outwardly cool.

All I could think was, I wish it had been Aaron instead.

"Come, lad. Come help ye girl with ey luggage," the cabbie said. Nate looked like he had just come from the airport too. One piece of carry-on luggage stood next to him. He looked thinner, and he appeared incredibly happy to see me.

He stood up and began to walk over.

"Your mom gave me your address and itinerary. I asked her not to tell you I was coming," he said, with a smile on his face I hadn't seen in a long time. He had an unmistakable modest air to him this time around. He grabbed my luggage from the cab driver and tipped him.

"Cheers!" yelled the cabbie before returning to the car and driving off with his window down.

When we reached the stairs, all I could blurt out was, "I sure wish you hadn't come." But in my usual complacent tone, it came out timidly, when in reality, I was angry. So angry. Did he know how angry I was? I unlocked the door and went inside with a heavy heart, still unable to look Nate in the eyes.

"I missed you so much, it hurt," he said, before grabbing both suitcases and charging forward after me, the door slamming behind him.

I pulled my luggage away from him and rushed into my bedroom, thinking—wasn't this what I wanted all along?

He followed me into the bedroom, his eyes pleading. "I want to be with you, Rach. It was such a mistake to have ever left." He came next to me and planted a kiss on my lips.

But I pulled back. All I could feel was anger. I didn't want him kissing me. It felt awkward, and I envisioned him being Aaron instead. I should have been happy. But I wasn't. I felt nothing. Most of me still resented him for leaving me when I needed him the most.

"I was a lonely wreck here in Ireland. Did you know that, Nate?" I blurted out in tears. The rain started hitting the windows like pellets of rocks.

He stood by me and pulled me from my waist, as he always did when he tried to console me. But I moved away. It thundered outside. It was the first time that I had heard thunder in Ireland.

"You broke my heart into a million and one pieces, Nate," I cried.

When I turned around, still sobbing, there he was, on one knee, with a ring.

He took my hand and whispered, "Will you marry me, Rach?" I took a step back.

CHAPTER 22

YES

I forgave Nate by saying yes. Because forgiving your partner was what you were supposed to do, right? We had been together for so long. He made a mistake, and so did I, except the "I slept with someone else, and still had feelings for this aforementioned someone else, while we were on a break" didn't exactly come out.

I had to stop thinking about Aaron. We had only met recently. What Nate and I had made up almost a third of my life. It must have been true love, albeit bruised over the years. Wasn't respect and friendship the underlying foundation of love—true love? Wasn't the "butterflies in your stomach" just so cliché, and only during the beginning of a relationship, anyway? Just ask any of the over 50 percent of divorcees out there. A quick internet search reaffirmed what I had suspected:

Your partner should make you happy. *(Nate sort of does.)*

Your partner should make you feel excited about life. *(Nate sort of does.)*

Your partner should make you feel secure. *(Nate sort of does.)*
Your partner should make you feel lucky. *(Nate sort of does.)*

Was it silly of me to marry someone who didn't give me the butterflies anymore? Who didn't give me this intense asthma-attack-like chest pain (even though my cardiologist would encourage me to stay far away from any such culprits)? Was it odd to feel these things when I thought about Aaron? How could I be "in love" with someone I'd only known so briefly? I forbid myself from doing so. I didn't want to develop feelings for someone else. It had always been Nate. My logic was greater than my heart as I suppressed any new feelings into an empty, bottomless void.

Nate and I were becoming *Nate and I* again during those seven days together in Ireland. We did cheesy things like take the Viking Duck tour in Dublin before stopping at St. Stephen's Green Park for a long afternoon walk.

Nate took my hand as we walked over a small bridge to the other side of the park. I became nervous for some inexplicable reason. He kissed me, and this time, it felt like the world had stopped moving. Was Nate truly back in my life? Were my feelings for Nate returning? Was the break the reboot we desperately needed to make our relationship work? "I love you," I abruptly cried out.

My phone started buzzing while Nate took his arm and wrapped it around me. It was Aaron texting me—again: "Rachel, hope you are OK. I haven't heard back from you. Don't make me come over there and check on you ☺." I quickly put my phone away and continued to ignore him. I needed to distance myself from Aaron and had stopped responding to him. The silence buried me like a sudden avalanche, causing incalculable loss to my heart. But I told myself this was just a crush. An infatuation. I would get over him. I had to get over him. I was going to marry Nate, and I was in love with Nate again.

So in love again that Nate was my plus-one to this weekend's Sunday roast. Liam, the most gorgeous man I ever laid eyes on and my human resources savior, finally invited me to his mother's home for Sunday roast. He would talk about it every Monday at the canteen.

"Where's my invite," I would balk back, as he described the perfect medium-rare, marbled roast beef his mother made.

"Fine, when you return from Germany. I promise," Liam said.

I was excited to be with Nate, and to be a couple again.

Sunday roast was a thing here. Liam tried teaching me about the holiest day(s) of the year, but all I heard was he could only eat fish on Fridays and abstain from being a carnivore for several more days before repenting to Father O'Connelly on Sunday morning, where his sacrifices and wrongdoings were forgiven, before subsequently being blessed to binge eat meat following service. This was my favorite part, and what brought us here this Sunday. I made sure I—*we*—were on time as it was our first roast in Dublin with Liam's family.

A petite woman with a striking resemblance to Queen Elizabeth opened the door, revealing a delightful, three-story Victorian home with bright-red bay windows protruding from the second floor. "Welcome to Ballsbridge. Come on in," she said in a sweet, dominating voice.

"I'm Rachel. This is Nate, my fiancé," I said, realizing that sounded weird to say. I unwrapped the shawl from around my shoulders and placed it on a floral sofa in the living room. Nate stepped in behind me, as I overheard an occasional "NOOO!!! EGIT!!! HOOF THE BALL ALREADY!" presumably from one of her elder sons watching a futbol match upstairs.

"I'm Nate. Beautiful home here, Ms. Gavin," Nate said, as he stepped inside and extended a bouquet of flowers for Nana. Afterward, he removed his coat.

"This is the fiancé, eh?" Liam walked by, inspecting Nate.

Liam escorted us into the dining room wearing a fluorescent, green futbol jersey with the word "Vodafone" on it, before disappearing into what seemed like a British-Irish-Soccer-Game abyss.

"Rach, is that your coworker? Why is he wearing a jersey like that?" Nate asked, his eyes shifting back and forth, and his tone becoming increasingly critical.

"I don't know. I thought Sunday roasts were a dress-up affair here," I said honestly, then added, "Look at the dining table, Nate." The table was set with fancy dinnerware and colorful Irish flowers in the center—a mixture of white and purple lilies perfectly bringing out the hue of the dining room. Nate was right; wearing a Vodafone jersey didn't seem appropriate, an absolute abomination to the fashion standards Liam held so highly in the office.

"We look ridiculous," Nate said, removing his tie.

There were tiny spoons and forks that looked more apt for a dollhouse tea party than an actual meal. Only Queen Elizabeth would know what to do with them. Why were there three spoons, anyway? In case I dropped two onto the floor? An extra just in case my third cousin from the best Chinese restaurant showed up?

Nate and I were the only ones sitting down at the dining table.

"Rach, where is everyone?" The sound of the telly could be heard from where we sat. It sounded like two different televisions. There was someone upstairs, still screaming because his beloved Irish team—from a county I couldn't pronounce—was losing (again). The others were in the den next door with the rest of the family, with lots of loud chuckling and cheering going on.

"Nate, I have no idea. Roast is supposed to start promptly in fifteen minutes," I said, and I could tell that Nate was growing agitated. He did this thing with his thumbs—tapping them continuously against each other—whenever he was annoyed.

"I'm starving, Rach." Nate pulled his chair in. A loud thump could be heard from upstairs.

"Me too. Now just be pati—" I said gritting my teeth before Nana entered the dining room, laying out a gorgeous roast beef with rosemary sticking out in the middle. It smelled delicious.

"Here, let me help you," Nate said, jumping out of his chair, jostling the Waterford crystals that were so perfectly placed on the table.

"Nonsense. Sit, please. You are our guests," Nana said. The *au jus* of the roast beef continued to drip into the large, oval dish.

"Jack, come downstairs!" Nana screamed. She placed a carving knife nearby, and slung a tea towel over her left shoulder.

"But Mammy! They're gonna score…I just know it…let me finish!"

"If ye don't come down, *right now*!" Nana screamed again, re-tying her apron and now sharpening the knife. Nate and I looked at each other, smiling awkwardly. He tapped my foot under the table, as if to say—*What the hell did we just witness?*

"But Mammy, let me be!" Jack screamed back from the upstairs. We heard another loud thump coming from his room, presumably.

"Oh, I'll let ye be…with a wooden spoon. We have guests downstairs. Now get down here, NOW!"

Nana started carving the roast and placed a perfect slice onto the plates, one by one, before reaching for the peas and potatoes and scooping a generous portion onto each plate. "Liam, Siobhan! Michel! Get in here!"

I placed the dinner napkin on my lap, and Nate followed my lead. He reached for the pitcher of water and offered to pour it for everyone. A group of thirty-somethings and Nana's 70-something-year-old husband Michel made the pious pilgrimage toward us, barging through the dining room door and sitting themselves down, a weekly tradition they've followed for decades. A tradition I *so* looked forward to.

"I dun want dem peas, Ma!" shouted Jack. He looked around, as if looking for a telly with his game on, but didn't spot any in the dining room.

"You will eat them, Jack." Nana banged the spoon against his dish with another scoop. Then, Michel went straight for the bottle of wine and began pouring a generous amount for everyone.

"Here, drenk up now; y'all need it," Michel said. He stood up and reached over to make sure Nate's glass was almost full.

Jack sat at the other end of the dining table, squirming in his chair and moving any sign of green peas into a corner of his plate before ripping into the unofficial mascot of Ireland—potatoes—and making hostile eye contact with everyone.

"Now hold on now, Jack. We must say grace first!" exclaimed Nana. She moved the silverware back to the center and placed her wine glass down.

Jack looked inquisitively at me, and I wondered if it was because I wasn't one of his siblings. He looked vaguely familiar, but most Irish people did to me. His eyes darted to Nate, who had finally looked up.

Nana sat at the head of the table, and like the archbishop leading her lower ranking officers of the archdiocese, said grace:

Bless us, O Lord
and these thy gifts
which we are about to receive
from thy bounty
through Christ our Lord.

Bless us, O God, as we sit together.
Bless the food we eat today.
Bless the hands that made the food,
Bless us, O God.
And please watch over these ungrateful
children of mine. Amen!

Nana pointed her fork at her husband and started berating him for raising their "useless" son who "did nathin 'cept watch futbol. You go ahn, dat bahy never ever even left de cooehntry in dirty five yers," she continued.

Her husband cut into his roast and stayed quiet. I looked down at my food. Nate sipped a glass of the full-pour wine he had. The other thirty-something-year-old children didn't say a word while tearing into their meaty feasts, as if they hadn't eaten in weeks.

"Look at ye. I should have taken me ma'ma's advice and not have married ye!" she yelled. Nana pushed her seat back. The sound of a kitchen timer went off.

Michel's eyes lit up. "Do you mean to tell me yooehr mammy tried to stahp ye frahm marryin' me? Why dedn't I lesten to dat wise wahman?! Gahd bless 'er sooehl!" he yelled.

"You know what ye problem is, Michel?!" Nana demanded when she returned to the table, her right index finger now pointing straight at him.

"Yes, I married ye, ye bird. Now go fly away, on ye broom!" he retorted. He reached for more wine. His children appeared used to their parents' weekly banter and continued to eat.

My cheeks flushed with embarrassment. I secretly laughed inside, trying hard not to snort a pea or spit out my alkaline Irish flat water. Nate kicked me from under the table, but I couldn't even look up at him. My mind suddenly shifted to any serious matter I could conjure up to avoid inadvertent heckling on my part. I forced my head downward toward my plate, unwilling to make eye contact, as the lovely husband and wife continued to banter back and forth like two dueling combatants, unable to reconcile their differences, mired in a shambolic household of futbol fans and one non-futbol fan during their roast. Was this what true love looked like after twenty, thirty, forty years of marriage?

"We have guests, Michel," Nana firmly asserted. "Nate and Rachel here are gettin' married."

"Oh, are ye? How lovely. 'Ahly jesoehs look at de size o' de ring!" exclaimed Michel. Nana forced me to show off the two-carat, round-cut diamond to the family. Michel took my hand, admiring it as I held out my hand.

"Somethin' ye never 'ot fah me, ye old bloke," Nana retorted. Siobhan scratched her knife against the plate as she sliced her roast, making an unpleasant sound like that of scratching a chalkboard.

"Maybe if ye ain't spent all 'dis mooney on Waterford crystals, I'd 'ah 'ave some left for ye." Michel took two gulps of wine before topping off his pour again.

Liam looked up finally and said, "Nate and Rachel 'ave been college sweethearts." He put another forkful of roast into his mouth.

"Ohh, isn't that lovely," Michel said. "Nana and I been together sense cahllege too, 'aven't we dahling?" he said as he drank more.

"Dis calls fahr a toast. To de lahvely cooehple, many joyaus retoehrns like ouhr marriage. Cheers!" Siobhan, Liam, and Jack reached for their glasses of wine, their mouths full, and raised the glasses before taking a sip. Nana, too, reached for hers. Michel continued to drink after we each took a sip.

I started to feel hot. My face was flustered and red. My stomach started churning too. Was there heavy cream or some other dairy ingredient in her roast? Or had I drunk too much? I felt like I was choking on an invisible ball of anxiety, and I didn't know why. I reached for Nate's leg under the table and squeezed it. He ignored me.

Jack interrupted my ball of uneasiness by pointing his fork toward me and asking, "'ey ye ever were at Temple Bar for the Liverpool game 'bout few months ago?" He went back to removing the peas from his plate. Nate looked up at me.

Oh my goodness, I thought. I *had* met Jack. He had the colors of the Irish flag painted on his face and had forced his Guinness on me. I had quickly pulled an Irish exit afterward.

"Um, I don't think so," I said with my head down. My stomach was churning and twisting into knots. I wanted to leave.

When Nate and I finally did about two hours later, I let out a loud, obnoxious belch on our walk back to Clontarf.

"Rach, what the hell was that?"

He turned toward me and took my hand.

I pulled my hand back. "I think there was heavy cream in that food...lots of it." I placed both my arms across my stomach as it continued to gurgle.

"I tried to get your attention to leave, Nate. Did you not feel me squeezing your thigh?"

"Oh, that was you?" Nate asked as if he didn't know it was me.

"I thought it was the sister trying to get some action," he added, looking up at a three-story Georgian home with a red door.

I turned away, clearly annoyed.

I looked up too. It read: "15 Marino Crescent."

"Rach, do you know where we are?" Nate excitedly exclaimed. He walked toward the white two-door coup that sat out front.

"Nate, what the hell are you doing? This is trespassing!" I followed him but stopped short of the driveway.

"Bram Stoker lived here, Rach!" He raised both arms over his head. I looked around to see if anyone noticed us.

My phone buzzed. It was a text message from Aaron: "Rach, I'm in New York City this weekend, and it's as chaotic as you described it. A taxi almost struck me. Then a biker almost struck me. Then a homeless guy almost robbed me. But here I am, sitting on a bench here in Bryant Park. Did you know they play music in the public bathroom in this park?"

Nate ran toward me and grabbed my hand while I was still holding onto my phone. I didn't respond to Aaron, or Nate. Nate looked me deep into my lactose-induced, slightly tipsy eyes, casting me under his Nate spell again as he opened his mouth and moved toward my lips with his protruding canine teeth.

CHAPTER 23

Waiting for Me

A package was awaiting me when we returned to the flat. It was from Aaron, and it was a jar of kimchi, bubble-wrapped and FedExed from Seattle.

Helping you find kimchi in Ireland.

Love,

Aaron

"Who's that from, babe?" asked Nate. He went into the other room to change out of his suit. A lump began to form in my throat, which I quickly had to swallow. The sun was beginning to set outside, and there was little light coming in through the bay window at this hour.

It's kimchi! It's from…my mom," I said, quickly wiping a tear away with the back of my hand. Nate emerged from the bedroom and placed a kettle of water onto the stove.

"Oh yeah, she mentioned you missed kimchi. I was going to bring you a jar, but I didn't want it bursting all over my carry-on," Nate said as he turned the stove on. He turned around and went into the bathroom, slamming the door behind him.

"We'll get some when we return to NYC together!" he yelled, but his words were muffled by the sound of the shower. It was getting chillier. The sound of the boiling kettle soon went off loudly and startled me. By the time I made it to the stove, water was splashing all over the place.

We were returning to New York City this week—together. His brother was getting married, although it was a wedding I was not looking forward to attending. For one, his entire family would be there. Judgmental mom Sue. Big mouth Uncle Joe. Gossipy Aunt Helen. And the cousins. *All* of his passive aggressive cousins.

But Grandma Lucetta would be there. I did miss her. I never mustered up the strength to return her call either. I don't know if it was shamefulness or running away from reality. She wouldn't want me returning to Ireland, and neither would Nate. I was marrying Nate. I didn't have a life in Ireland. I soon wouldn't have a job in Ireland either. I was marrying Nate, and soon I would face his entire family.

CHAPTER 24

Lucetta and the Wedding

"Can the bride's dress spell 'tramp' any clearer?" Grandma Lucetta whispered as she stood up, nudging at my arm as the bride's father walked her down the aisle. "Where are the clear heels?"

The bride, Brittany, wore a sleeveless, sequin, strapless dress so tight, every inch of her voluptuous body screamed—*I'm dressed for a strip club and not my wedding taking place at Saint Michael's Catholic Church.* Nate's grandmother, my favorite family member of Nate's—and possibly, my favorite person in the whole world—had this way of expressing herself by sharing every thought she had. She never quite gave me the shit I deserved for not returning her phone call, but she let me know how she felt in other ways.

"You're too good for my grandson. I know a nice, single bachelor for you—way cuter than Nate. You like Italians? Obviously, you do," Lucetta would always say, often in front of Nate. "Don't forget about your grandmother here when you're married. I don't care how many kids you have!" She gravitated toward me for some inexplicable reason. Though I never admitted to her my lifelong dream of going to Greece, because she'd give me an earful, for sure. "Greece? Greece!" she'd say. "It was called the Roman Empire for a reason...not the 'Greek' Empire!"

Lucetta was the eldest daughter of nine kids, born and raised in Naples, Italy. Her father was from Napoli, and her mother was from Palermo, Sicily. But both of her paternal grandparents were born in Palermo, so she considered herself Sicilian—a Sicilian immigrant growing up in Naples. It was a rough childhood, one "you pansies would never survive," she'd love to reiterate. She would remind everyone how Italians made the best of everything too. "The best pizza doesn't just come from Italy. It comes from Naples. My great uncle's Pizzeria Giuseppe Delizioso could not be replicated anywhere in the world. If you had a taste of one of these babies, you'd never flee the country...unless of course Mussolini was taking away your freedoms, and even then, it might be worth a compromise." She married at the age of twenty-six and had four sons by the time she was thirty-two. She had so many stories of her husband, Angelo, who died when Nate was still little. She'd often mention that she loved him—until he had a one-night stand with a woman half his age. After that, each night he'd arrive home and she'd slam the door in his face as if he was a Jehovah's Witness.

"Look at those hoo-has! Where's the rest of her dress?" she continued. I brought my index finger to my smirking lips in hopes she'd quiet down; after all, the bride was just a mere few feet away coming down the aisle. I wouldn't want this commentary to embarrass her.

Grandma Lucetta slapped my arm with her silver clutch bag. "You're too good to marry Nate. He deserves a tramp like his brother, and grandfather." The orchestra trio was playing Pachelbel's "Canon in D," and as the bride's father teared up, I couldn't help but wonder, was I in this relationship because I wanted to be closer to his grandmother? Because I was nearing thirty and getting married was what I was "supposed to do"?

"Carpe diem," Uncle Joe whispered to Lucetta, and when that didn't work, he said, "Hush, Ma," and stood tall next to her. By now, the father of the bride gracefully gave his blessings to the groom, Jeff. Jeff pulled her veil back, and the priest—who had a look of disdain as he peered at the bride close up wearing a tight, sequin dress in his church—cleared his throat. I imagined him wondering what diabolic spirit possessed this woman to wear this and if the groom was sure in taking thee as his bride.

"How about I *carpe diem* you by the throat, Joseph?" Lucetta said before slapping her firstborn son's bulky arm with her backhand.

"Ow!" yelped Uncle Joe, just as the orchestra stopped playing.

Grandma Lucetta sat down. We all followed.

Jeff began to read his vows to Brittany. "I promise to love and cherish you..."

"...Until the next thing comes along like your father, and his father," Grandma Lucetta mumbled with clenched teeth, tugging at my forearm hard. Brittany was tearing up and Jeff continued.

"...with faithfulness," Jeff continued. I squeezed Lucetta's hand.

"Joseph, did you fart? I smell something," Lucetta blurted.

Joseph fidgeted in front of us and turned his head to the side, pretending to ignore his mother.

"All the schmuck boys in this family! They inherit the wandering eye gene," Lucetta said. Uncle Tony turned toward his mother and whispered, "Oh, Ma, shhh! You're interrupting the best part."

"Are you the one with heavy flatulence today, Tony?" Lucetta said accusingly to her second eldest. "What'd I say about eating beans for breakfast?" Tony was the eccentric one, wearing purple velvet pants with a matching purple bowtie. He carried a colorful, stuffed toy bird the size of his palm and kept it in his left jacket pocket at all times, even naming it "Birdy." The family never quite could confirm whether he would qualify for the psychiatric ward of a hospital when he started showing these child-like tendencies, and then well into adulthood, speaking to his stuffed toy as if it were a person. Outside of this, though, he carried on a more or less "normal" life, graduating from college and even dating. He brought his latest date along to the wedding, a middle-aged Anglo Saxon named Raymond, who outside of the groom and groomsmen, was the only one dressed in an all-white tuxedo.

"*Ma*!" screamed Tony with clenched teeth, before reaching for Birdy with one hand and Raymond with the other. Brittany started to read her vows. All of Nate's cousins—Vincenzo, Franco, Giovanni, Luca, Alfonso, Agosto, Aldo, Antonio—were there too, in the rows adjacent to us. I'd swear I was at a private table at Rao's Restaurant in Harlem, waiting for the hosts of Lucky Luciano and John Gotti to join us, rather than at a wedding.

"I always told you, you could do better…but I see the way you look at my grand boy," Lucetta whispered out of nowhere as we witnessed the bride reading her vows. Lucetta was right, though. There was some powerful, gravitational force that always pulled me back to Nate, and I always searched for that feeling to be reciprocated within Nate the way it once was. I pictured myself trapped within a decade-old quest searching for a hidden treasure chest filled with love, faithfulness, and support buried in Nate's heart. At the same time, I desperately sought asylum from him. He was standing next to Jeff as his best man. Tall, cocky, proud, and never once did he look over at me. Were we settling with one another if we continued our relationship? Would we be "another divorce statistic" in the future?

I still wanted to travel the world. He didn't. He and I used to have the same dreams. We would talk about building a school together in a third-world country plagued by poverty and poisonous insects. Then, after building the school, we would backpack together and find ourselves, spiritually, all the while volunteering our time and staying with the nearby nuns.

But slowly, I felt him slipping away.

He stopped giving to charities, even though he had "all this money now." He became so addicted to himself, to his lifestyle, to his new body image, and to his new job. I didn't think I knew him any longer, because I *didn't.*

"Any schmuck who goes on a break with you, sweetie, spells disaster. I loved my Angelo...until I didn't. May you never experience that pain," Lucetta whispered to me, as the priest belted out, "Speak now or forever hold your peace!"

The room was silent except for a few people whose sniffles could be heard. Raymond placed his head on Tony's shoulder.

Something smelled foul. Grandma Lucetta continued to pinch her nose. Her suspicions were correct. I moved farther away from Tony.

"I'd like to tell the priest I saved a bunch on my car insurance...but would now be the wrong time?" Lucetta quipped.

The groom made a cross-like gesture against his body, followed by the bride. There was some chanting and praying in Italian. The only praying I did was for this to be over fast so we could all escape the smell of growing flatulence in our area that Grandma Lucetta so correctly identified earlier. There was some hand holding—and breath holding—and the priest threw some holy water onto the soon-to-be husband and wife (it seemed to me that he doused Brittany with extra holy water). Jeff and Brittany were soon pronounced husband and wife. We stood up and made our way outside the church, where a stretch limo was waiting for the bride, the groom, and the wedding party. But first, we had to stand in single file lines with rice in our hands and throw it at the couple when they emerged. Personally, I had never understood this tradition. That was a lot of wasted rice. We Asians eat rice. Didn't the Italians eat risotto, which was like rice? Why waste good food by throwing it at people?

Cousin Angelo took an entire bag of rice, and as soon as Jeff emerged with Brittany, poured it over them, with several getting stuck in the intricate jewelry holding Brittany's hair up. She didn't look pleased.

After an uncomfortable, thirty-minute ride to the reception with all of Nate's cousins squeezed closely beside me, I arrived at the reception to witness the photographer taking a hundred and one contrived photos of the groom dipping the bride in some variation of the pose they were just in.

"Now pretend to kiss the bride—all the cousins and groomsmen—one by one. Now, hold the bride up on her side. Now blow a kiss to the bride...."

"How many guys do you think she's used to touching her at once?" Grandmother Lucetta said snarkily, out from behind the photographer.

The photographer knelt to the ground, pointing his ginormous camera upward toward the group, and ignored her. "Now stare at each other, groomsmen and bridesmaids, pretend to be in love like the couple," he instructed next.

Cousin Angelo came over to me soon after photos were done.

"I hear you and Nate are engaged," he said. "Congratulations!" The other cousins began to disperse, mostly to the bar.

Congratulations didn't resonate with me. I should have felt in a more congratulatory mood, but I didn't. I felt rambunctious, and decided to embrace my "let me see how many white lies I can share with these cousins I didn't care for" mood.

"We decided to keep the baby this time. No one knows," I whispered to Angelo, as I sipped vodka on the rocks in front of him and slowly backed away. His face was perplexed, and concerned, and angry all at once. He was shaking his head and looked around, as if searching for Nate and waiting to condemn him for my irresponsible actions.

At the bar, I encountered Cousin Franco, who embraced me with a kiss on my left cheek, then right. "I heard the news, Rachel! When's the wedding date?"

"I'll have another vodka on the rocks," I told the bartender. The DJ started to play EDM music. Two unattended glasses of Aperol spritz began forming condensation on them. Nate's other cousins soon spotted us.

"It was the chemo. We don't know how much time Nate has, and we want to get married right away," I responded, sipping more vodka and looking at Franco. "Don't tell him I told you. He doesn't want anyone knowing." I'm not sure what got into me that night, but sharing different unbelievable, yet believable, lies to Nate's cousins seemed like the sweetest revenge for the family members I did not like even a little bit.

Cousin Vincenzo rushed over, taking my glass of vodka away from me. "Rachel, don't drink. This stuff, um…this stuff is strong." I always knew Cousin Vincenzo was the family rat, breaking their Castrorillus family sacred code of secrecy, and damning himself into family purgatory.

Cousin Antonio spotted me near the DJ with Lucetta. He rushed over. "*Congrazulazione*, Rachel. I hear the news. When iz the date?" I hid my vodka on the rocks behind me on a column ledge because it was clear he heard the false rumor of my impending pregnancy.

Lucetta turned toward him. "What the hell do you want, Junior?"

"Nonna Lucetta, I'm so happy for Nate and Rachel," he screamed, as he embraced Lucetta. Lucetta whacked him over the head with the Stella beer she had in her hand.

"Go get me another one, Junior!" she demanded. The DJ started to play a slow song, and the MC soon announced the bridal party, and finally, Brittany and Jeff.

Lucetta rolled her eyes. The bride came out with an even shorter dress. "I need beer. I like beer. I need more beer," she insisted.

"How about limoncello, your favorite," I suggested. Jeff grabbed his bride and began grinding on her in front of nearly five hundred family and friends.

"Vodka will do," she said as she grabbed it out of my hand and chugged it.

"There better be good food here…not the cheap, buffet-style food I eat in Atlantic City," she said, as she flagged a waitress down and interrogated her about the food that was going to be served. Lucetta wanted lobster, or steak, or lobster *and* steak.

"On the menu is a choice of chicken or tenderloin, or a vegetarian platter," the waitress said. More guests started joining the couple on the dance floor. I spotted Nate from afar with the other groomsmen.

Grandma Lucetta reached for more vodka.

"Can you believe this, Rachel? No steak. No lobster. The bride and her entire family are cheap beyond words." Lucetta was annoyed. "They're the kind of family who we know has money but would drive to a members-only club with their Mercedes S550 to save a few dollars on gas! Stingy miser bastards!" She sat down and began hoarding party favors into her pockets.

"What are you doing, Grandma?" Giuseppe approached us.

"Doing something to avenge the delight Brittany's family takes in saving a few pennies on this crappy food." Lucetta continued stuffing party favors into her bag when her pockets were full. Nate and I made eye contact.

"Can you believe they're not feeding the eighty-nine-year-old her favorite food here? Let's drink," Lucetta insisted. Nate walked toward us. All of his cousins were now congregated on the other side of the reception hall, drinking, talking, and looking over at us occasionally.

"Rach, let's dance," Nate said, pulling me away from Lucetta. My eyes were fixated on his as I searched within him—behind his corporate job, behind his new life in New York, behind his reasons for taking a break. I couldn't find anything. I knew "that treasure of love" still existed, but I wondered if I would ever discover it again. He leaned in and said, "I love you, Rach." I rested my head on his shoulders, unable to say the words back this time.

CHAPTER 25

Pizza and Kimchi

"You're engaged to Nate?" screamed Magda. We were sitting at the counter of my favorite pizza parlor in Flushing, Queens. I hadn't dared to share the news with Magda earlier, because I couldn't. I knew what her reaction would be, and it was unfolding exactly as I imagined. I had avoided her until now, and she instantly spotted the two-carat, round-cut diamond on my left hand as I reached for the kimchi in my purse.

I craved kimchi with pizza, a combination you'd embrace only if you were me. It was an act only Paolo, the proprietor of Glorious Pizza, famous for all its glorious pizza, would allow me to do with my own, smuggled-in-a-jar, kimchi.

"The wedding is set," I said. Paolo was tossing the dough of a pizza into the air with his lean, muscular arms.

"I'll take a plain, Paolo. Rach, are you sure you want to do this?" Glorious Pizza was the best-kept secret in Queens, which served as a rite of passage for any friends or family visiting New York City. I introduced Magda to it when we were college roommates, and we had been coming back ever since. They still churned out the ooey, gooey, melt-in your-mouth, thin-slice pizza you could only get in New York, and were the best cure for this lovesick hangover I still carried for Nate (and Aaron).

"It's what I always wanted," I responded back. But it was sort of a lie. I thought about Aaron now, a lot, and not Nate. Even this pizza reminded me of Aaron. Aaron and I shared the same lactose intolerance for extra cheesy, New York–style pizza. The thought of this whetted my appetite…for pizza and for Aaron. Aaron surely would have taken a Lactaid for this too, as I often had.

"It's what you *used* to want," Magda spat out, along with pieces of her pizza as she chewed it.

"I'm not returning to Ireland." I looked up at Paolo. The photo of Paolo and his pops and his grandpops was taped on the tiled wall behind him, as it had been all these years.

"Paolo, is it possible to love two people at the same time?" I asked, biting into the oily pizza I topped off with homemade kimchi. Magda paused and looked up, dumbfounded. I had never really told her about Aaron.

Paolo was taking out another one of his masterpieces from the oven when he threw his apron over his shoulders and turned toward me. "Ov course. I lov my daughter, and my son, and my waife all at same time. That iz three people."

"Yeah, but…you see, Paolo. There's this other guy…." I put my pizza slice down. Paolo leaned in. Magda almost choked.

"Other guy? You've been seeing someone else, Rach?" She put her pizza down too.

"Is it the guy who tutored you in Chinese?" she asked. The sound of the door opened. A loud New York City bus went by, and an officer sat nearby on a red leather barstool taped with brown masking tape.

"What happen to Nate?" asked Paolo. Paolo knew Nate too, because I used to bring Nate here. He turned to retrieve two plain slices.

"This other guy…I hardly even know him. It's insane. How could I possibly feel this way?" I bit into the slice of pizza again as it slid off the parchment paper and into my mouth. The oil dripped onto the checkered floor.

"Rachel, I met mai waife through arrange marriage and fell in lov with her, immeeeediately. Of course, it possible." Paolo began layering a new pizza with pepperoni, mushrooms, and peppers before moving it into the oven.

Something in me unraveled, as if layers and layers of badgering from Magda and now Paolo—who was busy topping off another pizza—subconsciously peeled away my exterior until the truth revealed itself at my core. The metamorphosis occurred when that revelation surfaced at the counter of Glorious Pizza with a slice of overly oily pizza dripping from my mouth: I loved kimchi *and* pizza. Why couldn't I love both? My Tiger Mom was wrong. I had always been in love with the idea of being in love, and I never put myself first—ever.

I was putting myself first from now on.

"Paolo, Magda, I'm going to go back to Ireland—this time, for me and only me! I have a job to finish there!" I exclaimed. The oily parchment slid off the plate and onto the floor as I stood. Paolo sliced his newest creation into eight exact slices. The officer continued eating his slice of pizza, unfolded, and ignored my immature blathering.

Magda looked up, surprised. I wrapped a slice of pizza to go and prepared to leave Magda and Paolo with hope and a bullish outlook on life.

"Finally, Rach. You chose you," Magda said. She folded her plain slice and bit into it.

When I finally got to Nate's to break the news, he didn't understand why I was leaving for Ireland so abruptly, which made sense because, throughout our whole relationship he didn't really seem to understand why I could *ever* put myself first.

"Babe, we have wedding venues to look at," he said, with a tone of disappointment. "I want you there."

"I can't be there with you." Not now, or today, or tomorrow. He wouldn't understand, and I couldn't share with him my revelation—not yet. I wanted to finish the assignment with Künt. I wanted my life back. I wanted to put me first, and I was determined to have my call with Morimoto-san.

"I'm going to pick out a cake without you." Nate's voice softened, like a child who didn't get what he wanted and, therefore, continued to implore.

"As long as it's not coconut," I responded while both of us giggled playfully trying to find light in the dull situation. Not coconut, not chocolate, not vanilla—there was going to be no cake. Because it was in that exact moment, that I also decided there was going to be no wedding. None of this felt right anymore. The spark there always was in the beginning was put out a long time ago, and I truly felt as if I was forcing myself to continue with it just because of our past and what I hoped we could be.

At last the giggles finally died down, and I took back a giant gulp contemplating everything I was about to say. *Breathe Rach, breathe. This is for you. Don't let your heart get in front of your head.*

"Nate." My already apologetic eyes met his. He stared back blankly, waiting for me to say something else, but I was still struggling to be firm. I slowly picked up both of his hands. "I can't do…" His blank gaze shifted, quickly distraught, as if he already knew what the following words leaving my mouth would be.

"I can't do this. *We* can't do this. I've changed; I've grown. I can't keep pretending everything is okay when it's not. That wouldn't be fair to either of us." Still stuck, I felt my eyes begin to water with every sound I projected. "It's best we just keep this, *us* as a beautiful memory. We don't work anymore—not the way we used to."

Nate shook his head slightly, then again more intensely in denial. "Rachel. Stop it. After all this? You're okay to just walk away after everything we've built for ourselves?" he responded frantically, trying to find a glimpse of convincement in my eyes.

"*Think*, Rach," he said calmly.

But that's the thing—I was thinking. I had been thinking. *This* was already thought through.

I hesitantly let his hands down at his sides.

"Thank you for everything, Nate," I said as firmly as I could before making my way to the door, fighting with every fiber in my body not to turn back. Still, Nate stood there in the dim apartment with the light of his laptop on the coffee table opened to a wedding venue.

With that, I boarded a flight back to Ireland. Now, I could feel my feelings. I had seven hours to do just that. There was no going back now. What's done was done, and I had to deal with it. I just really didn't want to. What if this was the biggest mistake of my life? This played like a bad song in my head, and I prayed the whole flight that feeling would pass.

CHAPTER 26

The Wedding

I called off the wedding exactly seventy-three days after Nate had proposed. I ought to have been relieved to finally be "liberated" from the "were we still in love?" purgatory status that Nate put us—*me*—in. I broke it off. I. Broke. It. Off.

My heart was heavy—really heavy—and broken (again). Nate was and would always be my first love, and all the possibilities of us growing old together in some foreign land, raising orphans and our own children behind a broken picket fence, played like an infinite loop in my mind.

I had to remind myself that this perfect life behind this perfect fence was in fact, not perfect. It shouldn't have hurt like this yet. It felt like a scene out of the movie *Saving Private Ryan*—which seemed to be on constant rerun here in Ireland—where I was paralyzed from a self-inflicted gunshot wound, my blood and existence drenched on the walls of what ought to have been my new life in Ireland.

I called in sick and stuffed myself with cake that Monday (Tuesday, and Wednesday). It was a delicious, four-layer, rainbow chocolate cake with ganache frosting custom made for twelve people, but more suited to one lonely me, moping and still devastated, unwilling to move beyond the perimeter of my bedroom. When the nice woman at Marks & Spencer asked if she should inscribe "Happy Birthday" on it, I nearly burst into tears, a lump forming in my throat.

Nate and I had been growing apart all these years and had already been holding on longer than we ought to have. Even so, I became a lifeless mess, as if a ventilator artificially keeping me on life support in an intensive care unit was suddenly pulled too soon by the person I had trusted all my life—me. It would have been a slow, peaceful death. Would that have been less painful?

There was no celebration. A funeral would be more apt—a funeral to put my past relationship to rest. To mourn it. To eulogize it. To tell it how much I loved it before bursting into uncontrollable, drowning-in-my-own-snots, snorting tears. Again.

"Dearly Beloved," I imagined an officiant saying, "our Nate and Rachel, 2010–2020 born on a beautiful spring day in Ithaca, New York, at Olin Library, were dearly loved, and survived by one aged hamster who refused to run on his hamster wheel anymore…and a grandmother who preferred if her would-be-step-granddaughter marry her friend's grandson, anyway."

That's where the cake came in. Cake was the only thing that made me sort of happy and resembled any kind of normalcy in my life. I couldn't do this, being alone. I didn't know how to "be alone." I was always that plus one; I was always Nate's plus one.

So now, Cake was my plus one. His full name was Chocolate Ganache Rainbow Cake. He was there for me. He was super sweet. He made me feel loved. He didn't judge me. Ever. Stuffing myself with it seemed like the most natural thing to do in bed.

My phone went unanswered for days. By Wednesday morning, Katharina and Sinead were at my door, banging loudly and calling out my name.

"Go away," I moaned, barely audible even for me to hear. They were here to perform a "wellness check" on me, and they came with a locksmith, who helped them barge into my flat, finding me sprawled out under the covers with pajamas I hadn't changed out of in days and chocolate cake all over the place.

"Good Lord. We've been worried sick!" they exclaimed. I reached for more cake.

Katharina hopped onto my bed and removed the cake, placing it on my nightstand.

"We even called Magda! She asked us to come physically check on you because you never called her back," Sinead said, wiping off the chocolate crumbs that had been littered all over the white comforter. She placed her hand on my forearm like a worried mother.

They pulled me forward and hugged me. I was not ready. I wanted to curl up into a ball and sob under a hand-woven silk blanket and not emerge for a decade. Why did I feel this way? Why did I feel so hopeless again?

I returned to the office where my badge unexpectedly still worked. I sat there, working, holding back tears, and trying my best not to let a big lump form in my throat when Keil came over with his coffee.

"Rachel, where ye been?" He stood at the entrance of my office, trying to get my attention. He sipped his hot coffee and waited for me to answer.

"Uhh, umm...been busy," I said, without even turning toward him.

"I had me wanker-in-laws over the house this weekend. They weren't even supposed to stay overnight, but it started to rain real hard and they couldn't drive back. I'd say it was an excuse for them to drink more."

This was too much irrelevant information I neither asked for nor cared about, so I stayed quiet.

"By the way, Happy Thanksgiving, Rachel!" he said. I looked up. Today *was* Thanksgiving. It didn't feel like Thanksgiving because here I was, three thousand miles away in a distant land without Nate or any family who would celebrate a coming together of pilgrims and Native Americans in the other foreign land.

"What's de matter, Rachel? C'mon." Keil folded his arms. The row of analysts nearby continued to type. One walked by, spilling some of his hot coffee as he looked up at Keil.

I sniffed, trying hard not to show any emotions. I didn't want to look up again.

"We are going out tonight, all ye us, to celebrate this yank holiday with you. We are grateful ye joined the floor." Keil moved in closer. "Isn't that what you Americans did—celebrate thankfulness by binging on high caloric foods?" Keil stood there, waiting for a response. I continued to ignore him.

That is what Americans did, followed by forming long queues outside of department stores in hopes of beating one another for the best bargain basement deals. But what would I celebrate this year?

Keil wanted to make it up to me. He also wanted to see what all the fuss with Thanksgiving was about. He wanted to live vicariously through me.

"But Keil," I interjected reasonably, "you do realize as a Chinese American, my celebration of Thanksgiving looked more like a scene out of *The Joy Luck Club* with mahjong, matronly aunties gathered around insulting each other before turning to me to say something like, 'I haven't seen you in a long time and how fat you've grown;' the dining table filled with traditional Chinese dishes like noodles and spicy tofu; and me, hiding in the corner from these aunties with my own bowl of white rice topped with fresh kimchi out of a jar."

Still, Keil didn't care about my particular experience; he wanted to overeat like an overweight American. The true spirit of the gluttonous American holiday would be "fun," he thought—with or without a twenty-five-pound turkey (or kimchi).

I didn't budge and must have refused Keil's offer eight-hundred different ways, when finally, he dragged me out of my seat and into his compact, two-person car that had the engine of a lawnmower. I had no idea where we were going, and I didn't care. Keil could have tied me up, kidnapped me, and driven off the Cliffs of Moher at that very moment, and I wouldn't have put up an Irish, bare-knuckle-boxing fight. At least I would have drowned with some heartbroken dignity.

Instead, we emerged onto Dawson Street in the city center. By the time I looked up, a large awning with a mural of a little Asian boy with a haircut resembling my childhood Tiger Mom–made bowl cuts read, "Wagamama." It sounded Japanese and looked more like a hipster spot you'd expect to see in Williamsburg, Brooklyn than in Dublin, Ireland. Keil promised it was "really" more Asian than the "Best Asian Food in Ireland."

Under duress, I went inside with him, and we were greeted by a loud, vociferous "Happy Thanksgiving!" that roared and echoed along a communal table. There they were: everyone, smiling back at me, holding up some sort of alcoholic beverage aimed at reviving my broken heart. Liam, dearest handsome Liam, was sitting at the head of the table impatiently imbibing far too many pitchers of something. Next to him were Katharina and Sinead. Adjacent to them were familiar faces from the office whose Irish names I still botched when pronouncing. Grainne and Siobhan from accounting. Maximilian and Shauna from helpdesk, who more often than not, ignored my weekly pleas for IT support. Phil, Deidre, Tristan and Niamh from Finance, who sort of "adopted" me since I was the only Key Account Management, non-sales, sales team member from Germany domiciled in the Dublin office. Even big-handed Hendrik was there, derisively laughing with Claire, the drunken recruiter whom I met in Rome and shared my love of Montepulciano wine and aged Reggiano cheese. I gave Claire a hug, who appeared already drunk (again).

Liam raised his half-empty, cold glass of beer, and in his most exuberant Irish voice said, "Thank ye, ye Pilgrims who landed in America on that historic day in 1600 somethin', for the Native Americans for bringing with them 'all those crops' and for giving this Irishman an excuse to go out with an American in Dublin on a rainy, random Thursday night."

He took a sip.

"Could the Vikings have reconciled over beer instead of invading and conquering the Irish?" Liam asked half facetiously.

Hendrik followed with a sip.

"Beer brings people together," Liam continued. "Could beer have stopped wars, helped procure peace treaties, and been used to feed families during famines?" Liam paused.

Claire let out a belch.

"If only Arthur Guinness had been born about a thousand years sooner, maybe, just maybe, we would have seen a very different outcome in Irish history, and there would be a regular gathering of Irish on a random Tuesday night, indulging in beer and carefully carved sheep stuffed with sweet potatoes," Liam finished with a chuckle.

Liam knocked his beer against the table. Everyone raised a pint of something to guzzle, followed by a loud "sláinte" before Hendrik jumped in with his heavy, stoic German accent, "I am dankful for being invited tonight, yah, with new Irish friends."

His hands suddenly didn't look so big. He didn't seem *that* mean either. For a brief moment, we were thankful even Hendrik was among us tonight, embodying the true spirit of the Thanksgiving holiday. Hoping he would heal, love, forgive, and no longer be the snitch he was.

One by one, with a beer in each of our hands, we went around saying what we were grateful for.

Graine teared up as she spoke, "I'm so 'appy to be 'ere. A year ago, I was in an abusive relationship and dedn't know 'ow to get ooeht." Katharina hugged her, then said, "I'm grateful we can come together on this Thursday and have plenty of beer."

Claire slurred her words and said something incoherent that the rest of us could not understand, "Oi'm 'ere! Oi love yer al'! Oi draink ter yer! An' turkeys!" Everyone still raised a glass with her to celebrate and drank.

Hendrik slammed his beer down with his big hands. He soon shot everyone with his infernal stare, telling us with his eyes he was "watching us," but he let out a gentle, "*Danke sehr.*"

Then, it was my turn.

"I'd like to thank…I'm thankful for…" A lump soon formed in my throat, but I found the strength to continue.

"I'm thankful for you all, for resuscitating my lifeless soul. For meeting Claire on that fateful day in the wine cellar of that tiny restaurant in the alleyway of Rome…"

Claire knocked her glass of wine back in my direction.

"For Liam, warning me about the belligerence of Ballymun. For Clontarf. Wonderful, coastal Clontarf."

Grainne reached for her beer.

"For the fresh Irish Sea air. For Keil not kidnapping me and driving off the Cliffs of Moher."

Keil interrupted with a loud, "Sláinte!" and raised his tall pint.

"For Aaron, who's somewhere in the European Union, and who I still think about often. For Keil and his tenaciously annoying tendencies to drag me out. For Nate."

Maximilian and Shauna stood up and let out a loud roar, hitting their pints loudly against each other as I continued to speak.

"For gathering around in this Sino-American-Japanese-Irish group slurping on noodles—which I have to say, are better than the last Asian place Keil chose—and restoring my faith and strength in love."

Liam followed and raised his pint. We all drank to this, and many more.

The Irish craic was exactly what this newly single, lonely, heartbroken, depressed gal needed, and my Irish friends gave me that lifeline on Thanksgiving Day in Ireland. We continued to eat like true, ample-sized Americans and ignored our everyday problems like true Irish patriots.

Yet, during this festive, come-together moment, something was missing....

CHAPTER 27

The Unexpected

Dearest Aaron,

I never expected to meet you, and when I did, you resurrected a piece of me that I thought I had lost a long time ago: me. I moved to Ireland to get away from everything. But everything I was running away from seemed to have caught up with me here too—literally and figuratively. They were my own battles and internal struggles of "finding myself," whatever that meant. I never expected to fall in love with someone again so soon. I didn't want to, because I had just gotten out of a relationship with the love of my life (I think) and thought I was going to marry him. And so when we got close—too close—I pulled back. I'm sorry for going dark on you. When you couriered me kimchi, I cried. I wanted desperately to return to Cologne with you again. I was in denial. But I wasn't running away from you, I was running away from me. I was too weak and too afraid to embrace the idea that love could once again find me.

Know that deep down in my heart, I want you to find true happiness. Please forgive me for being selfish, but I need space. I need time. I need to breathe. I need to find and reconnect with myself again. I am taking as much time as I need to nourish my soul and start growing again. All my life, I've sacrificed for others and now I must be—need to be—selfish. Shouldn't we all be selfish and strive for everything in life? Didn't someone once say that greed was good? I pray that one day our paths will cross again.

With love,
Rachel

I put the pen down and folded the letter. I subsequently unfolded it and typed it onto my laptop, leaving it there to sit in my outbox indefinitely as I grappled for days on whether to hit "send."

"I'll send it tomorrow," I would catch myself saying each night. But each day came and I was too unsure, too numb, not knowing the unknown. How did Aaron feel? Did he reciprocate my feelings? We had never even acknowledged *that night*.

After numerous nights accompanied by Gin and Tonic, I decided not to deliver the letter to him, even though my soul apologized deeply to him, hoping he somehow had the intuition of a higher being who could hear all my thoughts.

Part II

CHAPTER 28

The 30th Surprise

"Rach, Rach!" Magda lunged at me with an embrace so strong, I almost toppled backward. The cab driver who dropped her off waited until I answered the door before speeding off, his cigarette flying out the window and hitting the pavement.

Magda showed up at my flat that morning. I was confused. She just flew over three thousand miles and was standing at my front door at 6:58 on this Saturday morning in Dublin.

"I've been worried about you, Rach." She pushed her way into the flat with her things. I was still half asleep.

"Worried about me?" I responded. I almost forgot about the call I made to Magda last week. I called her when I was in a depressed, drunken, deplorable state, sobbing on the floor of my kitchen past midnight before I brought the infamous chocolate ganache cake into my bedroom to cry even more, interrupting her dinner that was taking place five hours earlier. I wailed and cried, telling her how sad I was in an incoherent English she couldn't make out before my battery died and we got cut off.

"I came as soon as I could. I didn't want to worry your mother, so I had your colleagues check up on you, and when I still hadn't heard back, I booked a flight over." That was the thing with Magda. She was a good friend—most of the time. When she wasn't berating me.

"Mags, let's go to Giant's Causeway!" I suggested, still half asleep.

Magda took a step back and dropped her carry-on bag. "So, you're OK now?"

"Mags, I'm fine. I've come to terms with my life…and with leaving Nate," I said.

I pulled out the sofa bed for my surprise guest. "A revelation just came over me. So, I know I'm not the best travel companion…"

Magda raised an eyebrow. "What's your point, Rach?"

"Let's go somewhere, just you and me."

It was awfully bold of me to say. I packed at the last minute, dropped my passport more than a handful of times, and never, ever, EVER did any sort of "proper research" of hotels or neighborhoods or cities for that matter. I'd blindly buy airfare tickets to something that sounded cool and would walk up to the first hotel in that city, praying it wasn't booked with some weekend music festival brimming with college kids dressed in bandanas and combat boots. I made the mistake of driving to Miami one long weekend, and with hotels hovering around thousands a night, I spent the night on a park bench. I never planned, but Magda did.

"Let's go to Belfast!"

"Belfast? What the hell is in Belfast?" Magda moaned.

It was one of those places that appeared on a list of "Things you might be interested in" on my newsfeed. I pulled open my laptop and showed Magda the sight of interlocking, vertical rock formations. They weren't any ordinary vertical rock formations—they looked like giant steps emerging out of the sea. Gaelic mythology said an Irish giant was challenged to a fight by a Scottish giant, but the Scottish giant fled in fright and destroyed the causeway behind him so the Irish giant wouldn't be able to chase him down.

"C'mon, I really want to go!"

"Did you sleep with that other guy—what's his name, Aaron?" Magda asked inquisitively, suspicious and locking eyes with me until I told the truth and nothing but the truth. But at the last minute, I decided to resist.

"I did...n't know much about Northern Ireland, especially since most of the Irish in the south didn't speak about it, and had never been." I avoided her question.

Magda moved closer, but I continued my history lesson about Northern Ireland. Northern Ireland was like the only child two parents embroiled themselves into a bitter custody battle over. It was not politically part of Ireland, although geographically it was. It belonged to the neighboring United Kingdom. Those siding with the Irish parent rebelled in the form of the Irish Republic Army and a hint of Catholicism by fighting for its freedom and a United Ireland. Those who remained loyal to their UK Parent fought back.

"You slept with Aaron, didn't you? When do I get to meet him?" Magda reached for her bag.

"Mags, it's my living-in-Dublin duty to tour Northern Ireland as its black-haired, visiting-from-abroad, American stepchild who is neither a tourist, an Irish citizen, or a UK citizen, but a permanent resident of Ireland with a PPS number that gives me a discount to a two-day 'Intro to Belfast' bus tour. C'mon, let's go together," I insisted.

"I have a surprise for you." Magda placed her luggage on a stool, then pulled something out of her backpack. She handed it to me before dropping her bag back down.

"I promise it's better than Belfast," Magda said.

It was a boarding pass that read, "Athens, Greece."

"It departs tomorrow." Magda unwrapped her knitted scarf and pulled down her hoodie. She held out her arms. "Happy thirtieth birthday, Rach! We're going to Greece together!"

It *was* better than Belfast! I was ecstatic. I'd always wanted to go to Greece for as long as I could remember. I loved everything about Greece. The crystal blue water. The beaches. The copious amounts of food. She knew that. I knew that. I soon forgot about Belfast. "Wow, Mag. This is incredibly generous.... But..."

"You're calling in sick. I don't want to hear it." She went into the kitchen and started the coffee machine. I wanted to go, truly. But how would I tell Künt?

I imagined the phone call to go something like, "Uh, uh, uh, I'm um, calling in sick," along with a string of fake coughs. This call would be followed by silence, and then followed by, "Ve are turning ov your access!"

I couldn't. How could I leave tomorrow and go?

After much coaching from Magda, and seeing the blue and white photos of Greece littered in her travel book, I picked up the phone the following morning and in a brief, rebellious, uncharacteristic moment, my voice channeled the almighty powerful Godfather Don Corleone, demanding directives in a sheepishly strong, deep tone to Künt, before finally ending it with, "So I won't be in this week," before abruptly hanging up and high-fiving Magda. It was the best Monday morning I had in a long, long time.

CHAPTER 29

Greece!

"*Kalos irthate stin Athina!*" the pilot announced over the PA system. *Welcome to Athens!*

Magda and I hadn't said one word to each other or looked at each other the entire plane ride. I couldn't be friends with her anymore, let alone look her directly into her guilty eyes without the urge to punch her in the face. Not after what she revealed to me exactly fifty-eight minutes ago. The tension between us escalated, and I, like a dormant volcano, erupted into Mount Saint Rachel.

I continued staring out the window, refusing to turn my head and acknowledge my thirtieth birthday gift from Magda. Instead of the giddy, "We're here, we're here, we're here!" I should have been chanting, I slumped back and wondered, "Why am I here? Why am I here? Why am I here?"

The plane sat at the gate for what seemed like an interminable amount of time, but was probably only twenty minutes. The seatbelt sign turned off and, like a department store that just opened its doors to a queue of anxious, ill-mannered shoppers looking to beat you up inside for the best Black Friday sales, the angry-looking Greek mob rushed to the overhead bins for their belongings, wrestling one another and mouthing off what was Greek to me.

Magda joined the mob and wrangled our bags out of the overhead bins. I still couldn't look at her. We made it out of the airport in one piece, and a portly Greek guy standing next to his taxi, cigarette hanging out one side of his mouth, started waving at me, saying something in Greek, as his cigarette quivered up and down with his lip as though it had been glued.

"*Ella, ella, ella,*" he kept saying. He let out a loud cough, the kind of persistent smoker's cough you'd hear from an emphysema-induced patient in the emergency room of Weill Cornell Hospital awaiting a double lung transplant.

With bated breath, we stepped into his cab and announced, "Hotel Grande Bretagne, *parakalo.*"

In the span of a year, I was in the backseat of a taxicab with Magda again, in a foreign land within Europe, with a foreign driver taking us to God knows where. But this time, I couldn't forgive her. I wouldn't. Would I get my own room once we'd arrive at the Grand Bretagne? I prayed to the Greek gods that there would be at least one available room left at a thirty-year-old friendly price. Alternatively, that Zeus would dispatch a lightning bolt on Magda.

Magda stared out the window, looking into the mountainous landscape. The sound of static Greek music came out of the car radio. I tried my best to make out the little bit of Greek unfolding in the highway signs in front of us, which I only vaguely understood from joining a sorority in college.

If it weren't for the trauma of being woken up by the sisters blowing sirens into my ear in the middle of the night, forced to march through the dense, dark, foggy woods of Buffalo, New York, blindfolded in pajamas, freezing in the middle of winter, chanting the Greek alphabet at the top of my lungs with seven other strangers-later-turned-best-friends, backward, forward, then backward again before passing out, I would not have made out the Greek letters emerging in front of us: *alpha…theta… yota…nu…alpha…*Athina! It would be thirty more torturous minutes in this car ride with Magda to Athens.

That had been the beginning of her envy. When Magda didn't win a bid to join the Greek sorority I had joined. She insisted I pursue joining the sorority without her, but she never liked those girlfriends and referred to them with every imaginable expletive adjective there was.

"*Milate aglika*?" *Do you speak English?* Magda recited from her travel book, obviously ignoring me from the mere inches I sat away from her. "Mee-late…ag-la-ka? Mee-late…ag-la-ka?"

"It's important to know at least a little bit of the foreign language," she proudly declared to the middle-aged, slightly bald taxi driver who looked like the father from a prominent Greek American movie about a daughter marrying a non-meat-eating non-Greek. He was too engrossed in the music playing to pay any attention.

Yes, Magda! I sarcastically responded in my head.

The Greek cabbie spoke then, ignoring everything Magda said. "Athina is wonderful city. Beautiful city I grow up in," he said in his heavy Greek accent, another cigarette hanging out of the corner of his mouth. We emerged off the highway and into the dense city center of Athina.

"That over there, where my *yiayia*—grandma—raise me." He pointed left, then right, offering a brief history of Greece and showing us where the Acropolis stood as he weaved the cab in and out of the narrow streets of Athens. Although I could only manage to make out a few of the scattered words that were supposed to make a sentence, I just smiled and nodded.

His eyes briefly met mine in the rearview mirror. I quickly glanced away, and became too distracted by the appearance of Athens to pay any attention to the "tragic fall out of Magda and Rachel." Surprisingly, the city was ugly. Really ugly—nothing like the picturesque blue and white city of the Greek islands in the photos of those travel books. I sank back a little in my seat. There was graffiti on top of graffiti *everywhere*. Buildings, ramps, highway signage, store fronts, gates, even trees—most vandalized in some sort of way. It made those that weren't marked look like the odd ones out, practically screaming to also be vandalized.

Clothes hung on flimsy clotheslines on the balconies of buildings that looked like they violated just about every building code that ever existed (maybe there was no Department of Buildings providing regulatory oversight here?). Just up ahead was wire fencing and boarded-up storefronts with more graffiti on it. Where was the beautiful city of Athens that the travel book so proudly proclaimed?

"I betchu not know the Gleeeeeks defeated the Italian army in 1940?" the cabbie asked, as he nodded his head proudly. I continued to look out as we passed another old building with graffiti on it and the cab hit a bunch of potholes.

"Dah-ring World War II, the Italian ah-rmy under Mussolini approached the border of Greece and say, 'Look here, give us passage. If you do not, we will invade you. You have the three hours to decide.' Prime Minister Metaxa—may he rest in eternal peace—as he interrupted and followed the Holy Cross Trinity in his honor, say, 'We no need three hours to decide. We give you our answer now. It is *ohi*, which means no."

Magda placed her travel book back into her bag.

"In fact, Mussolini go to the Hitler begging for help to overtake our country. The day is celebrated each twentieth-eighth of Octobre and is called Ohi Day," he proudly said.

"Please let this end soon. *Please*," I whispered, holding onto the door handle as the cabbie sped through another pothole.

"The Italian army much better equip and a much stronger army, more soldiers, and better weapons than the Greeks. This invasion was the Greek version of David versus Goliath. You know dat story?"

The cabbie came to a stop at a red light in a narrow alleyway with what looked like restaurants and bars. A homeless man with a long, dirty beard knocked on the window, and Magda almost screamed.

The cabbie continued to tell us stories. "The smaller Greek army come together victoriously, with their older weapons and significantly outnumbered by the Italian army, defeating the Italians!"

Magda moved away from the window toward me, shaking her head.

The cabbie started another story, which ordinarily, I would have found fascinating, but today, all I could think about was forming a small army to annihilate Magda. As we continued to sit in silence, the cabbie started again, "My father is from Sparta. Do you know the famous battle? Two hundred thousand Persian soldiers approached Thermopylae, also demanding passage."

This time, the cabbie stepped on the accelerator and emerged onto a bigger street near a square with an erect building.

"The Spartans born to fight. The Spartan vives, they raise men and tell their husbands and sons not to bother coming back if they don't win." The cabbie made another turn. There was a small crowd gathered a few feet away, presumably tourists.

"I think we're almost here," Magda said, rummaging through her backpack.

"They had winning spirit. The king of Sparta back then, Leonidas, said to the Persians, '*Molon lave*'; it means 'Come and get it' when the Persians say put down your arms."

My phone buzzed. It was an e-mail from Aaron:

Bonsoi, Rachel. I'm in Paris now, or as they call it, "Paree." It's my first time here, and there's something about this city that could only be Paris. They even have a name to describe this French phenomenon, "Je ne sais quoi." I'm in the middle of the street now, pulled over on a bicycle, with baguettes sticking out of a wicker basket attached to the front, gawking at the arc de something and being scoffed at in French by passersby. I've turned myself into a mobile cliché.

Nothing bothers me here, though. My tolerance is the highest it's ever been. Even the throngs of tourists viciously fighting to get in front of me don't bother me here. Neither do the obviously disingenuous panhandlers crying about not being able to feed their babies, or the hoard of immigrant entrepreneurs running up to showcase their collections of blinking Eiffel Tower souvenirs that I don't need.

I'm in Paris this weekend following an assignment for no other reason than because I wanted to be. On the other side of the souvenir-gawking tourist traps, elegant Parisian women are dressed in the most stylish outfits as if the streets of Paris are their personal runway. There is a silent pact with the city—once you step out into the streets, you have to wear something that "prettifies" you. This could be a scarf, a bowtie, a bold-colored shirt, a brooch—or a beret, which has enticed even me, a "hat hater," to pick up two fedoras (one in cobalt blue and one in black) from a sweet French street vendor who spoke English only "un pas" (a little bit) and gave it to me at the discounted rate of five euros each. Even he was wearing a jacket and a tie. Donning a fedora hat in Paris made me feel French: "Je m'appelle Aaron."

Speaking of cliché things, the song "La Vie en Rose" is playing just a short distance away by an accordion player along the Seine River. Couples brazenly made out with a bold French kiss (or perhaps just considered a "kiss" here) as they held hands and walked aimlessly, and strangers seemed to enjoy watching them.

That is actually a thing here too—"people watching." It is exactly as it sounds; you watch people. You look at them, and it's what embodies the café culture here. The old adage of "don't stare" has become "do stare" here.

I skipped the museums again today and instead, chose to gawk at gorgeous people while sipping pressed coffee and eating croissants (the most buttery, flaky pastries I ever had. I had two, actually, on my first day here). Then I bought three baguettes to go (is it considered a cardinal French sin to tear apart the baguette with my two front teeth and eat it while I type this message to you)?

I thought by today, maybe I'd want to go to the Louvre, or the Rodin, or d'Orsay, but I didn't. I just wanted to eat more French food and rent a bicycle. I even found a non-discrete butcher-like shop earlier, lured in by the dry meats hanging from the counter and an older gentleman who looked to be the owner, just as his father, and his father's father. He highly recommended the saucisson with what we ordered.

It did not disappoint. My favorite thing to eat in Paris so far has been the cheese. Brie, definitely brie, paired with a glass of full-bodied red Bordeaux wine, and a few slices of this highly recommended saucisson. There were all kinds of similarly vibrant looking hams and hard salami and other things next to the brie on that wooden platter the gentleman brought over to me. The cut-up baguette was still warm and went deliciously well with this fatty-like spread next to it—rillettes, the butcher rolled off so easily. And these wonderfully small pickles that were neither pickles nor gherkins. Corn-nee-khon, I learned, as I dipped one into mustard before devouring it in one bite. This was such a foreign concept to me—eating meats and cheese on a cut-

ting board—yet one I so easily embraced. I spent four hours there without realizing four hours had passed, debating with a young couple who sat next to me where to find the most decadent coq (au vin) in the city.

No sign of kimchi just yet, though. I'll keep looking for you. Wish you were here.

Hope you're well,
Aaron

I missed him. Something didn't feel right, and I suddenly craved cheese. I put the phone away and continued not to respond to him.

"They fought and fought," the cabbie continued, "until death did each of them part, dying in a bloody attempt to defend their beautiful country...."

How much longer would Aaron be in Europe? I desperately wanted to contact him, but I wasn't ready yet. The emotions of Nate were still raw.

"Are you going to ignore me this *entire* trip?" Magda asked. A group of teenagers walked by as the cabbie approached a stop sign. They laughed and spoke a foreign language.

"Yes," I replied. One of the teenagers climbed onto another's back and started taking photos of the city.

"Winston Churchill once said, 'Hence, we will not say that Greeks fight like heroes, but that heroes fight like Greeks.'"

There was an overwhelming sense of honor and pride in the cabbie's voice that evoked the victorious spirit the Greeks seemed to have. I may have witnessed this ferocious fighting spirit on the plane just earlier when the Greeks grappled with each other and vied for their luggage.

He pulled up near Parliament and offered us the following advice, "Be careful when you exit. They will knock you off your feet, those bike drivers." Magda reached into her pocket for the euros she had exchanged at the airport earlier.

"Over there, Syntagma Square, and down there Monastiraki towards the Acropolis, lot of pick pockets," he continued. "Hold your things in front of you like-ah this. Also, you need to learn the word, 'malaka.'"

The most important word you need to learn in Greece apparently is the word *malaka*. It was nowhere in Magda's guidebook because it translates into the American equivalent of "asshole." But it can be used in an endearing way between friends, family members, and even co-workers.

Malaka, it's been ages! Get over here and give me a big hug. Malaka! Happy birthday to you and a million more! Malaka! The boss wants to see you!

But it was also used as a curse word. Car drivers who cut each other off—*Malaka* (followed by a slow motion of the hand palm to their face)! A big, German guy giving you a wicked stare and telling you what you were worth—*Malaka*. A smoker smoking in the non-smoking section of a restaurant, *malaka*! The colleague that secretly laughed at you for not speaking his language and pretended to be your friend—huge *malaka*. Walk down the streets of Athens in any direction and you'd inevitably encounter *many malakas* (plural for malaka). The Greeks didn't discriminate either, because they had this word for women specifically too: "*malakismenis*." They were all over Athens too, giving me a disdainful look.

Magda paid the cabbie, and he helped us retrieve our belongings from the trunk. "Yasas!" he screamed, as he waved us goodbye.

A bellboy emerged from the hotel to help us check in. "Welcome!" he bellowed out.

"Do you have an available room?" I asked when we approached the front desk.

"Rach, don't do this," Mag said.

"Not together?" the young man asked.

"We are. The reservation is under 'Kim,'" Magda retaliated.

"Ah, Kim for two, yes I see. Your room is not ready yet."

"No, I'd like...I'd like my own room," I reiterated, now confusing Yianni, the young man helping us check in.

"I'm no longer with her," I emphasized. Yianni went back to the computer and started typing.

"There is no availability, I am sorry. Tomorrow night, I may have," he said, moving his head from my direction to Magda.

"Don't do this," Mag said.

"I can't believe you and Nate hooked up while I was in Ireland!" I shouted, in a moment of rage, pulling my bags. I couldn't bottle it up anymore.

"Rach, it's not like that. I was trying to win him back—for you." I dropped my bag off for the bellboy to take while I stormed outside to a corner vendor selling piping hot, crispy cheese pies.

Magda dropped her luggage off too and chased me from behind.

There were a bunch of scammers outside. I felt myself being stared at—the perfect target. That's what the cabbie really meant. Athens downtown was a whole lot of seediness surrounded by these scammers, thieves, and pickpockets. Like the vendor who gave me back change in Turkish lira and not euros. I didn't even realize until I tried to pay a bill and the waiter accused me of trying to cheat him. These scammers spoke Greek. But they weren't really Greek—at least, that's what the cabbie had been really trying to tell us.

I lost Magda, and while I did, I encountered an older woman wrapped in a headscarf. She stopped me and focused into my eyes, as if pulling my soul from my body, saying, "This Aaron will be your true love." Then she said it again, as if dusting some invisible energy over my head, and then held out her hand for money. But the rest of my money was tucked into a money belt wrapped deep below my waistline, under a shirt inside my shirt, not easy at all to fish out.

I only had a cheese pie, still warm and occupying all of my right hand. I shrugged and pretended to move on. Her child kicked me in the shin, reached for the cheese pie, and grabbed it out of my hand before running off.

"*Hey*!" I exclaimed as she fervently pulled me away, and I started limping forward with a hurt shin.

"Are you OK?" I heard a stranger say.

I picked up my bag that had dropped.

"They are everywhere. Must be careful."

I nodded.

I was just mugged—of a cheese pie—in the country I had always wanted to visit. But I was still too angry with Magda to grasp what was really happening around me.

I was mad, hungry, and disappointed—and my shin was throbbing. I fell victim so easily. They were cunning. They worked in groups. They said things that were kind of true. Scary even. How did this woman know of Aaron? Of all the names she could have chosen.

"I should tell the police," I murmured. There was some kind of Interpol police standing across the street with a rifle slung over their shoulders. Throngs of tourists continued to pass us by.

"And tell them what?" chuckled this stranger. "Excuse me… *Aglika*? Um, yes, this tourist here got mugged. No, not knifepoint. Suspect was about three feet tall with a Tickle-Me-Elmo t-shirt on and no older than age five years. He stole her possession right out of her right hand. It was a…*tyropita*."

I pulled myself together and left Syntagma Square slightly bruised. I settled into a nearby cafe. As I got comfortable at an outdoor table, a gentleman with gray spectacles and a purple handkerchief tucked into his jacket pocket pulled up a chair and sat next to me.

I looked at him. He proceeded to light a slim cigarette and cross his legs, making himself super comfortable in front of me—someone who was visibly super uncomfortable. He said something in Greek to the waiter.

"I'm sorry, this seat is taken," I let out. The gentleman exhaled his cigarette and turned toward me.

"Yes, it is taken by me. My name iz Giorgos, the owner of this cafe." The waiter brought out two cups of what looked like espressos for us and some Greek pastries.

"On the house. There are no other seats," he said. "Besides, don't you want to people watch and judge Greek passerby pricks together?"

"Is this Turkish coffee?" I naively asked, holding the tiny cup near my nose. He put down his cigarette.

"The Greeks and Turks, we may all look alike, but never call a Turkish a Greek, and never call a Greek a Turkish. Here, it is called Greek coffee. Not Turkish coffee. *Greek* coffee."

I knew the two countries had a similar hostile-reconciliatory history as the Chinese and Japanese did. Their histories were full of bloodshed, murder, rape, and attempted conquer. Once upon a time, most—if not all—Greeks were Turks prior to the Ottoman Empire invading their homes and forcibly dispersing them.

"I forgive you. I cannot tell between Asians. To me, you are all Chinese." He smiled. I pretended to smile as I chewed into a crispy, spinach-like pastry. A loud moped drove alongside the road, muting his laughter.

For two and a half hours, we sipped Greek coffee, ate Greek pastries, and people-watched—and people-heckled—together. I met my first friend in Athens and learned that he spent an equal amount of time in the United States. He was the antithesis of me—mostly polite, sophisticated, refined, funny—and an incredible distraction from Magda.

He was oil; I was water. He was gold; I was lead. He was baccarat silverware, and I was the annoying, do-it-yourself, self-assembly Swedish furniture. But most importantly, he listened to me. I just needed someone. *Anyone.* To listen to me vent. He would become the yin to my yang.

"She's a traitor. A traitorous whore. She was my best friend." I took a sip of clear liquid in a shot glass, which had made its way to the little café table via Giorgos subsequently giving orders to his staff in Greek.

Giorgos refilled both of our glasses.

"She's not a real…what you call…friend." He lit a cigarette.

My face was still grimacing in response to the shot, but I still reached for another one. "We were going to get married. Nate and I."

By now, I was sobbing to a complete stranger. Giorgos crossed his legs, as if he was my therapist who encouraged me to continue talking.

He shook his head in disappointment.

"She even helped him pick out the ring, and unbeknownst to me, slept with him that night." He handed me a tissue.

"Then she had the nerve to come to Ireland to surprise visit me for my birthday. This trip was more of an 'I'm sorry I fucked your fiancé,' than a 'happy thirtieth birthday' gift." I blew my nose loudly into the tissue.

Giorgos moved an ashtray that was on the table closer to him.

"How could she? How could she? How could he? How could they?" I heaved and reached for another shot.

"Join me and my family for the celebration of Greek Easter," Giorgos insisted.

"And then, they're all out of rooms at the hotel so I have to spend the night with *her*!" I slammed my head down against the table, crying heavily.

"*Ella*. Come. My mama and aunt will be cooking a Greek feast tomorrow." He blew out a puff of smoke. "Do you like lamb?"

"Greek Easter? As opposed to just 'Easter'?" I asked.

"Greek Easter. This year, it falls exactly one week after the Easter you know of. There is lots and lots of food and we roast a whole lamb." He moved the ashtray away.

"You need some lamb. A little bit of Greek dance and you feel all better and no remember this Magda or Nate."

I picked my head up.

CHAPTER 30

O' Lord!

If there's one thing I had learned so far from the Greeks, it's that they worshipped the five Cs: cuisine, camaraderie, churches, coffee, and cigarettes. Many of these I could not indulge in without feeling some form of culpability. It made me wonder whether the things I had considered "sinful" were in fact "soulful." Eat (a lot). Play (a lot). Pray (a lot). Drink (a lot). Smoke (a lot). The secret vices to living a long life? The Greeks seemed to know how to live, and live long they did, especially on their islands. It sure as hell made me feel a lot better, and for a moment, I had completely forgotten about Nate and Magda. The Greeks had this machismo aura of "livin' la vida loca" that the Chinese emperors expunged from my Asian ancestors. A Greek attitude so successful it birthed the best philosophers, produced the best democracy, honed the best mathematicians, produced the best poetry, delivered the best drama, erected some of the best structures in the world, saved a country plagued by deep financial despair, and fought wars no underdog in history could or would ever win. At the moment,

I wished I were Greek—much to the annoyance of my deceased ancestors, likely cursing me from the heavens in the wrong kind of Chinese—because I had the sudden revelation that I lived my entire life wrong, and I needed to conquer my world back, retrieving what those traitors—Magda and Nate—took from me, as if I was some kind of magnificent Greek warrior like Alexander "Rachel" the Great.

"Cake. I think they'd like this cake," I said to the emotionless cashier, who probably didn't even understand what I was saying. "I have a Greek Easter to go to. I think Giorgos will like it." I pointed to it and nodded, holding up my index figure to signal I wanted one.

The lady at the counter said something in Greek and proceeded to wrap it up with a pretty blue and white ribbon.

When I arrived at the sprawling suburban town of Kifissia thirty minutes north of Athens, Nikos, one of Giorgos's cousins, who struck a strong resemblance to Giorgos but was a little leaner and more handsome, let out a big, "Welcome!" as if we were distant relatives who hadn't seen each other in years, when in reality, this was our first encounter. He gave me a strong hug, followed by the obligatory Mediterranean mouth-to-cheek kiss on my left cheek, then right cheek, then left again—although I think he snuck an extra kiss in there. I pulled back quickly, feeling uncomfortable because I didn't like strangers touching me. But I followed suit, since I was pretending to be Greek that day. The first thing he offered me was coffee. Coffee? So late? But how would we sleep at night, I thought, but I wouldn't dare ask him. It was called a frappe, and I hesitantly accepted one as Giorgos spotted us from afar, flamboyantly flailing his right arm to catch my attention, complete with his own tall frappe in the other.

"Ah, I see you like our frappe," he said. His family was gathered behind him.

"Happy Greek Easter!" I exclaimed. Or was it just "Easter" here?

I hadn't even tried the frappe yet, but blurted out, "Yes!" Turns out, it was sweet and frothy, like a Frappuccino from that famous coffee place in Seattle—and equally addictive. My heart palpitated. My hands shook. My eyes blinked (a lot). I couldn't stop talking or thinking or wondering. I was wired and wanted to learn the Greek language that afternoon if someone, anyone—Nikos, Giorgos?—would just teach me. "C'mon, teach me some Greek words," I implored.

Giorgos gently ushered me over and brought me to his family of fifty, saying something to them. It was all Greek to me.

I stood there, silent and awkward with my arms against my hips.

The family continued to speak. One waved at me. Another offered her seat to me.

I tried to repeat what Giorgos was saying, but nothing but mumbo jumbo came out. The Greeks had big families, and lots and lots of friends. Friends became family. Family was like your best friends. Everyone was an "aunt," an "uncle," or third cousin, so the only way to really discern they weren't blood related was to ask them (or to look at the obvious non-Greek like me).

"Here is a chocolate cake," I said clearly, holding it out to one of the family members. He moved forward and examined it.

"Thank you!" Pavlo said. "I am Giorgos's cousin." Another one of Giorgos's relatives stepped forward.

"I am Pavlo. Nice to meet you." I looked at both of them, confused. The other relative looked just like him and had the same name.

Giorgos's fifty or so family and friends looked at me with equal intrigue—a friendly, curious intrigue. They were smiling, and probably wondering who I was. Where I came from—really came from (really, really came from). Talking back in broken Greek-English. I couldn't remember their names. They all looked the same to me. They all shared the same five Greek names too. Was this one Pavlo, or was that one Pavlo? No wait, Pavlo was that one who just said, "Nice to meet you." Then there were half a dozen female cousins named Argiro or Aglagia.

"Those two there, they are both Pavlo," Giorgos said, as if he understood my confused, blank stare.

"No, one was definitely Nikos," I responded with confidence.

Using my strong mathematical skills inherited by my Asian ancestors, I assessed there was a 50/50 chance someone was Argiro or Aglagia if they were female, and a 33 percent chance that someone was Pavlo, Nikos, or Giorgos if they were male (yes, my math skills were still impeccable even with all this caffeine).

I sipped my frappe in embarrassment, trying to identify any feature that could set them apart. Argiro was the one with the light mustache. But wait, Aglagia also had a light mustache. She had slightly more forearm hair than her sister, Argiro. Nikkos had a coarse, black beard covering a visibly double chin, but so did his cousin, Nikkos. Nikkos had a black mole beside his nose if you looked close enough. Pavlo (I think) had slicked-back, dirty-blond hair. I sipped more frappe and made long eye contact with Aglagia (Argiro?). I was confused.

Aglagia and Argiro looked equally confused. Nothing came out of our mouths, so we had a long conversation in silence, with our eyes fixed on one another. I was saying to her, "Thank you for the graciousness of you and your family." She seemed to say, "What's your name again? You all look the same to me."

Nikkos (or was it Pavlo?) came over to offer me a second glass of frappe and a glass of red wine. Red wine and coffee? Didn't the Greek gods preach practicing all vice in moderation? It was obvious the Giorgos family household had other ideas.

Greek evening dinners at traditional households resembled feasts to this non-Greek. Giorgos' household was no different. The matriarch—Aglagia or Argiro—were the chef-de-cuisine of the Greek household. She sets the menu, prepares the food, and sometimes permits the kids to serve. Post dinner, however, the patriarch whispers to unsuspecting guests—out of earshot of his wife of course—that he is truly the better cook. Oftentimes recruiting an unsuspecting and treasonous child to support the bold claim but all so very covertly. Then there's the Easter Sunday feast, the feast that brought me here today.

While the rotisserie roasting the whole lamb is the main attraction, the inventory of a large city's food pantry make-up the sides. This is the women's domain. Any Y chromosome-carrying barbaric neanderthal can place meat on a stick and spin it over a fire. Greek women prepare with finesse and tender love and much care the evolved fine cuisine that was in front of me. The list of what was on the table runs long and could feed a whole neighborhood food bank. This was the Easter Sunday feast looked forward to by observers and non-observers alike.

I couldn't wait to sink my teeth into the food. Argiro and Aglagia started to bring out the dessert: mountains of butter cookies, yogurt, baklava, a whole chocolate cake, and a tray of something smothered with globs of honey over it. I excused myself and brought my plate to a corner of the backyard.

For the Greeks, at least this Greek family, eating was as much a ritual as praying and smoking cigarettes—it happened often and throughout the home. I may have been up to my second frappe, but Nikkos, Pavlo, and Argiro were on their third, and simultaneously smoking so many cigarettes that the Surgeon General on the box might as well have popped out and joined them with a cigarette, giving up on his efforts to warn these three of the dangers of smoking.

Was this what they did on normal Sundays too? It was a different celebration here, one that honored Jesus Christ for dying on the cross for our sins (only, seven days later than the calendar I knew).

The abundant consumption of food didn't seem to be one of the seven deadly sins in their religion. I learned that a priest named Father Giorgos (different Giorgos) was in attendance here, with a cigar not-so-hidden in one hand and a glass of wine in the other. Was the priest just as guilty of this overindulgence of food and drink?

"Attending church at midnight is 'tladition,'" Father Giorgos said, taking a deep puff of his thick cigar.

Pavlo sat down next to me to explain the service. Easter is the holiest holiday for Orthodox Christians, which is the faith that seemingly all Greeks practice. Even those who have different ideas look forward to what the Easter Sunday feast offers. In the religion, Greeks who observe fast for forty days before Easter, some more stringently than others. The older people fast from all meat and dairy with the exception of crustaceans and mollusks. On Easter Day, the feast starts just past midnight upon the families' return home from the midnight service. Children, too, would be woken and dressed, standing in the rain or cold past midnight, reciting religious prayers in Greek and following the motions of the Greek priest, so pristinely clad in a cloak, motioning his right hand into a cross sign and saying, "*Christo Anesti.*" Then, one by one, each person would light a candle close to their chest and use it to light their neighbor's candle, again with more muttering of Greek words. To me, it sounded like some kind of secret society induction prior to all the food indulgence. At least, that's what I was understanding of his explanation.

Then there's Easter Day proper. The men tend to the whole goat and or lamb spits. They take turns rotating the whole animal at just the right speed. Some think it sacrilegious to automate the spit until they realize that an automated spit affords more time to drink and talk. Giorgos figured this out a long time ago.

I stood up and went inside looking for a bathroom. The Greeks were so religious that a small corner of the house had rosary beads, icons, and photos of ancestors that seemed to act as a church—or a shrine. Some fresh pieces of lamb were left as offerings, as if to say the Greek ancestors were there in spirit to join us in today's festivities. I left a small cup of Greek coffee too.

I wondered how the Greeks could be healthy, but they were. I'd read it was something about the healthy amounts of anti-inflammatory properties found in Greek food.

Even so, some of these dishes looked peculiar. "Margarita," was actually *magiritsa*, a gamey, lemony soup filled with chopped lamb's offal and greens. This would have made even the haggis-eaters proud. I should have felt at home with this dish, considering my Chinese ancestral palette of devouring other questionable animal body parts that I occasionally found delicious. But this "margarita" repulsed me. Pavlo egged me on but as soon as I sipped a spoonful, I spat it out. It was bitter, gamey, and more repulsive than the bull testicle I was secretly fed in Tokyo. I quickly excused myself.

The roast lamb finally finished roasting after about six hours on the spit. It was perfectly charred, perfectly seasoned, and went perfectly with feta. The giant beans drenched in tomato sauce and chopped up feta went down smoothly. I liked it. It was familiar. It was like rice and beans without the rice. It needed rice so I reached for the spinach rice with dill and feta. Then came the feta cheese a la carte. The smooth, rich feta was cut into thick one-inch blocks and smothered over the top of my Greek salad before it had been tossed in tablespoons of extra virgin olive and then drizzled with even more oil.

Feta cheese to the Greeks was their Achilles' heel, like kimchi—globs and globs of kimchi—was to my stomach. "A lot" was an understatement when describing the amount of cheese this family ate. Giorgos reached for a two-inch block of feta cheese and rolled it onto a toasted pita before dousing it with olive oil and oregano, devouring it like he hadn't seen food in weeks. My grandmother used to say, "Cheese makes you hairy," and so she never, ever ate cheese and discouraged us from eating it too. Was my grandmother right? Did slabs of heavy Mediterranean cheese correlate with Giorgos's intense amounts of body hair (there was a lot…)? Was my family's inevitable lactose intolerance a blessing in disguise? It was the weirdest combination of food I had ever seen. It needed something else. Kimchi definitely. Rice maybe? They had rice here. But who was I to declare it needed something else?

I excused myself and, in a corner, pulled out the smaller jar of kimchi I always kept in my purse. I unloaded a spoonful onto the feta cheese that smothered the lamb on my plate and let out a pleasurable sigh.

"What's that?" Argiro asked.

"Uhh, uh…" I pulled the jar behind me, hoping to hide it. But Argiro saw it and pointed at it again.

"May I try?" Like a devilish child caught red-handed by her parents, I confessed, opened the jar of kimchi, and laid a generous portion atop her lamb.

Argiro's eyes lit. She ran toward the family and started shouting at them in Greek about this red vegetable I had given her—"the Greek kryptonite" she later would describe to me in English.

Giorgos came over. Then Pavlo, and Pavlo, and Nikko, and Theia Aglagia. They gathered around like sharks do when they smell prey.

"What is this red vegetable, Rachel?" I pulled out my jar.

"*Aftos kimchi*?" Is this kimchi? They examined it and passed it along to their family members, as if it was going through an assembly line being carefully quality controlled.

Emerging from the large group was Theio Thanasis Markopolous (better known as Papa Markopolous), patriarch of the family, restauranteur, and owner of several olive oil production plants throughout Greece. He pushed his way through and had a taste. His eyes met mine.

"Where can I get more of this, how you say…kimchi?" he implored.

Papa Markopolous had just opened a chain of restaurants in Athens, but it was too traditional and needed more fusion. Athenians wanted nouveau Greek food, not traditional. He envisioned something like kimchi to be topped on his souvlaki and gyros—a flavor Greeks were beginning to embrace: spice.

I felt myself becoming more Greek in girth and in spirit. Two forearm hairs might as well have sprouted out from under my skin as I began to sweat. I was experiencing an unusual, medically inexplicable phenomenon in which my body began excreting sweat—a protein-induced sweat—from my overindulgence of the roast lamb. I reached for a cigarette, hoping it would suppress my desire to reach for more mouthwatering food, but my asthmatic cough from the secondhand smoke came back with vengeance.

We continued to eat, drink, and smoke like this for many more hours that day, taking just enough breathing breaks to make room for more food. The jar of kimchi was empty, and lay on the grass, turned on its side with the last drop of kimchi juice dripping out. The afternoon turned into night, and Aglagia offered to make Greek coffee for everyone. Coffee was the necessary narcotic here because it meant we could continue to sit there talking to each other in a mixture of English, Greek-English, and Greek, and letting out the occasional belch as we sat in a resting position waiting to get hungry again. Giorgos was fast asleep on a lawn chair, experiencing what I presumed was a food-induced coma.

A few mischievous kids were playing ball with each other unsupervised (how did they stay up so late? Was it the coffee?) on the opposite side of the courtyard. One, no older than five, ran up to me, pointed and yelled, "*Kinezoula*!"

I smiled back. He continued to point and yell, "*Kinezoula*!" until his *yiayia* approached him, yelling, "*Stamata*!" (stop)

I reached for more coffee, and one more piece of lamb, before raising my glass of red wine to say, "*Yamas*!" (cheers) to the strangers who ignored me before passing out in the corner too.

CHAPTER 31

I Summon Thee

An urgent request came in from Hendrik.Müller@WilHeltek Commerz.de with the subject "Meeting with Künt":

> Rachel, Künt summons you to be at the upcoming meeting with Morimoto-san. It is scheduled for Monday at 18:00. She expects you to discuss the prospective client's request for proposal.

I put down the phone and continued packing. Afterward, I scribbled what I could remember of Magda's family's kimchi recipe on a folded notepad lying face down on the nightstand. Unbeknownst to her, she had left it face up one day and I, of course, caught a quick enough glimpse that I memorized the ingredients: a big head of cabbage, a few bunches of scallions, garlic (lots and lots of garlic, I forget the precise quantity, but think about how much I would need in the event I was attacked by voracious, blood-sucking vampires in the middle of the night), some grated ginger, and the secret: a freshly squeezed lime.

I picked back up the phone and started typing. "Hendrik, I am tending to a family emergency this week. Please send me the conference line so I may participate."

I threw the phone back down.

My "family emergency" consisted of somehow figuring out how to mass-produce kimchi in Greece for Theio Thanasis and his restaurants, which were scattered throughout Greece. Giorgos volunteered to accompany me as my "personal tour guide" while we toured the family's production plants, trying to figure out if we could repurpose their equipment and make batches and batches of kimchi with it. It was a small price in exchange for my wisdom of kimchi (which really was lacking, but Theio Thanasis promised, "You don't need to cook; just show me the main ingredients and taste to make sure it's authentic."). Giorgos had to help with the family business anyway and check up on all the production plants, so "why don't you just tag along?"

Yes, why not? I reiterated to myself. I didn't come to Greece to learn about its rich history or tour their ancient ruins. Evidently, I came to Greece to introduce kimchi to the world's first purveyors of democracy and philosophy.

Giorgos picked me up promptly at 8:00 AM.

"We need cabbage. Where can we get cabbage?" I asked Giorgos, my new Greek friend.

"You dun worry." Giorgos was maniacally focused on the road, weaving in and out of traffic and going through a plethora of tunnels set up at the most random places—seemingly an excuse to collect additional tolls. There were no speed limits, and every road sign was Greek to me.

But yes, he was my new friend. It was the start of a friendship. Friendship, because he was short, plump, twenty-plus years older, a recent divorcé with a teenage daughter who was living abroad in Switzerland attending a super expensive private school with one of those highfalutin names too difficult and high-end for me to pronounce, and had a restraining order against his ex-wife (who I learned continued to stalk him with horseback riding bills because it was a "necessity that he had to pay for" for his daughter). Not that being short and plump made him any less desirable as a friend, but I would never, ever, ever, ever, ever, ever in a million years date "someone's daddy." It was one of my golden rules of dating. Plus, I really wasn't looking for anyone, and I still thought about Aaron.

But I realized the dynamics of us traveling together would soon come into question, because immediately, judging by the raised eyebrows of store owners and passersby, you could just hear the questions in their heads: *Were they father and daughter?* No, she doesn't look like us. *Did he bring her from Kina (China)?* But her English is too perfect. *Is she using him for money?* She is not dressed so well herself, and she is also paying for things with credit cards to her own name.

Business associate. I was Giorgos's business associate from the States who was here to identify additional revenue-generating product lines! It must have crossed Giorgos's mind too, because when I finally met the head of operations at one of the production plants in Kalamata, Giorgos introduced me, in English, as his colleague from "corporate" who was assessing the first lines of business. It was a win-win. I really didn't know the business well enough to speak, so my job was to "observe"—and eat.

I learned more about olives and how acidic olive oil could become if an olive was harvested a certain way, if there were delays between harvesting and extracting, if there was prolonged storing, and if it was processed on a certain month.

When Vassilis, head of operations, walked us through the production plant, he stopped in the area of the plant that was "experimenting" with different flavors of olive oil—rose, chocolate, basil, red chili pepper—and laid them out in sample-sized shots for us to try.

I'm not an olive oil connoisseur, but good Lord, upon dipping a piece of pita into each sample, my eyes lit up in a way they never had before. Oil to me had always been something you sort of coated your wok with before cooking food. It wasn't "supposed" to taste good; it was supposed to provide a quick function.

"For Gim-chee, to mix with the gim-chee. What you dink, *kinezoula*?" Giorgos tilted forward. His broad, uneven-toned shoulders moved with him. His hairy, olive-skinned, bulbous hand reached for another spoonful of this wonderful oil made naturally from the rich Greek earth before it was packaged into nice grande-sized tins.

I had never tried this rich, buttery, pungent, tasteful thing I was getting all over my palette now. Like fine wine, I began to recite the different flavors I had tasted to Vassilis: This one was fuller with a floral taste; that one really tasted like chocolate. The red chili pepper oil was just spicy enough, a little more tannic than the others but equally as full bodied—and just perfect for kimchi.

"This one. This one." I pulled the spicy red chili pepper oil away from the others. Vassilis turned toward Giorgos with eyes that said he won the lottery. A woman donned in a blue scrub-like outfit and wearing a clear face shield moved swiftly over to us, as if she had just concocted Frankenstein herself in an unorthodox experiment.

"For *kinezoula*," she said, before dropping two rows of neatly packaged chili pepper olive oil in front of me.

Vassilis went on like an infomercial to proudly explain the plethora of health benefits too.

"Do you know da Greeeeks use in da soap?"

I reached for another pita.

"Da Greeks use olive oil for moisturizer for skin and hair." Vassilis turned around to pick something else up. Giorgos proceeded to fill out paperwork. The same woman who had brought over the chili olive oil removed her face shield and sat down, saying something to Giorgos in Greek.

"It fights inflammation, Alzheimer's disease, cancer-causing agents, heart disease, lowers blood pressure, and improves brain health too. Did you know dat?"

It sure taste good too. I soaked it in and anxiously waited for him to announce some 1-800 number I could quickly dial to reserve my order today, but I stayed quiet and nodded as he went on to tell us about the multi-generation, family-owned business. Apparently, if any of the olives tasted off in their plants, or were processed too early or too late, they would toss it all out, until they perfected the perfect batch.

I couldn't get over how good the olive oil was. It would go into my collection of memorable *first* foods in my life, like the first time I had Reggiano cheese in Italy, or the first time I had Sunday roast in Ireland, or the first time I had pizza from Glorious Pizza.

Giorgos returned with a heavy bag filled with large olive oil containers and handed it to me. "For you," he said.

CHAPTER 32

Island Hopping

Giorgos and I caught a ferry from Piraeus port early the next morning. We were on our way to Mykonos to meet Theio Thanasis and his restaurant partner. Mykonos was the Hamptons-meets-Ibiza-style Greek island full of sexy silver foxes (one believing he was a better-looking George Clooney than the next) and oily, buff gay men dancing around in short-shorts, flossing their flock of rugged, gray chest hairs, and rocking linen shirts they knew they looked sexy in. And partying relentlessly. Nonstop. All day. All night. Every day. Every night. These men thought they were Greek gods but, in reality, they were just goddamn Greeks. But the goddamn Greeks came to Mykonos to do business too, in between their daytime, nighttime, nonstop partying antics. They were important in their own eyes.

Let me distinguish between an important person and a not-so-important person. The important person was someone who hailed from the upper echelons of society—"old money," if you will. This includes dignitaries; highfalutin professionals (like the infamous lawyer O.J. Simpson hired); socialites (the more they donated to not-for-profit charities, the more important they were seen as); A-list actors (this excluded once-upon-a-time A-list actors who now only starred in those ultra-cheesy movies featured around the holidays with a predictable plot about a boy falling in love with a girl he suddenly meets, unless they made a sizable donation to an important not-for-profit charity and thereby, put themselves into the socialite category); career politicians; and successful entrepreneurs (of course this didn't include the hot dog vendor that opened up across the street from the other five hundred hot dog vendors; rather, the person who invented the first electric car would certainly qualify).

One of Thanasis's restaurant partners was at the famous Pinky Beach, where he was waiting for us with Magda (ugh, yeah, she ended up tagging along too). After spilling everything from A-Z about Magda to Giorgos, Giorgos "insisted" that she tag along too. Giorgos and I were to meet them there and pitch this partner the "kimchi" idea.

"She kan take ride with my un-cle. He pick her up." Were they the Greek gods of reconciliation too?

"Who iz diz, *koukla*?" Theio Thanasis reached for Magda's hand and kissed it before opening the car door for her and retreating to the other side.

"*Oxi*." I said no, rejecting his insistence and squealing like a toddler not wanting to eat my vegetables as equally as I detested Magda.

"She is you friend."

Was she? Would a friend sleep with your ex while you were on a break with said ex, then surprise you on your thirtieth birthday to tell you that she slept with your ex while you were on a break with said ex?

Magda was there when we arrived at Pinky Beach, wearing about a bottle of sunblock on her face and a long, white linen covering her high-waisted, polka-dot bikini. It was like pulling teeth with three pliers introducing her to Giorgos. Even though I still felt Magda deserved to have her head shoved deep into the hot grainy sand, in order to take in the perks of the islands and the fact that the Greeks would soon be eating kimchi, our squabbling would have to wait for later.

"Magda, this is my new friend Giorgos I met back in Athens." The music started growing louder as a shirtless, chiseled-looking, twenty-something tatted up with Chinese characters (he likely couldn't read) jumped onto a makeshift stage and started DJing. He put on clunky-looking Bose headphones and moved his right hand swiftly against the equipment below him.

Magda turned her head toward me, likely filled with shock and confusion that I was even speaking to her with such politeness. The corners of Giorgos's round, aged face turned upward as his eyes grew smaller.

"*Yiasou*, Mugda!" he said, letting out his hand and grunting louder and louder before the music could consume his voice.

"*Yiasou, yiasou*!" she said hesitantly, placing her hand on his.

It just so happened that Greek island hopping was a must do, and Mykonos was at the top of every tourist's list (next to seeing ancient ruins, of course). People came here to party and throw their fists up in the air to American hip hop and R&B music, as they were doing so around me. It wasn't even noon yet.

"*Olright peddia*!" Giorgos exclaimed, clapping his hands together as he aggressively let go of Magda's. "We have few moments before Papa Markopolous's partner, arrives. Let us get into the water!"

But I didn't want to go into the water. I wanted to lay down like those Greek island pleasure seekers over there.

I learned there were two types of Greek island pleasure seekers here: There were those who declared themselves superior, and like Superman, proudly ripped open their shirts with two hands simultaneously for the world to see their coarse and curly-haired Mediterranean chests, dunking their entire bodies, SPF-free, into the clear, blue waters of the sea, then lying flat in the sun for hours until they were slightly less charred than a roast chicken. Women followed suit closely too, taking everything off as they sunbathed to achieve the perfect no-tan-line tan and a shade slightly less dark than night.

On the other end of the polarity, there were those who continually sought refuge from the sun. They hid under giant sunglasses and larger-than-life umbrellas, hats, trees, and awnings. They used bottles and bottles of SPF. I fell into the latter category, along with some of the *yiayias* and the occasional tourists seen posing with their hands holding up peace signs. If a civil war were ever to break out between the two groups, I would be relatively safe because everyone respected their *yiayia*, and the *yiayias* would preside victoriously over their overly tanned brethren.

I had on a big, ostentatious hat—the kind you'd find at the Kentucky Derby—and applied half a bottle of SPF 50 to my face. With Giorgos not being able to hold in his laughter just to the right of me, I could still feel my skin peeling and red, sunspots appearing everywhere, while the *malakas*—and *malakismenis*—slipped into calming comas around me, letting out deep snores. Magda was already in the clear Aegean waters and had the facial expressions of a child finally finding their lost puppy.

Giorgos and Theio Thanasis followed suit.

There was something magical about just lying there on a Greek island. Something that made you happy—genuinely happy—and healed your soul by just being there. Take the old man we saw on the roadside earlier. He was perfectly happy sitting outside on a hard, rickety, wooden chair for God knows how many hours, making even the most fit derriere sore. He lit up a cigar and spread his legs out onto the pavement—occasionally with black and white striped kittens sprawled near his feet in similar leisurely positions—sipping his frappe, smoking and knocking back *ouzo*, not necessarily in that order.

I even felt some of the tension between Magda and I slip away under the Grecian sun (although, let's not get carried away; my blood continued to boil under that ninety-eight–degree heat). It reminded me of how my uncle used to utter the words "fulfillment" at the family table. "You must live a fulfilling life." But aside from the minor inconvenience of potentially being burnt by excessive sun exposure, and your best friend turning out to be a pathological liar, I never understood what that meant until nearly two decades later. There was a fulfillment here not obvious in Athens or any other part of the world. I knew the fulfillment and contentment would only grow as Giorgos took me all over the country to introduce my kimchi to people he knew.

Life on the Greek islands seemed simple and fulfilling, without a care in the world except for ensuring there was enough *ouzo* on the table. There was no set time to do anything. No schedules. No dinner time or breakfast time. No time to go home. "Greek time" was whenever you felt like it. Greek time meant sitting idly on a beach, swimming and relaxing under the sun, or hanging out at some café, sipping Freddo espressos and talking like a gossipy teen, a cigarette in hand.

I tried really hard to relax with my giant hat under all that sun and not think about how unimportant I was while Magda swam and the partygoers around us danced and smoked. But thoughts continued to consume my sad attempt at relaxation. Magda and I were neither important nor freeloaders, but middle-class wannabes from New York City who had heard so much about Mykonos. When I shared with her the vision of me being Giorgos's family's "Kimchi Girl," and their goal of wanting to add the spicy cabbage to their menus throughout Greece, she chuckled.

It took so much out of me to even look at Magda again.

"Kimchi? In Greece? That's the worst idea I ever heard," she said, rubbing more sunblock over her freckled face.

I leaned back and turned away with the oh-so-familiar lump that frequently formed. No words came out.

She didn't make it easy to forgive her. I struggled being there with her. I struggled trying to relax. It took me thirty years to finally make it to a Greek island, then another several hours to acclimate to the idea of sitting idly and soaking in the sun. Magda's betrayal hung over me like a dark cloud on the pristine beaches of Greece.

I tried to shift my focus. I daydreamed about John Stamos running toward me, slowly, with a Greek yogurt in his left hand, whisking me away from the blue shores of Mykonos with his right, before dipping me under the Grecian sun with a deep, French-Greek kiss. Just as I would begin to relax, feelings of guilt ambushed me like a group of Greek warriors fleeing from the Trojan Horse and attacking me, headfirst, as if I were prohibited to relax under the Grecian sunset. They arrived like an army, shooting spears of shame at me.

What are you doing here? Did you prepare for your meeting? Have you been practicing your Chinese and Japanese? Did you do something productive today? What will you do to become important?

I'm not working today, I told myself silently. *I'm taking the day off and helping this nice Greek family with their restaurant business.* Then my preoccupation with the upcoming sales call with

Morimoto-san would take over, making me feel guilty over choosing to be idle instead of working. Then, I worried whether I had enough money to pay for the Mythos beer I just ordered because I forgot to exchange euros. Next, I pictured my parents at work this very moment; they didn't have time to "sit and be idle." And finally, I wondered whether the giant weird-looking insect—only visible on this island and flying just crossed my legs—was poisonous.

Will it bite me? Did you put on insect repellant? Did you put on enough SPF? Is this why you skipped out on work this week—to sit idly on a beach, hoping that someone in this strange, foreign land would go for your kimchi, waiting to be bitten by a poisonous insect, and getting skin cancer?

God damn it, yes! I'd yell internally, fighting back. *OK, not the skin cancer or poisonous part, but I do want to sit out here, with all the wildlife under the Grecian sun.* The angst within me began to die down, but only by the late afternoon, as if my internal Agamemnon victoriously won the battle against my anxiety (or hopelessly gave up in its weak efforts to).

I finally fell asleep, sprawled out like a baby who just drank a bottle of breast milk and collapsed in the middle of the living room, arms and legs completely spread apart. I was happy, and joined the other *malakismenis* in an indulgent sunbathe while Magda continued her swim.

But no sooner than fifteen minutes later did I wake to the beginning of a horrendous sunburn across the half of my body exposed to the sun, despite the repeated applications of SPF 50. Damn my light Asian skin!

Good job, Rachel. See what you did.

I sat timidly at the corner of the daybed the rest of the afternoon in an effort not to get anymore sunburnt than I already had, when a couple of important Greek foxes spewed all kinds of Greek next to me, laughing, and drinking, until they coughed, then laughing some more, drinking some more, and smoking until they coughed more.

A short while later, a prominent actor (definitely important) from a well-known, late '90s movie about an upper-society girl and a poor Irish boy who fell in love on a doomed ship—the biggest of its time—heading across the Atlantic for America around 1912, sat on the daybed near me. I LOVED that movie! I was enamored and speechless. I couldn't believe he was a few feet away sipping *ouzo*, resting on his right arm, and talking about his summer plans so casually with these other people.

"Magda! Magda!" I tried waving at Magda to get her attention, but she was so enamored with the Aegean Sea that she couldn't hear me.

The giddy teenage girl came alive in me, obliterating any feelings of shame. I suddenly forgot about the pain of my sunburns and of Magda. I couldn't contain my excitement. I smiled and stared at the actor for a few awkward minutes before he looked over and smiled. I reciprocated with an awkward wave and head tilt, before retreating back to my corner and making an internal vow to rent every single one of his movies to rewatch.

"Rachel, this is Leo, Theio Thanasis's restaurant partner. I've told him about the kimchi." Giorgos made the introduction as he reached for a glass of *ouzo*.

I couldn't believe it. A smidgeon of happiness overcame me.

He turned toward me. "Do you have any I can try?" he asked, before reaching for a cigarette.

"We didn't want to wake you," Giorgos said. "You were fast asleep and snoring." Giorgos lit the cigarette for Leo. Theio Thanasis emerged from the waters of the Aegean and sat down, soaking the day bed.

As a matter of fact, I had brought with me one of the last jars of kimchi I had. It was tucked in my beach bag. I pulled it out and twisted the cap off, waiting to see if anyone would flinch from the smell. They didn't.

I took a plate from the middle of the daybed that had a half dozen keftedes left on it and laid a spoonful of kimchi next to it. Leo took it.

He laid his cigarette on the ashtray. He slowly chewed on the kimchi I gave him, inquisitively nodding his head back and forth. He sipped his *ouzo* and let out a barely audible burp.

"It's spicy. But I like it. It goes well with the meat. What did you say your name was again?" He reached for another cigarette and sprawled his manly, muscular legs in front of me.

"R...R...Rachel." The words struggled to come out as I sat straight up.

"Can I have some more?" He let out a puff of his cigarette and reached for more keftedes. Thanasis refilled his ouzo.

I passed the opened jar of kimchi to him. A few drops of kimchi juice fell from the jar and hit the clean daybed. Between sips of ouzo, and with one knee bent forward, Leo leaned back on the daybed, pulling the kimchi out of the jar and tilting his head back as he consumed more, like the Greek god he was. The only thing missing was someone fanning him nearby and dropping grapes into his mouth. Hopefully one day, I thought deliriously, that would be me.

"You bring more for my restaurant." Leo dunked his already eaten fork into the jar of kimchi and ate directly from the jar, with bits and pieces falling back in. He lit another cigarette.

"That's why we are here, Leo." Giorgos and Theio Thanasis pulled themselves closer. "We need your help to find ingredients to produce this."

"What is the main ingredient?" Leo hadn't noticed it was fermented cabbage. He spread more out on a pita and washed it down with another sip of ouzo.

"It's cabbage." The music grew even louder, and I was distracted now by Magda, semi-topless and dancing in the middle of the dance floor making out with some Greek silver fox near the DJ. I reshifted my focus.

Leo sat up. "You must go to the island of Zante. There is cabbage there! They also grow it up north," he added.

A smidgeon of happiness overcame me. A Greek island with cabbage? Apparently, the Greeks ate cabbage too. The older generations fermented it during the warmer months and like squirrels, buried it and let it sit idle until the winter months when it was scarce. The most traditional dishes were served with rice and feta cheese, then covered with a generous dollop of lemon sauce. You rarely encountered these dishes in the cosmopolitan cities like Athens because it was a time-consuming process, and Athens was too trendy for food you'd find grown on the Greek islands.

"Then we must go!" Giorgos turned toward Theio Thanasis and nodded to him in agreement.

I was happy again. The only prescription depressed people should ever be written is one to come to the Greek islands. Too many people I knew back home saw a therapist for one relationship or career suicide problem or another (guilty!). Most of us were on some form of monoamine oxidase inhibitor or other antidepressant that was too difficult to pronounce or too expensive for our own out-of-pocket expense.

The true remedy ought to be frappe, cigarettes, and ouzo. I now aspired to add kimchi while lying in the sun getting redder than red and waving at important A-list actors—not necessarily in that order—to the list. It's not a bad way to live and may be the only way to live.

Magda also joined us. I was hoping she wouldn't.

CHAPTER 33

Zante

We found ourselves back in the car with Giorgos, who was indulging in some prepackaged kimchi, while driving uphill endlessly on a curvy, bumpy mountain road. As night was falling, my ears popped, as if we were ascending in an aircraft during takeoff. We passed a wide landscape of farmland accidentally closed off by one flimsy fence, and I pulled out a paper map from the glove compartment, trying to make sense of the Greek letters in front of me. My sorority diversion in college was finally paying off.

"Giorgos, over there! You should have turned back there!" I screamed, folding the large paper map over. He dropped a glob of kimchi on the steering wheel, then abruptly turned back toward the farmland and around a bend where we encountered a pack of dogs jumping and chasing our vehicle for what seemed like miles.

"Where is this bed and breakfast?" Magda demanded, clearly frustrated and scared. By now, it was dark outside. We had also lost all phone signals, and the roads on this tiny island were narrow and rugged.

Papa Markopolous was fast asleep in the front passenger side.

Giorgos let out a loud sneeze, almost knocking the half-jar of kimchi from the arm rest. "It's going to be the most magnificent place you'll ever stay at."

"Mag, he's right. I looked it up and could not find a trace of this place in any travel book or travel channel."

Giorgos had heard about this place from a friend. That friend had brought him to the town's taverna, and the owner happened to be the second cousin of the owner of this inn. You had to be "in the know" to know about this place. It wasn't in any of the Greek guidebooks that Magda touted. It was also next to a farm.

A farm that grew fresh cabbage.

Magda took another sip of the cold coffee, still sitting in the cup holder from early this morning. We were both exhausted.

When we arrived in the small town of Skinaria, I shook Theio Thanasis. He fought back with a loud snore. Magda and I got out and checked for dogs, while Giorgos went inside to check us in.

Magda and I didn't speak. We were too tired, and I was still too angry.

Moments later, Giorgos came back out.

"*Kinezoula, aftos*...give me the kimchi. Kimchi. Now," Giorgos demanded in the middle of the night.

I returned to the car, retrieved another jar of kimchi, and slammed the door. Theio Thanasis wasn't even woken up by the loud noise.

It felt like a rural family home we walked into and interrupted, and not the bed and breakfast I so looked forward to after having seen the vivid images. Truth is, I couldn't even make out our surroundings because it was so dark. The two people inside at the concierge were smoking and exchanging laughs in loud, hoarse voices. They looked at us, confused, as if they forgot they ran a business here. They continued to look at us. We looked at them. No one exchanged words for several minutes. Were they wondering if we were lost? How we found them? Why two Asian girls with messy hair, sweatpants, and bags strung over their shoulders disrupted their "craic" of an evening? Did we just waste a whole day traveling through Greece, almost being attacked by a pack of vicious canines, to come to a bed and breakfast Steve Ricks said was "the most magnificent place on earth" only to find the most un-magnificent place on earth?

"Yas. Kan eye hellllp yu?" the one with the gray, coarse beard asked. The other one tapped his cigarette into the ashtray—which already had a half-dozen or so cigarette butts in it—and didn't even bother looking up. In the background was some Greek music coming out of a radio with lots of static.

Giorgos interrupted and said something in Greek to them. Their demeanor changed immediately.

"Yasas! Come in. Come in," they said. An older woman soon emerged from the backdoor and pulled up two seats for us. She pointed toward my bag.

Giorgos opened the jar of pre-packaged kimchi and scooped out a spoonful. The two continued to have a conversation in Greek, nodding their heads ferociously and pointing toward the window that showed nothing more than darkness.

They continued to speak in loud Greek, when Theio Thanasis stormed in saying, "*Poise enai…*" before everyone erupted into laughter. They pulled up another chair.

At some point in the night, I passed out in that chair, only to be woken up inside a white, stone-washed windmill by the slam of a door. Magda was next to me. I don't recall at what point we even walked over here. We must have been drunk on ouzo—and kimchi. It was an old windmill that had been converted into two rooms overlooking the Ionian Sea.

By morning, a perfect sunrise occurred outside our window against the picturesque backdrop of the Ionian Sea perched perfectly below us with the most magnificent view of the earth. Behind us was a farm, which neither of us could make out when we arrived in the middle of the night.

I spotted Theio Thanasis from a distance, hunched over in the fields and picking something up.

Giorgos entered our room without even a knock. "Galz, get ready! We must go pick cabbage."

"I didn't come to a Greek island to pick vegetables from a farm," Magda retorted. She got up and threw two colorful swimsuits onto the bed.

"I'm going swimming." Magda started stripping her pajamas off with both of us still in the room. The sunrise crept into the room too, hitting my forehead and making it difficult for me to even look up.

"Magda, you frend here, have opportunity to make kimchi for za Greeks, and you selfish, self-absorb, call yourself a frend? Gamóto," Giorgos's deep voice echoed against the white, stonewashed walls.

She turned around, uninhabited in her ways. "Let's ask Rach. It's her birthday today."

That's right. It *was* my birthday. The big three-o. But it didn't feel like my birthday, or a milestone celebration with birthday cake and balloons and friends showering me with presents. I still felt twenty-nine and had almost forgotten.

"Mag, I want to pick cabbage. I want to pick it with you by my side and I want to make kimchi together...." *You traitorous bitch*, I added to myself only. A cloud of tension erupted between us.

Looking between us, Giorgos stormed out of the room and said, "I will see you downstairs in five."

Magda pulled me out of bed and threw open the balcony door, dragging me outside. "Look at that, Rach. It's the Ionian Sea. You won't get that back in Ireland, or New York." I pulled away and went back inside. Magda put on her sunblock and reached for her flip flops.

"I'm not picking cabbage on this magnificent Greek island," she said firmly. It was obvious in that moment I had to ditch Mags. It was something I ought to have done years ago. But some impulse—and someone by the name of Giorgos—insisted I forgive. But what was that wise saying? Better late than never?

"Enjoy your day, Mags." The door slammed behind me as I sprinted after Giorgos and Yiayia Mahi, the innkeeper. A warmth of hot, Ionian Sea breeze hit my cheeks as I ran after them.

"*Éla,*" Yiayia Mahi shouted toward me while I was hunched over gasping for air and finding brief solace on a railing. I secretly hoped she wouldn't turn around to realize how far behind I still was.

"This isn't a walk, it's a goddamn hike to Mount Everest," I shouted to Giorgos, finally catching up with him (but only for a moment). I took deep breaths and clutched my now thirty-year-old chest.

This was a hard climb that no aerobic video or virtual spin class could have prepared me for. I was no athlete and was not even a little bit athletic. I was out of shape. I knew this because I would rank last out of hundreds taking the same (beginners) spin class. These other species of people religiously trained to be in marathons. They participated in triathlons. They biked or ran ten to twenty miles…a day…with ease. They lifted weights. They rollerbladed, swam, hiked, climbed, danced for miles and miles—and enjoyed it. They had a level of endurance and perseverance that would take just a couple months of training before they headed to the Olympics if they wanted to. Giorgos sped ahead.

I was wheezing too heavily, unable to respond, but wondered how a seemingly healthy twenty-something (thirty-year-old) fell so far behind a seventy-something-year-old. Richard Simmons's aerobic voice of "you can do it" coupled with Ally Love's "C'mon, C'mon, 4…3…2…1" presided in my thoughts, except defeat finally overcame me when we reached the bend of a mountain, and a whole other side that still needed to be scaled stood in front of us.

My mobile rang. It was Salzberg. Dietrich Salzberg, Chairman of WilHeltek. My inability to breathe was just exacerbated. My wheezing became even heavier. Why was he calling me? He was firing me. He was firing me before I could victoriously emerge on the Key Account Management team. Hendrik must have told him about my refusal to take Morimoto-san's sales call. I didn't want to pick up. How would I explain my family emergency?

Despite my concerns, I picked up.

"See, Rachel See," I answered in the most even voice I could muster. "Hello…?"

"Iz this Rachel?"

"Y…y…yes. Hi…"

"Vell, HAPPY BIRTHDAY TO YOU, RACHEL!"

I was taken aback and couldn't respond.

"Today iz your birthday, no?"

It was, but I was still in shock.

"Hallo?"

"Wow, what a pleasant surprise, Salzberg. That is so nice of you."

"I hope you enjoy your day doing something nice."

"Danke-sur."

"*Éla, éla*!" Yiayia cried. The old woman was now so far out of sight, her voice was but a mere echo. I leaned against a tree, sweat dripping from my forehead, craving water and wondering what just happened. I took in a few deep breaths. Salzberg, what an outstanding leader. Not once had my former partner Stu Pitt, esq. ever wished me a happy birthday in the entirety of my tenure on his team. Here I was, thousands of miles away, relative newbie, and at a company seemingly run by even meaner people, and the chairman of this multi-billion-dollar global conglomerate took time out of his day to call and wish me a happy birthday.

I picked myself back up.

The field had looked a lot closer from the second floor of that room. Around the bend and down a set of carved stone steps was Giorgos, adjacent to a couple of sleepy black and white kittens sprawled atop a row of grass.

Sneaking in two puffs of my rescue asthma inhaler and applying a handful of SPF 50 to my face, my endurance was briefly restored.

When we finally reached the top, the old lady was sitting near Theio Thanasis, who had a bushel full of what looked like cabbage.

This. This is what we endured life, limb, and respiratory ailments for. Cabbage. Cabbage in Greece! The old woman smiled a calm smile, as if reflecting a prophet sent by a Greek Messiah to induct us into her monolithic cult.

She handed me a basket.

"How'd you get here so quickly?" I was still out of breath, and leaned over, pulling the basket up.

"I take donkey," she explained. "Only two euros." Theio Thanasis set aside another full bushel of cabbage and then stood up. Next to him was an elderly, portly woman with dark hair that bore a striking resemblance to Yiayia Mahi, who was just as diligently picking cabbage.

"You could take a donkey up here?!" I breathed more heavily. My beady eyes glared at Giorgos, who dropped his basket.

"You make good exercise, *kinezoula*," Giorgos bellowed in his deep monotone voice. He soon darted away into the fields. It was a hot, late spring morning. Temperatures didn't usually reach thirty degrees Celsius at this time of year, and there wasn't any central air conditioning—*anywhere*. The Ionian Sea was still cold.

Yiayia Mahi knelt down, pointed to the portly, elderly woman, and said, "My sister, Agnes." Mahi reached for an empty basket too.

"Where are you from?" Sister Agnes asked with a perfect English accent. Actually, it was an Australian accent, but to me, it all sounded the same. She attended university in Australia, before voluntarily moving back to the Greek island where she was born and raised, to care for her aging parents and to eventually settle with her own family.

"The United States," I said, rolling up my sleeves and starting to pick the first head of cabbage.

"Where are you really from?" Agnes moved another two baskets toward her. She was quite skilled at picking cabbage.

"New York City." The heat was getting to me. I'd only been at this for about ten minutes. Sweat dripped down my forehead, wiping away any evidence of the previously applied SPF 50.

Yiayia Mahi began to speak to her in Greek, presumably explaining to her "where I was really from." The Greek word *kineza*—which meant "Chinese woman"—was used a few times. Agnes nodded as if to say, "Oh, that makes sense."

But she jumped up in excitement instead. "You are the Kimchi Girl! We heard so much about ye!" I stopped and looked up.

"Kimchi, isn't that Korean? But you are Chinese?"

"Kimchi Girl," I repeated, liking the way that sounded. News traveled fast in the Greek community. After eating, smoking, and drinking frappes, their favorite pastime here must be gossiping. It was even more prevalent on the islands, where television or what a New Yorker would deem a "real job" didn't exist. Apparently after Greek Easter, Giorgos's mother shared it with one of her cousins, who shared it with her sister, that she had "the most amazing spicy vegetable" and wondered "vhere she get dat?" That cousin asked around. Someone mentioned to that cousin that there was this one farm in Zante with the freshest growing cabbage. That farm happened to be the one we knelt over, picking the freshest growing cabbage in the whole country.

"There is a Greek wedding t'morrow night, mate, and we want to have kimchi as a side," Sister Agnes said. Logistically, I wondered how we would be able to pull this off. Giorgos had packed the spicy olive oil; there were fresh lemons, ginger, garlic, and peppers all over this island too.

"But the cabbage needs to be fermented. There's not enough time." Thanasis let out a loud sneeze nearby. Giorgos stood up to take a break.

"Not a problem. You will go to the island next door." Agnes pointed at a distance, showing me the outline of what looked like a mountain—but was really another island.

"There, you will find Larysa of Larysa's Taverna in the town of Fiskardo. She sells the island's most famous lemon cabbage dishes in the winter and has fermented cabbage. Take these bushels to her and trade."

Theio Thanasis and Giorgos started speaking in Greek to each other nearby, and we started in on the next step of our journey.

CHAPTER 34

Kefalonia

I didn't think there could be a more stunning island than the one we were just on. But there was. It was called Kefalonia, sometimes spelled "Cephalonia," but equally botched in pronunciation by a foreigner like me. We were on a mission to find Larysa of Larysa's Taverna in Fiskardo. The island was about an hour away from Zante and was certainly uncharted territory for all of us. Andonis, our ship captain, picked us up at the port of Zakynthos. I didn't bother telling Magda, though, who was God knows where doing God knows what. We packed the boat with about ten bushels of the freshly picked cabbage. Captain Andonis wasn't happy.

There was a noticeable pride in Kefalonia that didn't exist in any other place I had seen in Greece—a pride that seemed to scream, "I am the best Greek island!" Captain Andonis started weaving in and out of the Ionian Sea with his feet—he had hands but preferred driving with his toes—at the wheel of the boat. He sat at the headrest of the seat so he could see out into the sea more clearly, swiftly maneuvering turns and passing by hidden beaches and caves when we reached Kefalonia, proudly showing off and speaking Greek much louder than the other Greeks and reminding us for the twentieth time he was born and bred on the "best Gleek island."

"*Éla, malaka*, Larysa's Taverna. *Poise*, take us here." Giorgos fled toward the back of the boat, before succumbing to the late day sun on the deck above.

I hid in a shaded corner and put on additional sunblock. When we reached Fiskardo, we stepped into a colorful seaside town bustling with tourists speaking English. Theio Thanasis and Giorgos each grabbed a bushel of the cabbage at a time, while Captain Andonis tied the boat down.

"I wait here." The captain held his hand out to help me off the boat, before retreating into the den of his boat for presumably a siesta nap.

I examined the map Agnes had given us; circled in a large red marker was "Larysa's Taverna."

Theio Thanasis stepped into a local Greek supermarket, speaking in loud Greek and asking for Larysa's Taverna. She looked up, and in excitement, pointed at me, "Gim-chee girl! Gim-chee girl!"

She had been expecting me. So was Eleni and Aprhodite. She—Katerina—the supermarket owner, personally walked us the one hundred feet or so to Larysa's Taverna. It was the last restaurant that lined the serene bay of Fiskardo. Outside the taverna was an elderly woman sprawled on a wooden chair, cutting fresh zucchini flowers that fell neatly into a large basin between her worn feet. She introduced herself as the owner of the taverna, Larysa, but not *the* Larysa. *The* Larysa was her granddaughter, who would be upstairs momentarily.

Theio Thanasis and Giorgos let down the bushels of freshly picked cabbage near her, and all three of them began yelling Greek words at each other. Grandma Larysa closely examined the cabbage, lifting up one leaf, nodding, placing it back down, before repeating it again to the next leaf.

Moments later, a young, thirty-something woman emerged with ripped jeans and a white cami. She extended her hand, and in perfect English, stated, "You must be Kimchi Girl! I'm Larysa."

Giorgos scrutinized her up and down, as if to signal with his unwavering Greek spirit that she couldn't possibly be *the* Larysa whom Agnes and Yiayia Mahi were pointing us to. But she was. We followed her downstairs to a cavernous room. In front of us was four hundred square feet of fermented cabbage.

She explained that they didn't always make fermented cabbage. But her late great-grandmother stumbled upon it accidentally at a time when she needed to preserve food and make it last longer. They paired it with rice and a lemon sauce during the winter. Now, because her restaurant was so busy during the holidays, Agnes prepared the cabbage ahead of time.

She accepted our bushels of fresh cabbage and we left with a cart full of fermented cabbage.

CHAPTER 35

The Big Fat Greek Wedding

"Rach, I'm sorry. I've been a selfish bitch." Magda wasn't at the beach, but back in our shared room, awaiting my return. "It's your birthday. I put on some extra sunblock if you want to pick cabbage in the fields now."

The grandfather clock in the room bellowed out a loud noise, interrupting the diatribe that was going through my head.

"Put this on and make use of your Korean heritage." I threw Magda an apron. "We're going to make kimchi."

I didn't have time to go off on a tirade and tell Magda everything she had done to wrong me. Using the fermented cabbage Larysa had so generously traded us for, there was only about two hours for us to make kimchi for about one hundred wedding guests tomorrow—something Papa Markopolous wanted us to do to "test" the fermented cabbage to see whether it would be good enough for his restaurants.

We met Yiayia Mahi, Agnes, Theio Thanasis, and Giorgos at the inn's kitchen. Joining us was a clan of about twenty other Greeks, all bearing some relation to Yiayia Mahi and Agnes, with strikingly similar names and facial features. Giorgos and Agnes acted as the translators. I didn't cook, but before I could admit defeat in leading this pack of twenty-something in conjuring up the thing that made me known as "Kimchi Girl," Magda stepped up:

"Grated ginger. C'mon. You. There's about five pounds of ginger in front of you." She pointed to Agnes's niece, who acted quickly on the instructions.

Like a drill sergeant, she went down the line of ingredients and delegated instructions to each of us. Magda spread the task out amongst all of us. Within minutes, we had about twenty something sous chefs, chopping, slicing, peeling, mixing, before Mags and I poured out the fermented kimchi. I pulled out the large containers of chili pepper olive oil since we didn't have fish sauce. Theio Thanasis attempted to surreptitiously sneak some into his mouth when Magda stopped him, and like the sort of army sergeant she was, was ready to make him give her twenty pushups for being disobedient. She didn't, but he stopped sneaking bites.

By the end of the night, we had a large batch of edible, Greek-influenced kimchi for about one hundred people. Not bad for a group who had never made kimchi before.

I was exhausted. Picking fresh cabbage all morning, and then island hopping to pick up barrels of fermented cabbage, was finally catching up with me. My legs gave out, and I collapsed onto the bed, protesting the strenuous work this vacation had burdened me with.

"I have a surprise for you," whispered Magda, and then a short, strong, stocky middle-aged man—with what appeared to be big, strong hands—entered our room carrying a big bag. I guessed that he was from Germany. But I was in neither a striptease sort of mood, nor did I want a male stripper when he commanded me to "remove my shirt."

He started to set up a massage table in the living room. He sprayed the air with fruity-smelling essential oils that did not complement the sweat his armpits were emitting.

"Friedrich is the island's best masseuse. I met him on the beach earlier, and there was about a two-hour wait." Fully on board with this turn of events, I plopped myself onto the massage table face down and let Friedrich rub lavender oil on me. Magda stepped away.

"Tell me vat kind of mazage vu like." He rubbed his hands gently together and raised the massage pillow until I was comfortable.

I laid there, face down, seeing his stocky, hairy toes escaping from his overused flip flops.

"Please beat me up. Strong massage. Back. Legs. Arms." I was *sore.* I thought that is how Atlas must have felt when he had been condemned to carry the heavens, except I was bearing the burden on my two scrawny shoulders with underdeveloped muscles. I closed my eyes.

Friedrich acquiesced and proceeded to beat me up, one muscle at a time. First, with his elbows. Then, with a quick slap, alternating each big hand against my tense shoulder blades. I felt like Japanese cattle being tenderized to perfect Kobe beef texture before he summoned me to turn over. Then, he turned his attention to my head, where he kneaded my skull with the tips of his stocky fingers, stimulating nerves I didn't even know existed up there.

I fell asleep. It was a great way to end my thirtieth birthday.

I awoke to the sound of clamoring dishes and Magda's voice. It was 5:00 PM I had been asleep for almost sixteen hours, and no one bothered to wake me up! It was the night of the one-hundred-person wedding, and Mahi and her family were outside setting up. As I walked outside, Giorgos pointed at me and laughed out loud.

"Get the kimchi over there." He continued to laugh. "You no wake up…like in a state of coma." I picked up a heavy tray of our homemade kimchi and walked it to the buffet table.

"Here, luv, have a frappe." Agnes passed me a tall glass of the frothy, caffeine-laden elixir. Magda was behind her, picking up decorated chairs and placing eight at each table.

Yiayia Mahi invited me and Mags to the wedding. She wanted us to be "eligible bachelorettes" for the groom's nephews, as I understood it. Not really anyone's date, per se, but an "accompaniment," because there were so many boys in the family she was hosting. Theio Thanasis and Giorgos invited themselves because Greek weddings on Greek islands "are open to da whole dam village!"

At the wedding reception, the elderly Greek women immediately swarmed around me and Magda, inspecting us like two rare, yellow jewels and inquisitively asking if "we haf boyyy-frans" and whether we've eaten. They inspected our bodies, touched our hair, and wondered if we were good enough to be pawned off to their single man-children who still lived in their parents' homes.

"Stamatis! Come here! *Éla* do!" one with a deep voice said. A group of young, chiseled, Greek thirty-somethings seemed to multiply at the sound of their matriarchs summoning them.

Giorgos was watching from a distance, but was too distracted by the kimchi he was devouring to bother coming over to save us.

One medium-bodied Greek son came over. He was shy and waved at us. He was thirty years old and had already endured a nasty divorce, one his traditional Greek family did not approve of. They had prayed to the Greek gods of fertility for forgiveness.

Then Stamatis came along.

"Hah-low," he said in a deep voice. He was wearing an almost fully unbuttoned button-down shirt and chewing on some of the kimchi we made. He had a thick beard, and even thicker chest hair that caught some of the kimchi he dropped.

"You make dis?" He swallowed a handful of kimchi he grabbed with his big, bare hands, and washed it down with a hearty slice of feta cheese. The kimchi that fell on his thick chest hair was so distracting that I could not answer. "Kinezoula?"

Then more of these men came over. Their mothers seemed to think a *kineza*—like me and Magda—would suffice for their boys to reproduce the chiseled bodies of their young, Greek sons on this small, Greek island with a little help of ouzo.

"You mas meet my son first." One aggressively pulled on Magda's arm.

I looked up. It had become like survival of the fittest for their moms—may the one with the cleanest arm hair win us over for one of their Greek sons.

"*Oxi, malakismenis*, my son, first. He more handsome and gif you stlong babies. Stlong, like bull," another one intervened, knocking away the other bullish woman who so closely clung onto Magda.

Magda pulled away and went to the bar, where she discovered ouzo. She drank ouzo while I danced with another eligible bachelor named Efrem. Then I drank some ouzo and danced with someone who looked like Efrem, but was named Stelios, before throwing up just a little bit, and then deliberately breaking a few plates before going back to dancing and stuffing myself with Greek infused olive oil kimchi. I had never felt so free! I broke another large dish—

"Oppa!" everyone yelled. Then I joined the children and started smashing wine glasses and clanking forks against more plates. Everyone was having fun.

Pappou Nikko was the most badass of them all. He ignored every one of his doctor's orders by following the mandatory Greek wedding rituals of drinking, smoking, overeating, and ultimately throwing his cane and fedora to the floor, opting to instead spin and clap to the Greek music that came on.

"Spicy cabbage. Gif me some of dat spicy cabbage!" He spun on the dance floor, and the groom tossed a spoonful of kimchi into his mouth. He promptly spat it out. Evidently spicy was not his thing.

His family cheered and jeered, and like a fraternity inducting its newest member, his son tilted a bottle of champagne over Pappou's mouth to cool him off and wash the kimchi down, forcing Pappou to tilt his head back to guzzle the champagne. So much of it flowed off the side of his mouth, it was as if he was having a seizure—foaming with Veuve Clicquot and remnants of spicy hot kimchi juice.

Yiayia Mahi soon joined him, and in a similar fashion, snapped her fingers to the beat of the traditional Greek music as both her arms were extended outward and her feet stepped forward, one at a time. She received the royal treatment of having champagne poured down her throat too. She started grabbing hands, and soon enough, everyone was linked up one by one—even me—kicking their left, then right foot, then stepping back, then forming a circle around the bride. Theio Thanasis was fast asleep on one of the chairs, but Giorgos enthusiastically grabbed one of the women and wedged his body into the circle.

One by one, a Greek family member stepped into the middle of the circle and did some dance, like that of Yiayia Mahi's. Paper money started raining in the air. Hundreds of single euro bills were laying on the floor, and the smallest kids snuck into the circle to pick them up. The craftier ones placed chewing gum under their shoes and casually walked over the dance floor.

This went on all night, until at the end of the evening, Pappou Nikko was rushed to the island's only emergency room. He had suffered a heart attack. The medical center appeared closed and had a handwritten sign on its door that said (in Greek), "At night, ring the buzzer." Inside, it looked like a 1960s, Cold War–era, socialized hospital. There were dry chemicals splattered against the walls, peeling off most of the paint. Tiles were coming off, used needles and medical gloves were strewn visibly in a corner, and a blanket was covering what looked like a used portable toilet seat (but hey, it was free medical coverage—for everyone!).

"We should have gone to the beach today." Magda's whiny voice could be heard over the music that was playing over the radio. Mascara was running down her eyes, and she was holding the Herve dress—that I had lent her—on its side.

The one doctor in the hospital finally greeted us, a cigarette hanging off his lower lip. He pulled up in a ripped chair and took Pappou's pulse. He listened to his heartbeat carefully with the decades-old looking stethoscope.

"Overexert. Ventilator," were the only words he uttered that I could understand before he rattled off Greek to the family. There was clamoring back and forth between the doctor and the family.

Pappou attempted to get up, but let out a loud, exasperated cough that seemed to hurt his ribcage.

"No more spicy cabbage for me!" he exclaimed.

CHAPTER 36

Going Home

There wasn't any time to say bye to our newly formed Greek friends, so we left them a note atop the remaining bushels of fermented cabbage that Theio Thanassis would use for his restaurants. Then we raced onto a ferry with our rental car, and what should have been a three-hour drive to Athens from Kyllini port was achieved in under an hour. Magda jerked the rental car into the "no standing" zone of Athens International Airport and shifted the gear of the Audi A3 into park.

"C'mon, let's go! Our flight leaves soon!" she yelled, jumping out of the rental and leaving the keys in the ignition.

"But, but..." I lagged behind, but there was no time to ask questions or worry about the Hertz rental car that was illegally left outside. Mag's flight to JFK was imminent. We were in Greece, and the Greeks viewed laws as suggestions—especially when the sign read "no smoking." Nevertheless, I looked back and whispered "sorry" to the security guards as they turned their backs and we rushed to our gates to return home.

• • •

A package awaited me when I returned to Dublin. It was from Nate.

> "Dear Rach, Grandma Lucetta died last week. We scattered her ashes by the ocean just as she requested. She wanted you to have this."

I dropped the note to the floor. I was in disbelief. She was gone? She…was…*gone*? The palpitations of sorrow started fuming through my veins, with the memories of Lucetta causing me to drop to the floor and cover my face with fresh tears. I never got to tell her how much I loved her. I never got to share with her the futile attempt of my latest lasagna or that the Greeks had liked the kimchi I made them. I never got to tell her thank you for making my life better. The inability to express my feelings was a byproduct of Tiger Momism—no hugs, no "I love you," no sharing of emotions the way Lucetta so freely had. I recently saw her, happy, healthy, and complaining about her "*mammoni* (momma's boy)" deadbeat sons who still lived in her home at the ripe age of fifty. "They need to get out already!" she'd say at every holiday gathering. "Those bottom-feeder sons of mine. What did I do to deserve this, Rachel?"

Lucetta died on a Wednesday, while I was having the time of my life in a territory she most certainly would have disapproved of. I imagined her indignation: "Greece? They have nothing on the Italians! There are two kinds of people in the world: the

Italians, and those who *wish* they were Italian!" Her infectious laugh was vivid as I recalled what she would've said.

I opened the package to a scrapbook of all of her recipes, handwritten, with a brief story of where they originated from. Italy, of course. All across Italy—from Milan, to Rome, Florence, Naples, Sorrento, Capri, and even Sicily, where Lucetta's grandmother was from. All of Lucetta's best memories, eighty-three years of favorite places and nostalgic recipes passed down from her family, stuffed into a bulky, forty-page photo album. There was a letter enclosed on the first page:

> *Kiddo,*
>
> *I'm a very sick woman. All of Palermo always thought so, but alas, I'm succumbing to some form of rare blood cancer that I can't even pronounce. The doctors told me it was serious, but all I heard was, "blah, blah, blah." I didn't share this with any of my schmucko sons or bottom-feeder daughter-in-laws. I didn't want anyone knowing, because, well, my schmucko boys would have restricted me from eating my favorite foods: pizza, pasta, prosciutto, and limoncello. And what is life without pizza, pasta, prosciutto, or limoncello (especially limoncello)? The doctors insisted I immediately start intensive chemotherapy. I told them, "You might as well inject me with a lethal dose of hate and death now!" I wanted*

to live my last months my way, and so I did, eating all the pizza, pasta, and prosciutto I could.

Nate told me about the breakup, kiddo. Sometimes, if you're lucky in life, you come across a great love. One who moves you to become the best version of yourself and even volunteers to do the laundry (this one is important, and speaks to a real man doing things for his family, so take notes). I love you and I'll miss you most of all. I never thought I'd meet another great love like my Angelo, but I did, in the form of an introverted Chinese American girl named Rachel.

On page 38 of the photo album is the recipe for my grandmother's traditional Sicilian meatball soup. There's a couple of ingredients not written down, and I need you to take notes. You need extra virgin olive oil—the good kind, from Sicily. It's a secret, but the best olive oil doesn't come from Italy, or anywhere else in the world; it comes from Sicily. Don't ever, EVER let those overbearing Greeks tell you otherwise about their "Kalamata olive oil." I'm gonna say it again: there's a reason it was called the "Roman Empire" and not the "Greek Empire." Make sure you use high-grade, first-cold-pressed olive oil from Sicily. Then, put your love into mixing it. Manifest the best thing you could ever make as you peel the freshest leaves of oregano, pour in minced garlic, and fold the chopped parsley into the meatballs. I used to always think of Angelo when I made this dish.

Now go! Don't lose this. I'll be watching over you, kiddo. And dear sons, if you don't get this to my beloved Rachel, may the spirits of Angelo and Lucetta curse you for the rest of your lives with ugly children from your tramp wives and in the afterlife!

I smiled. Then cried.

Near the album of recipes Lucetta left was an old CD with my favorite Italian song on it: "Con Te Partiro" by the great Andrea Bocelli. I played it in her memory.

I continued to cry. *Hard*. My soul was paralyzed by the Italian words this Italian tenor opera singer bellowed out. Lucetta loved Andrea Bocelli. Two Christmases ago, Nate and I tried to surprise Lucetta with front row tickets to a live concert, but it was sold out.

"Grandma, we tried getting you tickets to Andrea Bocelli," Nate said, as he handed her a Christmas card with a gift card from the both of us instead.

"I told you we should have gotten them off Craigslist," I berated Nate in a loud whisper.

Lucetta accepted the card and chuckled as Nate and I were going back and forth.

"You two should have told me you wanted tickets to Andrea Bocelli. I know Andrea—" she started to say, but was interrupted.

"You know Andrea Bocelli?" Nate jumped in.

"*No*, I know Uncle Andrea Tortellini, who knows Andrea—" Lucetta continued.

"Uncle Tortellini knows Andrea Bocelli?!" Nate gasped.

"NO! Uncle Tortellini knows Andrea Rigatoni, who knows Emos…"

"Emos Tortellini?" I asked, not knowing who that was but logically trying to weave together the connections.

"Close, my dear. Emos Bocelli. Andrea Rigatoni is Emos Bocelli's cousin. His cousin is Andrea Bocelli's personal chef. I could ask him next time to help me get tickets to Andrea Bocelli's concert."

With each lyric belting out, I continued to wallow hysterically. Nate's family scattered her ashes along the Long Island Sound, one of her favorite places where she'd like to sit outside and just stare, for hours, into the water. I realized all this time, my mourning was misdirected at Nate. It was Lucetta whom I cherished and missed. I wasn't ready to say goodbye. It wasn't time to say goodbye, despite how the song continued to say so over and over again. Not now. Not in a lifetime.

"I'm so sorry, Lucetta. I'm sorry I visited Greece before Italy!" I clutched her recipes tight toward my chest, and with my head tilted down, continued to cry.

CHAPTER 37

I Quit!

My phone started buzzing. It was Hendrik. *It was Hendrik!* Today was my call. In a surreal way, I didn't care. I had just lost Lucetta and felt my entire world had coming crashing down.

I picked up the phone.

"Morimoto-san, *arigatou gozamasu-shita.*" I greeted Morimoto-san, Hendrik, and the team before telling Mr. Morimoto in Japanese not to pursue the opportunity with Künt and the team.

Dear Mr. Morimoto. I want to be honest, as our culture requires us to be. Künt and her team are horrible people.

There was silence. I could envision Hendrik holding his pen at a forty-five-degree angle, fidgeting and wondering what was just said in that big conference room with Künt and the other team members waiting for their next instructions.

They overbill their clients, they overpromise and under-deliver, and they are just awful human beings.

A thunderous roar could be heard from my window.

What you seek—a "trusted partner for your solutions"—is not something you would find with Künt.

I stood up and pulled down the window shade.

I say this as a warning for you to heed and in good faith, for you to find a team you would be happy to work with.

The rain started pouring, hitting my windowsill with loud bangs.

I feel it is my obligatory duty to share with you the truth behind their proposal.

I hung up after he thanked me.

Hendrik called me immediately. "Rachel, ve didn't get zee sale from the Chineze morimoto-zan," he said, expecting me to somehow care and apologize profusely.

"Japanese. He's Japanese." I wanted to hang up the phone. A draft email confirming my resignation letter had sat in my Outlook box for weeks, after my last status meeting in Germany.

Even though I struggled with feelings of unfulfillment toward my job, I was scared to hit send—and scared not to. I wanted more.

Did I have enough money?

What about health insurance?

I really ought to be saving.

What would my resume look like?

How would I explain this gap in unemployment?

Did I really want to travel alone?

The answer was an astounding, "Yes, I want to live!" I wanted to see the world. Nothing could hold me back. I had always been responsible. I had always gotten passing grades. I volunteered at a nonprofit tutoring low-income kids. I saved the children on weekends and spent my childhood summers working. I studied, studied, studied and worked, worked, worked. I was dependable, and always did what I was expected to do.

I once had childhood dreams, and it was Lucetta who helped me look deep enough within myself to find them. One Thanksgiving eve, she'd said, "C'mon, kiddo. I know you hate law. Pretend you had a million bucks...which you ain't ever gettin' if you marry into this family, that's why it's pretend." Lucetta, with a knitted blanket over her shoulders, chuckled while we looked out into the sunset.

I had simply pulled my knees into my chest and sipped my hot chocolate.

"Now, what would be the first thing you would do?"

I pondered again about the possibilities of what I would do if I had a million bucks. The answers were buried somewhere behind adulthood, responsibility, fear, anger, and next to love. *Writing. Travel. Painting. Cooking. Singing. Science.* Nowhere in there was "assistant administrative analyst to the Key Account Management team at WilHeltek Commerz."

With thirty-five thousand euros in my bank account, I took a deep breath and submitted my resignation to Hendrik by email. Then I dropped off my badge and laptop at the campus and sat outside to inhale the wet, Irish sea air. It smelled of freedom and fulfillment. It was so early in the day that no one else was around. No one was there to witness my giddiness or sly smile, both of which would've made me look like a crazy person.

For the first time in my life, I felt alive. Like a newborn kicking and screaming who had just exited the womb of her young mother after nine months; the chains of Hendrik and Hilda that had been shackling my soul were cut loose and I could do anything. *Anything.* Finally, I'd be backpacking through Europe—alone—with the one love I should have always remained faithful to: Adventure.

CHAPTER 38

Italia Encore

All roads—or at least, the most recent road—led me back to Roma. I found myself full circle, holding a Frommer's travel book and Lucetta's recipe book in my hands, while standing in the epicenter of where my adventures first started. I stared up at the Italian heavens and proclaimed my love for this country by shouting, "Grandma Lucetta, I've come to Roma!" beside the historic ruins of the coliseum. Moments later, though, I found myself being shoved by anxious foreigners sharing an awful lot of similar features to me offloading a tour bus nearby, their bulky cameras in tow and speaking a foreign language I kind of understood.

I stopped by the Trevi Fountain this time to finish what I had started, after being berated by Grandma Lucetta when she learned I had only tossed two coins into the fountain.

"Rachel, tossing two coins into the fountain is bad luck! It means you'll fall in love, but it doesn't mean you'll marry!" she had said, raising both hands in the air as if to summon the Italian gods to watch out for me. I had flinched when Lucetta told me this, as I was boasting about my first adventure to Rome with Magda. We had stopped by this wonderful water fountain with chiseled sculptures of unknown gods who had abs even Superman wished for, before we each threw in some coins and made our own wishes.

"Three coins—you must throw in *three* coins—to find love, and to marry," she instructed me.

"Lucetta, when I return, do I throw in just one more coin... to make up for the third I missed last time...or do I start all over again, and throw in three?" I asked, seeking wisdom for any technicality that may disqualify me from the heavens that would mark my destiny.

"Throw in another three! The gods wouldn't mind some extra money." So I did. I threw in three coins this time and closed my eyes.

That evening, I also ventured back into that little alleyway with the "8" on it. It was one of the best places I had found in Italy, and when I shared it with Lucetta last year, she'd said, "Take me there one day."

So I did. With Lucetta in tow, in spirit, I knocked. Vincenzo didn't recognize me, but welcomed me in the same way with his familiar baritone voice, whisking me away to the back of the dining room. This time, there was no Irish recruiter dancing at our table and no girlfriend to share the most amazing buffalo mozzarella caprese salad with. It was all mine! Just me, myself, and I, getting drunk off Montepulciano wine and eating the melt-in-your mouth Vincenzo specialties until my stomach rebelled by way of acid reflux.

This was no time to order another drink, but I had to. I said a prayer to Grandma Lucetta before taking a sip of limoncello and whispering, "For you." My stomach, heart, and soul were somehow simultaneously content. I wish I could have told the late Lucetta about the ticket sale I couldn't pass up: airfare tickets were going for two hundred thirty-nine euros from Ireland to Italy—roundtrip. Surely, it was a sign from her to "just go" (or…a very pricey Google algorithm ad the company bought).

This airline could not give two shits if its passengers were fully seated and buckled up before it began taxing on the runway. ("Imagine this: it's 1965, and there are no such things as seatbelts," Lucetta used to say when Nate and I insisted she buckle her seatbelt.) The flight attendants were standing around chatting with each other, unconcerned, walking through the narrow aisles and brushing by passengers who were trying not to fall over as they placed their final overhead luggage in the bins. Instead of offering a helping hand, they turned around and gave a dismissive look at the passengers still standing as they whisked by them.

There had been no announcement of any kind that we were imminently taking off—at least that I could comprehend. No "welcome aboard," no redundant demonstration of buckling a seatbelt by the uninterested flight attendants. It felt like we were intruding on their own cliquey, private party, and we had to apologize if we interrupted them. If something did happen on this flight, the flimsy seatbelt or life vest that was presumably under my seat would not be able to save me. I told myself that was true of any flight, really.

I wasn't religious at all, but that day, my right hand began the motion of the Catholic Holy Trinity cross on my body: *In the name of the Father, the Son, and the Holy Spirit, Amen.* Luckily, the Italian pilots we surrendered our lives to for three hours and thirty-nine euros landed us in Milan—safely. Praise the pilots of this frugal-friendly commuter airline, and the Pope (wait… wrong city)!

I didn't get to say goodbye to my Irish friends either, unless you counted the hasty seventy-five-word text message I sent to each of them: "I quit WilHeltek Commerz u guys. I quit so I could sit in some cafe eating pizza and prosciutto and pasta in Italy by myself and to honor my late grandmother."

I was fortunate enough—or maybe just pathetic enough—to be able to pack up my life from Ireland in exactly eight and a half standard-sized boxes and ship it to my parents in New York while I traveled. I chronicled my journey along the way on my amateur blog for the world (or handful of friends) to see and vicariously live through me.

My nonexistent itinerary resembled something like this: fly into Milan. Eat. Tour the Piazza del Duomo. Admire the centuries-old iron and glass vault-like ceiling with Leonard Da Vinci's Sistine-like Chapel painted above me. Take an overnight train to Venezia. Be serenaded by handsome Where's-Waldo-looking gondoliers navigating the Venice canals before taking a train to Firenze. Eat; tour the Uffizi museum and see the titan *David* in person. Then, travel to the town Lucetta grew up in in Naples, before returning to see Pompeii, Capri, Sorrento, and Positano, and sailing into the sunset of Palermo, Sicily, to honor Lucetta's heritage. My one-way flight back to JFK International Airport was scheduled two weeks out from today. Only two weeks to indulge in pizza, pasta, prosciutto, and limoncello.

Was it enough time to properly honor Lucetta? I hoped so, because I was living for her. There was no other agenda. I would be guided by curiosity, culture, and cravings, with Lucetta's recipe book as my divining rod. Every experience would be a story authored by me. I could already see Lucetta smiling at me from above and saying, "I'm proud of you, kiddo. You're finally putting yourself first."

There would be no early morning bus tours beginning at the crack of dawn, unless I wanted there to be. I could sit and stare at people all day while sipping macchiatos if I wanted to. I could spend an entire day at a museum, although I didn't know how long one could really stare at that naked *David* statue. "Oh, trust me," Lucetta had said, many years back, "if you get to see the extraordinary *David* in person, you'll wanna spend all day staring at that naked statue."

I could get lost in this timeless city until I found the perfect bench to eat a double scoop of pistachio gelato with machismo men—and women—loitering and hollering "*Ciao bella*" as they passed by. It would be up to whatever I was feeling, or craving; finally, the freedom to create my own day every day, to eat anything I goddamn wanted to, because well…I was wearing very loose sweatpants (practically sacrilege in this mecca of fashion).

The first thing I ate in Milan was a heaping plate of hot spaghetti. "Al denteeeeee" of course. This was *the only* way to eat spaghetti, according to Lucetta. They made it by hand in house, tossed in butter with shaved black truffles on top, which came recommended by my cute, Italian waiter. The truffles would be "*delizioso*," the handsome waiter said as he raised his right forearm, flexing it and praising the Pope when I asked him to have the kitchen make me their best in-house specialty. "Truffle season," he declared. "Good enough for Vatican City to eat." I scoured the recipe book Lucetta so carefully bound for me. Where were these truffles? There was not a single mention of truffles, so I sat there with some hesitation.

When the young waiter returned with a half-bottle of moderately priced DOCG labelled Chianti wine, he uncorked it slowly and carefully. Then he poured a little into my bulging glass while he patiently waited for me to give it a swirl and a taste; he stood tall, his chin in the air and a white dinner napkin folded in half, hanging from his forearm and ready to wipe the neck of the bottle. He seemed anxious to see if I would approve of the red ambrosia he just poured into the glass.

I really ought to have known because I took Cornell's Intro to Wines class—the *most* sought after elective at Cornell that, when annualized, indebted a middle-class family and prompted a phone call from your Tiger Mom, who yelled at you for the additional expense of the required equipment (one hundred dollars for four tasting wine glasses). Professor Avery explained the best climates to yield the most tannic of grapes for most of the three-hour lecture, before distributing the wines and making us sniff, and swirl, and hock in our throats…the real reason newly minted twenty-one-year-olds took this wine class (to get a little buzzed).

The only thing I remembered before becoming completely inebriated was: "Denominazione di Origine Controllata e Garantita"—or DOCG—a classification in Italy that indicated it was of the highest quality of wine from the protected region of Chianti. It was enough knowledge for me to remember after all these years to score a great bottle of wine, and to impress the connoisseur. With a quick sniff and a firm nod to the waiter, he proceeded to fill the glass with a generous overpour.

The waiter returned to present a strange, black "rock" for me to smell.

"The truffles are hidden deep in the mountains, and dogs or pigs have the right nose to hunt these delicate 'mushrooms' out. In front of you is Burgundy black truffle."

Oh, praise the Italian truffle lords! It was so aromatic. I inhaled, sighed, then inhaled again before he stripped the truffle from me. My inner soul demanded he leave it whole on my plate. I sat back and fell into a trance. He completely ignored my silent, telepathic demand before returning with the plate of spaghetti and proceeding to motion the aromatic black mushroom against a grater until they were perfectly shaved thin atop the spaghetti—or as I learned, pappardelle, thicker and flatter than spaghetti. It was soft and stretchy too, like it had just been beaten and wrestled to the ground by an Italian gladiator fighting the death of its enemy.

I closed my eyes, and in a silent prayer to Lucetta, asked, "Did you know about this thing called truffles?!"

I didn't think my meals in Italy could get any better. But they did. This was the best thing I'd ever eaten. Possibly better than kimchi....

I didn't even know the name of this place! That's the thing with Italy. The best places to eat at were the ones that didn't have much signage or advertise their hours. Menus in English were limited. Manners were optional, and whatever you do, do not ask for spaghetti and meatballs, chicken parmesan, breadsticks, or Caesar salad here. These were foods created by Americans and strictly forbidden here. The emperor would roll over in his grave if he saw the paltry salad using his name!

It felt like Lucetta was with me as a petite woman with similar gray hair and a red and green apron stood in the kitchen with her hand on her hip, giving directive orders to her sons.... Then, *congratulazioni*, you've found an Italian gem. Kind of like that inevitable afternoon I popped into what smelled like a delicious alleyway—there was something about the best restaurants in Italy being hidden away in alleyways—near the Duomo. An older Italian man was sweeping the floor by the entryway when I entered and pointed to the analog clock attached to the wooden wall in the back, "*Un' ora, arrivederci.*"

God, I miss you, Lucetta. I wish you were here. It feels like you are here, sniffing these unfamiliar large shavings of truffles and concluding with me they may be the best thing we've ever had.

"*Ritorni in un'ora, arrivederci,*" the Italian man retorted loudly, standing in front of his restaurant. Using my middle-school proficient Spanish and desperately trying to remember any Latin I learned during my mandatory pre-SAT Latin classes, "un'ora" sounded like "una hora"—one hour. Rientro, rientro…I could just hear my former Latin teacher, one of the only Latin teachers left in the entire five boroughs of New York City, stand over me with a ruler in her hand, declaring once again, "Latin wasn't dead!" as we dreadfully sat there, conjugating verbs from masculine, to feminine, to neutral, to its respective m/f/n plural form: *alumna, alumnae, alumnus, alumni.*

"Return in an hour!" was what I had gathered from my dead Latin. I returned in "*essatamente una hora,*" and was the first person to be seated in what felt like their intimate living room.

My waiter was the only one in there who knew a little bit of English, and told me his mother cooked all the food onsite, as their family had done so for the past half a century. When the kitchen ran out of food, or if they were too tired, or had a special holiday to celebrate, or their other son was getting married (as I learned he was the next day), they would close the restaurant. No announcement, signage, or social media postings, which explains my encounter earlier in the day.

I could just picture Lucetta, nodding, and saying something like, "Well done, kiddo, you found a great gem. Even I would visit this place."

CHAPTER 39

Venezia e Firenze

I made my way to the next city mentioned in Lucetta's recipe book, and was bum-rushed by an army of smoking Gondola drivers. They wore black and white pinstripe shirts more suited for a jail cell than the streets of this beautiful city, and each vied for my attention, trying to outbid the next when I showed the least bit of interest in a solo, romantic ride through this northern city. The price was 120 euros for a fifty-minute tour, more for singing, plus a mandatory tip, one man said, declaring his prices in a voice slightly more tenor than the great Andrea Bocelli himself. Another hollered in broken Venetian English, "One hundred yuros for yooo, *mi bella*."

It was a small fortune considering the water taxi was only four euro fifty. But I was told not everyone passes the gondola driver exam (yes, there was such a thing that required hundreds of hours of training, excellent navigational ability, and a physical stamina that made gladiators look weak). I relented and went with the guy with the extra red ribbon tied around his waist, who agreed to "only" eighty euros and forty minutes. But as soon as he started singing, I wanted to pay him another eighty to stop.

He let me off by Piazza San Marco, where I found more vulturistic restauranteurs trying to lure me into their restaurants.

"Come, *mi bella*! Authentic Venetian food," one said, before another jumped in to tell me the same exact thing. Rows and rows of restaurants—that looked more apt belonging to Little Italy, New York—were littered across the side streets of Saint Mark's Square, each one delegating a cute host or hostess to preside over a chalk-boarded menu outside, trying to seduce unsuspecting tourists like myself inside with their claims of "authentic spaghetti and meatballs."

In Lucetta's recipe book, she mentions dried cod being the staple of Venice. "Only the most authentic place in Venice would offer '*baccala mantecato*.' If they're trying to entice you in with their cries of authentic spaghetti and meatballs, run! Run for the seven hills of Rome!"

Needless to say, I left Venice empty-handed—almost quite literally, since I used up every last euro I had on the expensive gondola ride. My next stop was Firenze. Firenze—beautiful, beautiful Florence! I heard so much about Firenze from Grandma Lucetta. She used to swear up and down the Mediterranean Sea that "you came to Florence for the meat. The meat first (I wasn't sure if she was stating that literally or metaphorically) and then the arts!"

I found a corridor of little shops with countless slabs of raw meats and salumi hanging in the windows. The city felt like an endless carnivore's dream filled with T-bone steak, otherwise known as "*bistecca alla Fiorentina*" here.

I entered a shop where only Italian words were exchanged by angry sounding Italians:

"*Ne prendo uno*!" shouted one customer.

In Lucetta's recipe book, the Italian salumi must be eaten thin: "It's the only way to eat Italian meats," she wrote. "Make sure it's sliced thin, THIN. Shave it until it breaks your fingers if you have to."

In my best attempt, I motioned to the butcher for him to slice "some of that dry-aged beef" super thin. He drizzled something on it and wrapped it up for me in a bunch of wax paper to go. I squirreled away and found an unassuming corner outside. Making a bench out of a windowsill, I unwrapped what the master butcher had cut; some of the liquid dripped onto my pants as I bit into the meat. It was just incredible.

And now, I wanted something *dolce*—or sweet. Something big and dolce. But when I caught a glimpse of the person staring back at me from the reflection of the nearby window, I barely recognized her. She looked a little bit happier but also grungier. I hadn't washed my hair in days, my sweatpants were baggy, and I alternated between the very loose white Hanes t-shirt and a yellow Old Navy shirt. Would Lucetta call me drab?

"Rachel, you're looking a little drab today. What the hell did freshman year do to you?" Lucetta asked, when I visited her that summer after I acquired the prerequisite "freshman fifteen."

It felt as if Domenico Dolce and Stefano Gabbana crept up next to me from Milan, looking me up and down, scrutinizing my unflattering (lack of) style and urging me to sneak away from Firenze to shop at the luxury outlets that were only a half hour and a seven-euro, round-trip bus ride away. Go shopping, in Italy?

Domenico and Stefano followed me, and eventually, their confidantes Gianni (Versace), Giorgio (Armani), Salvatore (Ferragamo), and Mario (Prada) appeared in their powerful suits, joining the others in the intervening heckling. They formed a circle around me, puncturing me with criticism while I tried to enjoy my stracciatella gelato in my baggy sweatpants, blowing invisible smoke of condemnation at my face: "You are in Italy, bella! And you will one day return to New York City. You mustn't wear that. You need bedder fashion choics, bedder shoez, and bedder belt! And that hair?! How will you ever return to profession?"

"Leave me alone!" I screamed at them silently. "I sent Guccio Gucci home with the rest of my stuff. I'm having delicious gelato!"

But they wouldn't go. So I relented.

There was only a little bit of gawking at *David* that day before I discovered the god-awful, hours-long line waiting to get into the Uffizi, so I turned around and purchased a round-trip ticket to Tuscany instead. I didn't revel in Tuscany for the rolling, Italian hills, or the vintage wines, but spent the rest of the day in an outlet mall that resembled Woodbury Common Outlet in New York. I came back with nothing but a cute Gucci clutch bag and a little bit more dignity.

"There, are you happy?! I get to carry a clutch with my athletic wear now!" I bragged. I looked down at the glass counter as I berated my self-pity silently. The clerk wrapped it up nicely and placed it into a gift bag with tissue paper sticking out. I admired it for a few minutes before I took it out and threw away the wrapping. I was about to board an overnight train to the south of Italy, a train ride I told Messrs. Dolce, Gabbana, Versace, and their friends they were not welcome to attend.

I awoke in an uncomfortable position on the train to three strangers leaning against each other in the same car, speaking a language that wasn't English or Italian. It smelled of body odor; one of the women had her calloused, yellow feet out and kept closing the cart door whenever it rattled loose. The air smelled of gorgonzola. Outside the cart were a few passengers strewn on the floor, fast asleep on their backpacks. It was a sold-out train, and all seats were "first come, first serve." It was cheaper than the "quick train" tickets that came with a reserved seat.

In my regretful effort to save thirty euros, I later spent three hundred euros on a chiropractor. I endured neck pain, fought nausea, and left myself exposed to any airborne illnesses these bacteria-laden strangers were carrying. I reached for the door and opened it, again, this time waking the tired woman across from me.

"*Mi excusi,*" I said. She fell back asleep, this time elevating her bunion foot, resting it on the seat next to my knee.

I pulled my backpack closer to my face, wishing I had on a face mask like the ones they wore in Japan (envisioning the clean bullet trains with full service). There were so many thoughts running through my head, and I had to pee so badly, but was reluctant to with all my belongings because I'd likely lose my seat (and belongings). There was only three more hours, *c'mon Rachel, let's recite the Greek alphabet forward, backward, over and over again. Take deep breaths through the mouth....* I was completely alert and barely moved from my stiff, upright position the remainder of the trip, all the while these strangers loudly snored around me, with the bunion foot even rubbing my left elbow.

I learned another valuable lesson: never take the cheaper, local trains—ever! The ride is usually more than twice as long and results in severe muscular and emotional pain. But soon enough, I arrived at the town where Lucetta was raised.

CHAPTER 40

Napoli

When the train pulled into the station, I could not wait to get off. I hadn't brushed my teeth or gone to the bathroom for several hours, let alone enjoyed any fresh air. I emerged into a gritty-looking city that was nothing like the photos of the picturesque southern Italy dipping into a light-blue seaside that were bookmarked in my Frommer's book. The air here was questionable too.

But I was there for Lucetta.

There was garbage and other litter covering the streets. There were packs of gaunt, stray animals following me, begging for food. Clothes were draped outside rickety buildings. Perhaps most surprising was the fact there were no traffic lights anywhere.

Lucetta, this is where you're from?! I wondered. I stared around me, looking for any public place that might have a bathroom.

"Hey, it builds character," I could picture her saying before smacking Nate over his head.

I waited, and waited, only to get cut off again by mopeds and other speeding vehicles that barely had enough diesel in them to go up a hill…yet were loud enough to leave me running back in fear to the corner where I had just stepped off from when I thought the road was clear to cross. I stood there, letting an indefinite number of motorbikes and cars pass me when an elderly Italian woman (*Lucetta, is that you?*) couldn't wait any longer. She took me by my wrist, rambling something in her language while she *walked me* across the street, pointing to the lines drawn in the street while she continued to talk in her language.

As if the road were a sacred ocean and she were Jesus, every vehicle stopped, and we finally made it across the street. I nodded my head in a gesture to thank her, but she hurried about and continued on her way when she let go of me, still rambling with her bony forearm in the air and probably cursing me out.

Lucetta, I see the resemblance! At any crosswalk, I had to weave in and out quickly, as if I was in a Mario Kart video game dodging obstacles thrown at me, or otherwise, find an old woman who had the profile of Lucetta to kindly walk me across.

As if my arrival couldn't get any worse, when I reached for the map in my Frommer's book to get directions toward my hotel, a couple of teens tried snatching my purse while speeding by on their dirt bikes. Luckily, the purse was on me tight in a crossbody way so that I was able to pull it back from them. I jerked forward, raised my forearm in an upper-cut-like manner, and put my left hand on my forearm, a sign they sure would have understood when they looked back laughing.

I didn't like Naples. In fact, I hated it (sorry, Lucetta). It triggered this irritable, angry, impatient, high-stress she-devil overflowing with a boiling lava of negativity. I was awful. Naples was awful. This was worse than any of the worst neighborhoods I'd ever been to in my life, and I dreaded thinking about the two more days I had left here before venturing forward toward Sorrento, Positano, and the Amalfi coast. Naples must surely be a test, the mandatory rite of passage, the hellish freshman year of high school of getting beaten, bullied, and made fun of before making friends and being invited into the "cool" circles that defined sophomore, junior, and senior year. Surely, the rite of passage that made Lucetta who she was?

I had no interest in exploring Naples.

"If you ever make it to Naples one day, kiddo, you must find Giuseppe's Pizzeria. It was founded by my great uncle in 1923," I remember Lucetta telling me.

I looked up.

"It has the best pizza in the world," she would say, balking at me whenever I shared with her my favorite pizza came from a hole in the wall in Flushing, Queens.

I left the room and approached the expressionless receptionist. Her attention was fixated on a reality show centered around a panel of judges with their backs against an amateur nobody who hoped to be good enough for them to press a buzzer to turn around and agree to coach them: "*Il prossimo abbiamo angelica da roma e canterà…*"

"*Giuseppe Pizza, doh-veh*? Where?" I asked, wondering if kneeling on both knees and kissing the almighty's hand for her forgiveness would prompt her to turn toward me.

She finally peeled away from the television, placed her cigarette in the ashtray before her, and circled a few restaurants nearby on the map in front me before turning back.

"Which one is Giuseppe's?" I demanded with no response.

The very thought of my *first real* Italian meal in Italy last year sent my soul fluttering and craving more. Sometimes, if I was in bed by myself, tossing and turning, I would close my eyes and pretend I was in Italy again, tasting a bowl of fresh mozzarella dripped in Italian olive oil in front of me. Weird, but it made me happy, and it was probably the reason Lucetta gave me her family's recipes and no one else.

"But I don't cook," I'd tell her.

"Oh, you will!" Lucetta would say.

Armed with nothing but my New York caution, I was bravely making my way through the not-so-quaint, chaotic streets of Naples—when suddenly, a loud *plop* of something hit the ground inches behind me. Startled, I looked back and it was a pile of garbage. Someone from the apartment above just threw their trash out the window. Out the window! I was mortified. This is where people, children, and pets were walking. What in the world was wrong with people here? There were at least twenty other garbage bags littering this street too. Was this the slums, or was this a city with an obvious sanitation problem? Naples felt in every way a third-world country, complete with unsanitary hoodlums and a lack of adequate transportation signs anywhere. Did Naples really belong in Italy?

I almost turned around right there, but just a few steps away was the local pizzeria Lucetta had told me about all these years: Giuseppe Pizzeria dal 1923. I had made it too far to turn around, even if I'd just realized I didn't have my Lactaid pills handy. I internally apologized to those around me in advance; then, I went inside.

My stomach grumbled. To my pleasant surprise, I wasn't spat on, beaten, robbed, or verbally abused here. Three tattooed men, dressed in white aprons and covered with flour, stood near the oversized wooden oven and looked up at me. One so nicely reached for an English menu and threw it onto the counter toward me, complete with a stone look on his face.

It smelled delicious inside, and everyone seemed to mind their own business because they were stuffing their faces with different variations of personal-sized pizzas. Just as quickly as the garbage hit the ground inches from me, moments ago, the margarita pizza went in and out of the oven. It was super simple: just tomato sauce, mozzarella, a couple slices of basil, and a generous drizzle of Italian extra virgin olive oil over it. This was the country's pizza, as I later learned, a tribute to the then Queen of Italy, Margherita of Savoy, and prepared with the colors of the Italian flag represented on it.

The pizza guru topped it off with a drizzle of more olive oil before bringing it over to me, and my soul instantly connected with it. Holy fuck, did this blow any New York City pizza out of the water. *I'm sorry, Glorious Pizza, for cheating on you, but Grandma Lucetta was right all along. You weren't that good for me and I could do better. I never thought I would admit to having pizza more incredible than yours, but you see, this was completely unexpected. I wasn't even looking for it. It just sort of happened, and I couldn't stop myself. I'm really not that sorry either, because I'm about to stuff myself with a second pie.*

If the Napolese could ever make it up to me for their rude attitude, and the whole "raining garbage near my head" incident that I barely dodged, it would be their amazing pizza. I would almost forgive them and would even consider coming back to Naples. At only 3.5 euros a pie, too, it was a bargain. I gave the boss here ten euros and told him to keep the change.

I returned again in the next couple of days, and both times, felt slightly more welcomed and equally as satisfied with the pizza I wouldn't be able to get anywhere else in the world. The locals got used to me, but I still preferred to scurry to a corner table on the third floor and eat in quiet solitude, chewing loudly with my mouth full, closing my eyes and occasionally letting out a loud burp at the end, a sure sign in certain Asian cultures you've enjoyed the meal (the louder, the stronger the compliment to the chef) because clearly, I enjoyed this meal very much.

I hadn't even left, and wanted to return already. I was enjoying all this alone time. I wasn't afraid. I wasn't crying (finally!). I wasn't wondering what the rest of my life would be like without *someone*. Even though Lucetta was gone, her spirit was felt through the magnitude of Italian ingredients erupting inside of me. Nowhere in the world could I find explosive flavors the way I did here, in this non-discrete place near a dangerous alleyway in Naples.

What was even more surprising, though, was what this experience was doing to me. Lucetta had been right about life. Live it on your own terms. Love on your own terms. Explore on your own terms. Never, ever, ever compromise for others. She was also right about this pizza too. "Damn good" was an understatement.

She had ignited a thirst for discovery for the first time in my life. The thirst to try new foods. New places. Meet new people. To cook. To actually want to cook! I could never, *ever*, be a master chef, and would always be more prone to microwaving a frozen dinner or eating kimchi out of a jar. But I examined the pizza now with curiosity, folding and unfolding, wondering about the specific cheese that was used and what the perfect amount of olive oil was. Flipping through Lucetta's recipe book each night made me hungry and crave something my soul had wanted for years.

The breakup no longer hurt. Or at the very least, it hurt a hell of a lot less. So did the thought of being on the outs with Mag and Nate. The thought of being without Aaron hurt less too. I felt myself falling in love all over again during this trip, only this time, it was with myself.

CHAPTER 41

Pompeii

Lucetta always told me about a place near Naples that was "*affascinante*" and a "*devi vedere*"—fascinating and a must-see. It was called Pompeii, a short thirty-five-minute train ride from the Napoli station.

To my astonishment, I recalled that Mt. Vesuvius erupted on August 24, 79 AD (though that date was later contended by historians), burying the beautiful city of Pompeii and its more than ten thousand citizens. That had been the first question on my high school Latin exam and worth ten points. Remembering that fact felt like a small achievement. The rest of the exam was easy, as if I had lived life as a Pompeiian and knew exactly what was at the center of Pompeii (the forum), their favorite pastime activities (outdoor plays, painting, jewelry making, and being spectators of violent entertainers killing their targets), and how long the flourishing city was heartbreakingly buried in near perfect condition by the disastrous devastation before being discovered by archaeologists (two thousand years).

Seeing all this in real life for the first time in my life—artifacts, mosaics, bodies, and even loaves of bread cast in near-perfect condition—asphyxiated me under a cataclysmic sadness. What were their last thoughts as they tried in vain to shield themselves from the pyroclastic flows of ash and pumice stones they ultimately perished in?

Was my own life in New York City, which felt similarly burdened by a layer of volcanic lava and ash, still intact for me to rediscover it a year later? Would I go back? I had tried to take refuge in Ireland, Greece, and now, Italy. Would I emerge from this journey unscathed? Would I emerge at all?

I wondered if I could ever go back to New York. Today marked 365 days since I resigned from the international law firm that left its own crippling scar in my heart. A scar mostly concealed behind the allusion of a happy, spiritual getaway to Ireland, and now, here. Would I be happy in New York…or would I arrive in a gurney, ready to be taken to a morgue?

CHAPTER 42

Pizza

I wanted pizza—again.

No, we are seeing something new today!

I never thought I'd say this, but I wanted to go back to Naples—for pizza. I was tired from all the walking around and exploring. I needed to rest and eat.

Let's spend the day resting and eating pizza! I want to go back to Naples for Lucetta's pizza!

I lost my internal battle, because according to Frommer's, Grotta Azzurra—which literally translated into "blue cave"—was a must see. It was accessible only from Capri Island, which was a nauseating ferry ride from Naples. That meant I had to skip Naples and the pizza today.

There were hordes of tourists everywhere, carrying their backpacks and cameras all attached to them with flimsy straps, waiting in line with me for the next small boat that would take us into this cave.

It was hot too. Very hot. The sun was beaming down, and unlike these other tourists, I was severely unprepared. No hat, no water, no sunscreen. All of those things I had accumulated in Greece and prematurely packed and shipped back to New York. Now I was forced to briefly lie on my back as we entered the narrow passageway among twenty-something other boats to the cave, and in those brief minutes, enough scorching sun hit my face to give me a sunburn.

But the cave was really, really pretty. Pretty soon, I had forgotten about the painful sunburn and wished to jump into the clear, blue water in front of us (even though I couldn't swim). Our rower—Mario or Luigi—gave a brief history of the cave, and pointed "over therrrre" where the sunlight entered to cast the blue hue into the water.

When Mario, or Luigi, dropped us back off onto Capri, I somehow made my way through a maze-like alley and stumbled upon a cooking class that had just begun. Through the window, I could see the master chef raise a big lump of white cheese, then throw it down before carefully slicing it. He caught me intensely staring at this, and gestured for me to come in.

I did.

"*Chai-neeze? Take un a'pron, j'oin ussss,*" he said.

Spontaneously enough, I did.

"Twenty euros," he said.

I took out whatever loose bills I had and handed it to the chef. The class of six, mostly tourists, some who looked like me, weren't the least bit distracted and continued slicing the mozzarella cheese carefully placed in front of them. I took an apron, wincing at the movement thanks to my sunburn, and sat next to an English couple.

"Today, we make *insalata caprese*, and ravioli," the chef reiterated. I picked up a knife and a cutting board.

The English couple next to me was following the chef's instructions intently before the wife started criticizing her husband's technique. "You sliced the mozzarella too thick."

"I like things thick. I married you, didn't I?"

She dropped her plate. "Albert, don't you start. I have a knife in me hands!"

"Settle down, settle down! The secret ingredient to cooking is love," said the chef.

I followed his instructions and sliced a plump, ripe tomato into four even slices, and placed the quarter inch thick caprese over it.

"Love? If mai wife really looved me, she wouldn't have brought me here. I wanted to go to the beach today."

I reached for the Balsamic vinegar and sprinkled it over before adding a couple teaspoons of olive oil over it.

"Where ye from?" he asked, directing the question at me.

"New York," I responded, smiling back at the English couple.

I was *cooking!*

CHAPTER 43

The Best Place on Earth

Frommer's said some of the best views of southern Italy were along the coastal ride toward the cities of Sorrento and Positano, which was on the way to Sicily—where Lucetta's parents were from. She used to tell me and Nate about their village just outside of Palermo, the farm she grew up on, and the three brothers and sisters she grew up with. She had even told us about the time she married and left everyone behind, which was about the time she was thirty—ancient in Sicilian years, apparently, because her father reacted with an "About time!" in Sicilian.

But I should not have sat in the window seat. The tour bus picked me up at 7:00 AM and began zig-zagging its way towards the Amalfi Coast. It was not a peaceful drive. It was dangerous and stressful. It felt like a bumpy climb to the top of an endless rollercoaster that would come crashing down any moment, no seat belts in sight, and a wide-open view of where we'd end up. Cars were driving backward too, as they couldn't compete with such a big bus taking up all four meters of the two-way road.

I didn't want to die here with forty other strangers, some sleeping and completely unaware of just how dangerous this ride was, although the backdrop to my death would be "one of the most beautiful in the world."

I imagined the inscription on my tombstone: "Here lies Rachel, beloved daughter, friend, born April 7, 1991–May 7, 2021, born in New York City and perished in a bus crash near the beautiful coastal shores of the Amalfi Coast, survived by her loving parents, and a cute cat who probably won't miss her."

So I prayed.

Dear Lord,

I repent and truly am sorry for all the horrible things I did in my life. I'll never kick rescued kittens again. I'll never squish bugs again. I won't yell at tourists or cut people in line. I'll help the elderly and the poor, even if they're really not poor and pretend to be. Please, please, PLEASE get us safely to our destination.

Eventually we arrived at a beautiful seaside town. There were bright yellow lemons the size of my palms hanging from the port-side trees. I wanted to take one…but would I get arrested? I took two. In Grandma Lucetta's recipe book, she described the massive lemons you could only find in this picturesque seaside town. The latitude, and the climate in which these lemons grew, made the flavors more intense. I reached for one more and stuffed it into my backpack.

As I got lost and wandered through the narrow alleyway of ceramic shops and handmade shoe stores, a young mother sat against the wall, her breast out, feeding her newborn. She looked up at me, saying something in a language I didn't understand, and moved an empty cup toward me.

I think this was the Lord's way of telling me to pay up on my debt, so I happily obliged and gave her two euros, said a healing prayer for her, and disappeared into the plethora of tourist shops to pick up a few refrigerator magnets to remember Sorrento, Italy.

CHAPTER 44

Sicilia

I caught a ferry the next morning from Naples. When the ferry reached Palermo after being at sea for eleven hours, I felt sick. It was an overnight ride, and this time, I had my own room—with a bed and a vent—but I awoke with a fever and sore throat. Maybe it wasn't such a good idea to eat all that pizza in Naples (but surely worth it). I hailed a taxi into a quaint part of Palermo and arrived at a bed and breakfast. A sweet old couple greeted me and showed me my own apartment on the third floor of their home. It was perfect—and so close to the city center, although I couldn't do much but lay in bed the rest of the afternoon.

What's the saying—feed a cold, starve a fever? The sweet nonna knocked on my door later that day only to find me emerging in pajamas, drenched in sweat with the bed's throw over me, and sniffling as she shook her head and said something, putting her hand against my forehead the way my mom used to and muttered, "*Febbre.*"

She disappeared, but quickly came back with a vial of *olio di oregano* before transferring it to a spoon and telling me to take it. Oregano? Like the stuff I used to sprinkle on the margarita pizza at Giuseppe's?

"*Olio di oregano*?" My head tilted. My body began to shake.

She nodded and put it closer to my mouth. I took it. It burned as I swallowed it, letting out a loud cough. She left me a couple liters of water in the flat.

I woke up later from a three-hour nap and felt good. *Really good.* The fever was gone, and so was the sore throat. Whatever Nonna gave me was better than Tylenol, Emergen-C, Airborne, or any other over-the-counter medicine that would have been in my backpack. I was ready to venture out into Palermo.

I realized there was so much to learn from elderly women with ancestral roots in Italy. How to live life. How to eat. How to love. And now, how to heal. In fact, I decided right then to never travel without the oil of oregano again. It was like a magic healing potion that treated anything and everything in its purest form: respiratory colds, toothaches, eczema, warts, cuts.... As a plus, it acted as a DIY pizza topping too! It replaced my small bottle of kimchi.

I shared the name of the town from Lucetta's recipe book with the sweet nonna and asked her about it. Her eyes beamed.

"Curcuraci. *Curcuraci*!" she exclaimed loudly and started pointing to herself. A young man who looked like Nonna and was reading behind her emerged.

"Our familia is from Curcuraci," he said in understandable English. "There aren't many of us from Curcuraci. How do you know of it?"

"My grandma Lucetta Cucinotta—well, I was engaged to her grandson, Nate—is from there," I explained.

"Cucinotta?!" yelled the nonna, who looked like she had just seen a ghost.

"Nathan Cucinotta is my cousin," the young man said.

Part III
Epilogue

VENI, VIDI, VICI. ARRIVEDERCI.

Life in New York was never the same. It wasn't awful, but it wasn't spectacular either. Yes, I was single, and living in a modest, 850-square-foot flat by myself on the Upper East Side. I had my own in-unit washer and dryer, a rare commodity and considered to be dwelling in the upper echelons of society—or one that my landlord had installed in the apartment because her hip surgery prevented her from walking down flights of stairs to the laundry room. I climbed the corporate ladder at a not-for-profit law firm where I actually enjoyed the work and thrived.

But that wasn't why everything felt different.

The Rachel I used to be was no longer present. The people who had once been my friends had made their way out of my life and turned to strangers. It started getting tiring reading all the "newlyweds" and "new addition to the family" posts on social media. As I watched rom coms until my eyes were dry, some of my former girlfriends were feeding their restless babies. Nonetheless, when I awoke in the mornings and stared myself in the mirror, I realized all of the superficial things most people go through huge efforts to rush into, didn't necessarily mean ultimate happiness. I had no problems going through the stages of life at my own pace.

Despite all this, there was a certain heartache in me when Magda dropped off. Magda. Mags. Even after I was willing to close the wound in my heart regarding the incident with Nate, the most unspeakable thing a friend can do took place. My dearest "Mags" had progressed onto the next joyous chapter of her life.

It happened exactly a year ago, when I opened an unassuming 4x6 envelope in the mail that announced, "Mr. and Mrs. Kim request your presence at the wedding of their daughter, Magdalena Kim." I dropped the wedding invitation. I hadn't seen Nate since I broke it off with him and after Magda had sworn up and down it had been an utter mistake. She had been apologetic to me in one hundred different ways, swearing it would never, ever, ever, *ever* happen again.

That had been a lie.

She did end up with Nate, and she actually came over to my apartment soon after I relocated back to New York to share the "wonderful news" with me without even an ounce of regret or acknowledgement that he had been the love of my life for a third of my life.

"Rach!" I opened the door to an enthusiastic Magda that afternoon. It was unexpected, as all visits from Magda were. She barged her way in with a couple of bridal magazines.

"Pick one, Rach."

I was confused and stared back at her.

"Which bridesmaid dress do you like?"

Magda picked up the *Marie Claire* magazine and flipped to a page that was carefully bookmarked with a post-it note. She pointed to the deep violet, ankle-length satin dress from Vera Wang.

"This one? Or…?"

As Magda pulled open the other bridal magazine, she flashed a two-carat diamond ring on her left hand—the same one Nate had once proposed to me with.

"You're getting married…to Nate?" My face smiled uncomfortably as I proceeded to look for words—any words—to say to her. "Wow…congratulations."

"I knew you'd be happy for us, Rach. If it weren't for you, Nate and I would never have found each other."

Except, I wasn't really happy for them. I secretly resented them both.

"Will you be my maid of honor, Rach?"

No. Never. Nein. Absolutely, not, you horrible, backstabbing, scum of the earth, two-faced human being…. Except, the only words that came out of my mouth were, "Of course!"

Magda jumped at me and lunged her arms around my neck, screaming until my left ear suffered a mild eardrum rupture.

"I can't thank you enough. Who knew we two would *ever* get engaged?" She chuckled. Then I chuckled. I couldn't bring myself to tell her the truth, which was harboring inside of me and causing my blood to boil. Watching two people I once loved and cherished more than the air I breathed announcing their marriage numbed me. So, I continued to fake chuckle until the word "Congratulations" was uttered out of my mouth again.

The following months were filled with dress fittings—lots of them—and my reentry into the spirals of depression. Magda wanted *the perfect* dress for herself and for her four bridesmaids, which meant we were dragged to every designer wedding dress store littered throughout Manhattan like puppies with our collars forcibly placed too tightly around our necks. By the eighth fitting, which Mags was "sure" was the one, she leapt out of the fitting room.

"Well?"

Mags's sister was oohing and ahhing, and their mother pulled up the back as she made comments in Chinese that it was unsuitable. It was a low-cut dress, too low, and Mags's C-cup breasts were overflowing like popovers out of the hip-hugging, mermaid sequin dress.

"Well, Rach? What do you think?"

"Where's the rest of the dress? Did the designer run out of fabric?"

Magda flinched.

"It's perfect for you! Nate and his sister-in-law would love it!"

Magda happily squealed and picked up the train of the dress, running back into the fitting room and declaring, "This is the one."

I dreaded each day more, as it was one day closer to their wedding. Why did I ever agree to be their maid of honor? Tomorrow was the rehearsal dinner, and the thought of seeing Nate with his family again made me uneasy. I hadn't seen them since our own engagement. I couldn't sleep that night, still pondering what I would say and how I would even start the maid of honor speech:

Mags and Nate, I love you guys and I'm so incredibly happy for you.

This was a lie.

Mags and Nate, there couldn't have been a better couple to have met during college and to be getting married.

Actually, there was.

Mags and Nate, things happen for a reason. And the events that led up to this moment were meant to be...

Nope, I didn't mean that either. I didn't know why I was feeling the way I did. I mean, I was over Nate. I didn't want him. I had moved on. But it felt as if an old, healed wound had reopened and salt was being poured on it, then pierced and prodded when I was surrounded by Nate and Mags's wedding nuptials 24/7.

I wanted to be fine on my own again.

THE REHEARSAL DINNER

Nate's mom opened the door and threw her arms around me. "We missed you," she said. The home had a familiar smell to it—like Grandma Lucetta's cooking, except Grandma Lucetta wasn't there. It was Nate's mom's attempt at the old-school, rustic, southern Italian fare. Lasagna. It was definitely lasagna, or her attempt at lasagna. There were photos of Lucetta throughout the living room, and a fresh bouquet of white lilies adjacent to a 1960s, black-and-white photo of her.

"I've missed you too." That was the truth. I embraced her back.

Nate's cousins soon marched in: Vincenzo, Franco, Giovanni, Luca, Alfonso, Agosto, Aldo, and Antonio. His brother came down with his wife, Brittany, who was wearing a dress too short and too tight for her voluptuous body. Some things never change, I thought. They each embraced me.

"Rach! So good to see you!" In a weird way, it *was* good seeing them too. Then, Nate and Magda entered the room, holding hands. I reached for a shot of limoncello.

Nate tapped his glass with an appetizer fork to get everyone's attention.

My beloved friends and family, thank you for joining us at our wedding rehearsal!

I moved backward.

If I could tell you how I first fell in love with Mags. It was freshman year of college, and when we first laid eyes on each other in the wrong college dorm room…

College dorm room? Like when he and I first met?

The rest is history.

I reached for another limoncello. Those who *really* know the story, stayed awkward and quiet, like me. Jeff and his cousins clapped loud and blew an occasional whistle before they dragged him away for shots of hard whiskey.

I reached for a third (or fourth) limoncello and walked over to pay tribute to Grandma Lucetta.

"Please Grandma Lucetta, please give me strength." My head was tilted forward, and my eyes closed as I silently repeated this over and over in my head.

THE DAY OF THE WEDDING

I threw myself out of my sorrows and put one foot in front of the other as I walked up the block from my Upper East Side apartment and plopped myself into the neighborhood pub on First Avenue, the maid of honor dress in tow.

"Whut ye having today, luv?" Paul, the Irish bartender, asked. The '70s hit "The Boys Are Back in Town" was blaring one decibel too high, and I was forced to lean forward and shout into Paul's left ear.

"A Guinness!" I shouted, then looked up to examine what I would have next: tequila, scotch, or vodka, all of which was so neatly displayed behind him. I leaned back against the chair, distracted by the soccer game that the pub was now live streaming from the EU that soon clashed with the music. My maid of honor speech was playing like a loop in my head.

A small group of mostly young-looking Irish expats let out, "*Ohhhhhh*!" as the Shamrocks lost the ball again. I reached forward for the tall, dark, frothy glass of Guinness that Paul had topped off.

"My best friend is getting married today...."

"Well, congratulations to your best friend!" Paul poured a new glass of Guinness for the newcomer who had just entered.

"...to my ex-fiancé."

He looked up.

"...and I am their maid of honor." I downed my Guinness.

Paul put down the glass he was filling. "Luv, are ye OK?"

"I'm not." And there it was. I wasn't OK. Again. I started bawling in front of Paul, in front of a half-dozen futbol watchers, and close to the stranger who moved a bar stool over in the opposite direction.

"I've lost them, you know? And I'm supposed to get my hair and makeup done at the bride's in an hour." Paul handed me a tissue.

"I don't even like either of them anymore." So, why did I feel obligated to still be friends with them, let alone be their maid of honor?

"I'm not going," I said suddenly, with a demand for another Guinness.

Paul slammed another one down. "Damn right! Don't go."

An epiphany erupted over me as if a heavy, dark cloud started to move out. I shouldn't go to Nate and Magda's wedding. Why should I?

My phone soon started buzzing incessantly with texts:

Rach, where are you?

Rach...

Rach, are you OK?

Over one hundred text messages from a panicking bride later, I looked down at my phone expecting to delete one more. But it was an email:

Date: 6/07
Time: 11:52 PM
Subject: Hi

It's been ages. Not even sure if you remember me, but we worked together back in Dublin. I even taught you a few words in Chinese. I'm going to be in New York and would love to catch up over coffee (or the best Chinese food in town).

-Aaron

I blinked a couple times and took another sip of Guinness.

ACKNOWLEDGMENTS

Thank you to Anthony Ziccardi, Michael Wilson, Aleigha Kely, Sara Stickney, Devon Brown, Luke Gard, Holly Pisarchuk, Rachel Hoge, and the entire Post Hill Press team for EVERYTHING. Words can't express my gratitude.

Thank you, Doug Deckert, for your unwavering support.

Thank you to Gerard Schriffen, Don Mazzella, Ann Marie Sabath and the Writer's Circle at the Union League Club for hosting those, "So you think you can write?" events, which inspired me to put pen to paper.

Huge thank you to fellow author and friend, Mary Adkins. Without your AWESOME coaching, I would not have made it across the finish line.

Big thanks as well to my many colleagues and friends who served as an inspiration and made writing this so much fun: Scott Shay, Ami Kaplan, Alyson Stone, Carol Beaumier, Helen Lundström Erwin, Mariann Sisco, Davidice Wong, Nora Chan, Jean Lai, Michelle Lai, Stephanie Fisher, Pamela Chew, Megan Yee, Evelyn Gong, Yani Martes, Monica Kline, Flora Lampou, Liz Mo, Mei Li, Diana To, Julia Park, Christine Tsai, my sorority sisters, many other college friends, Sarah McSharry, Joerg Schultze-

Lutter, Marcel Dekker, Gareth Bond, Jessica Melore (†), and many more.

To my big, loving Greek family: the Maroulis', the Rogopoulous', the Ziozis', the Karageorgious', and Hercules Kontas (†)—yamas!

To mom, Baba, Pat, Ethan, Kaitlyn, Sook Sook, Aunt Lily, Vic, Vin, Grace, Jasper, Elliot, Bun-Bun, Timmy and the entire Look and Eng family for your unconditional love.

Finally, to George and Sofia, my adventures wouldn't be half as much fun without you. Thank you for the stories and keep em' comin'!

ABOUT THE AUTHOR

Monica Hahn Photography

Raquel Look is an Asian-American woman with a background in consulting, living between New York City and Palm Beach. She's spent time in Ireland, Greece, and Italy, all locations in the novel. She's also worked at a large international law firm and drew on that experience in writing Rachel. This is her first novel.